MONTGOMERY
MANOR

THE HAUNTED BOOK TWO

ALLIE
HARRISON

Cover Design and Interior format by The Killion Group
http://thekilliongroupinc.com

DEDICATION

To Rachel, Ben, Stephanie & Dex
With Love

CHAPTER ONE

Meg Falkner shivered, but she wasn't certain whether the weather or the cold unease that ran through her caused it. She watched her husband. "Are you sure you want to do this?"

The wind blew an eerie sound all about her, whistling in harmony with the beating crash of surf against the rocks of a nearby cliff.

"Yes, I am." There wasn't a hint of uncertainty in his expression or his voice.

Meg drew in a breath that in no way warmed her, and ignored the icy bite at her lungs. "What if it doesn't work out?"

"We've already talked about this." Quint Falkner's deep blue eyes sparkled through the cold, misty air reminding Meg of a moonlit night full of stars. "We can do this."

Meg wished she believed him, but they were about to take one big, scary leap of faith. She didn't think any amount of preparation would be enough.

Quint met her gaze and gave her a soft, reassuring smile.

Despite his smile, Meg felt the icy fingers of fear touching the back of her neck. There were just so many questions, and even though Quint had answers for them before, the questions still swirled through her thoughts. "I can't help it, Quint. I'm worried. This will be so much work, and my store already keeps me so busy. I don't know how much of this we can do together. I think you'll be doing most of it alone."

"Meg..."

"I just need to know you're sure."

His gaze still held hers. "I'm sure," he replied without hesitation.

She stared at the hulking edifice before them. Montgomery Manor. "This huge, old place is liable to crumble around us. The upkeep alone is going to take everything we have."

"Even if we do nothing else, the restaurant that's already in the North Wing is doing well enough to pay expenses." He sighed.

"We still don't even know why Mitchell Greensburg left it to you," Meg muttered. "I didn't know he was a distant cousin."

"*Us*," Quint corrected. "He left it to us. And neither did I. Maybe he liked my construction work. I fixed a door for him a long time ago," Quint put in. "Come on, Meg. Cousin or not, Greensburg left this place to us, there's no other family left to take it. Either we take it and try to make a go of it, or we take the offer Greensburg's manager, Brad, made for it. I'm not selling it to anyone else. It's as simple as that."

Meg stared up at the monstrosity of a house. She took in its carved ornate architecture, its many balconies, decorative gray stone, columned front porch, and gargoyles perched on each corner as if to keep guard. It was beautiful and frightening at the same time. "It's rumored to be haunted."

Hell, it *looked* haunted.

The sun attempted to pierce the frosty clouds and shine down upon the old house. She wanted to groan. The idea of moving in to a supposedly haunted house and trying to make it into a profitable bed and breakfast while simultaneously updating the present restaurant, sent the lingering chill around her into the pit of her stomach. It didn't look as simple as Quint made it sound.

"Are you afraid, Meggie? Because I've never known you to be afraid of anything besides snakes. After all, you took a few boxes of books and turned them into a doing-very-well business."

Meg let out a breath, unaware she'd been holding it. "Yes, I admit it, I'm afraid. The house scares me. It will take me weeks just to learn the layout of the rooms."

Quint looked up at the house. "I know it's big and I know it's going to take a lot of work, but we've worked things out money wise. We just have to take it slow and steady, do it bit by bit while we expand. It's not like we owe on it. We inherited it. It's already ours. As we finish a section, we'll open more rooms up to the public. We'll get the ball room in order and rent it out as a banquet hall for weddings and things like that. We could even do floral classes in the conservatory. We can't lose here. Party rooms, game rooms, dinners, weddings, showers. We could create a space for any need. I've got so many ideas." His voice rose with every sentence. He was filled with enthusiasm, he sounded like child ripping open Christmas presents.

He turned back to Meg. "Don't let its size scare you now."

"Aren't you just a little scared?"

"No."

"What if it really is haunted?"

"I'm not afraid of a few ghosts, either," he argued.

She looked from Quint to the house. Forget it had flowerbed after flowerbed that would require a permanent landscaper every spring. Forget they needed to install a handicap ramp beside the twenty steps leading to the front door.

Despite Quint's admonition, the size and the idea of a *few* ghosts did scare her. She was used to a small ghost-free two-bedroom house.

"If this doesn't work out, we could be in big trouble, and it could haunt us for a long time."

He chuckled. "Funny play on words."

She laughed with him, but her unease remained. "I know. But it's true. That's why I'm a bit leery of doing this."

He laughed more.

"This isn't funny. I know for certain our little two-bedroom house isn't haunted. I don't have to worry about a single ghost closing any doors and hearing any chains rattle."

"Meg, I've been all round this house in the past two weeks. I assure you I haven't seen any signs of ghosts or heard any chains rattle here, either. But I do see potential. We can make this something grand. I know this all seems scary. Were you scared when you opened your bookstore?"

She didn't point out that there was a massive difference between her opening a small bookstore and running a bed and breakfast with over two dozen rooms. His smile eclipsed his face, and his hand over hers squeezed tight. Excitement burst from his every pore. She hated to shoot him down with her fear. The fact was her store was doing very well, but it had started out small and grown into what it was today. As the largest single family house in four counties, Montgomery Manor was by no means small. "I didn't have to worry about any ghosts moving books in my store."

"All right, I'll admit," Quint met her gaze again, but bright sparks of exhilaration filled his eyes, "it's a pretty big project to take on. And yes, it's true there are rumors about it being haunted, but you can't deny that this would be steady work, a lot steadier than the construction business, and I can do most of the repairs myself."

"That's true," she agreed slowly.

Quint gave her a determined look. He still held her hand. To her surprise he raised it to his lips and gave her two butterfly kisses to the back of her hand. "I know you're worried, but I don't want to do this without you. If you really don't think we can make a go of this, fine, I won't do it. I'll can the whole idea. I'll talk to Brad about the offer he made for it. But just remember, I never discouraged you when there was something in the store you wanted to add or change. And I never stood in the way of your opening, either."

That much is true, Meg thought. Quint wasn't much of a reader, and he didn't come into her bookstore very often, but he'd never tried to stop her from fulfilling that part of her dream. Nor did he tell her how to run her business, unless she asked him a question. If she didn't give him the same opportunity, he would resent her. The guilt alone would eat her alive.

"And I promise if we see any signs of anything out of the ordinary, we'll sell it. I don't want you being scared."

She smiled at his offer. "Thank you. Just tell me you think we can afford to do this, that we can handle it." She had to be certain. She looked up and saw a familiar fire in his dark blue eyes.

The wind blew a dark wave of his hair near his ear, and Meg fought the urge to brush it back with her fingers. He grinned at her playfully. "Please trust me on this. Yes, we can. Together, we can handle anything."

"How can you be so certain?"

"Meg, I just am. I've studied the numbers, and I've looked at the house. I want to do this with you. Please trust me."

"I do trust you." She looked up at Montgomery Manor again. Framed with dark, heavy clouds threatening rain, it appeared far from welcoming. The branches of the leafless trees around it blew in the wind, morphing into long, skinny fingers reaching out. And did she see a curtain in one of the upper windows flutter with movement? Who or what watched them from that upper dark room?

Meg fought down another shiver.

Quint reached out and brushed her cheek with the back of his fingertips. "I know we can do this. Besides, I dreamt about it last night. I feel like the place is calling me somehow. Let's just try—we always have the option to sell it to Brad later, if he still wants it."

"What changed your mind?" she had to ask. "Up until two weeks ago, you were all for selling it and walking away with the cash."

He stared directly into her eyes for a long moment. "Greensburg left it to us for a reason. Owning it and keeping it, giving it a shot is the right thing to do."

Meg stared back at him. For a reason she couldn't fathom, his words, his voice didn't sound like the Quint Falkner she knew, the Quint Falkner she'd married. His voice was deeper, and the slight grin he offered her was crooked and out of place. His dark hair was longer than he usually wore it, and it blew around his face in the wind. It even curled at his collar. Just two weeks ago, he hadn't cared about keeping the house; he was excited about having money in hand. He'd even mentioned something about taking some of the money and going on "the cruise of a lifetime."

"So tell me why you're now having all these questions."

Before, he hadn't wanted the house. Before, she hadn't needed the answers. Before, she wasn't standing in front of the house, looking up at it, seeing how creepy it looked with the clouds looming above it.

She didn't point out *she* still wasn't getting *any* real answers.

"I just feel that now we're to the point in our marriage, and with my business, that we finally have time for each other. I don't want to give that up." It wasn't a complete lie.

"We won't," Quint promised. "I know this will keep us—at least me—busy for a while, but it won't last long. And I'll be the boss, so I can take time off to spend with my wife any time I want." Again he kissed the back of her hand, and his grin teased with the hint he wanted more.

Did that mean he still planned to take her on the vacation of a lifetime? She was afraid to ask.

She forced a smile. "How mad was Brad when you told him we'd changed our minds and decided not to take his offer?"

"Not too much when I told him to stay on as manager and gave him a raise." Quint looked toward the front doors. "Come inside and meet the employees I plan to keep on. Then I can show you some of my ideas. You won't be sorry."

A strong gust of cold wind stung her cheeks.

She looked over at her husband, wishing she could match his enthusiasm. A large, icy raindrop landed right on her nose, and, despite her heavy, wool coat, she could no longer fight back a shiver. Absently, she pulled up her hood and tucked in the wisps of hair that pulled free of her clip and blew about her face. She studied the huge house before her. With its twin towers and many rooms, it was a castle. Meg stared at another one of the upper windows. The gauzy curtains looked for a moment as if a person stood there and watched her. Then it was just a window, just curtains.

It was going to take more than just a little work. It was going to take a lot of her time, even double or triple of Quint's. They stepped into the foyer onto a hard wood floor, and she looked around at the decorative carvings.

Quint leaned close. "You've been here before, haven't you, before you and I learned of the inheritance?"

"I enjoyed lunch in the restaurant a few months ago."

"Were you afraid then?"

She thought about it. "No, not at all? It was a very nice lunch."

"Did you see any ghosts, feel any cold spots?"

"No. It was welcoming." But then she hadn't owned it, either.

"How does it feel now?"

"All right."

"Tell me you don't see the potential." Quint put his arm around her and held her to his side. "Envision new lights, an old-fashioned check in desk with mail or message sorting boxes, plants, fresh paint, maybe a fountain.

"Oh, it does have character." She was glad her whispered words didn't echo. And listening to his ideas, she looked at the foyer with new eyes and she saw its potential.

"My goal is to keep the restaurant and a few rooms of the Bed and Breakfast running while I do renovations, then open the rest little by little. All the other rooms were just locked up."

"That's sad." Meg looked up at the huge grand staircase and pulled in a heavy breath.

"Yes, it's time to open the whole house."

Perhaps she wouldn't be sorry, after all.

CHAPTER TWO

Two months later...

The roses were beautiful, perfect red blossoms with long stems in a elegant vase, decorated with a red velvet ribbon. Meg set them on the counter and reached for the card.

Dear Meg, All my best for the grand opening of Montgomery Manor.

There was no signature. The handwriting was straight print and not familiar. She wished she knew who sent the roses so she could thank them. She leaned forward and breathed in a long whiff of their heady aroma. It was a wonderful touch of spring even though spring was still weeks away.

The door chimes jingled behind her and Evan Townsend, her sole employee, strode in with a book in his hand.

It was a leather-bound edition of Charles Dickens', *A Christmas Carol.* The book took her attention from the roses and their mystery sender.

Meg held the book with the gentle touch she would've used to caress a newborn baby. "Oh, my. I don't think I've ever seen a copy in such excellent condition. It's definitely better than any other copy I have to offer." She flipped through the pages. "And it doesn't smell musty or moldy. The pages are yellowed a bit with age, but the type is still crisp and legible. Where did you get it?"

Evan shrugged. "I can't tell. What do you think?"

"I think if you keep making finds like this, I'm going to have to give you a raise," Meg muttered, not taking her gaze from the book's perfect pages. "This is quite a gem. Come on, tell me where you found it?"

"I never kiss and tell." He gave her one of his easy grins.

Evan had only been working in Meg's *Treasure Hunters* bookstore for four months, but had already, on numerous occasions, proved to be a true book lover. Also, when it came to finding and recognizing literary treasures, he had the nose of a bloodhound. Meg was glad he worked for her instead of one of her competitors.

"Yes, I know, you don't." The kiss part she knew nothing about. What she did know is that he told her next to nothing about himself or where and how he obtained the books he brought her. The fact he'd been able to organize her shelves and her computer index even better than she could, and find rare books were just a few more reasons she liked him. Also, the fact that women flocked into her store, not to find a book but to check out her dark-haired, muscular assistant, didn't hurt either. The women came in to stare at Evan, and Evan always managed to sell them a book.

"In fact," Meg met his gaze, "do you even kiss at all? Do you have any social life, or do you only live for the next brilliant book find?"

He continued grinning. "I kiss." His dark eyes sparkled with laughter, but his voice dropped an octave. "Would you like to see for yourself? I could show you by example."

Maybe, if she wasn't married. The thought jumped in even before she could stop it. "No, thanks." She hoped her voice sounded light.

The truth was, if she didn't get a kiss soon, she very well might give in to the offer, and not because she wanted to, but because she *needed* to.

She tried to push the idea aside. She hadn't had a kiss, a real kiss, or a touch or a hug or anything, in what seemed like years. It seemed like years, but in reality it was just two months, the same two months since Quint decided to remain the proud owner of the Montgomery Manor. The same two months he decided to work there every waking moment. The same two months he refused to let her see any of his work since that first time she'd been there to meet the employees.

Yet, those two months seemed like forever.

But now, she thought of Quint and the simple act of a kiss. The wait was over.

Tonight was Quint's Montgomery Manor Grand Opening. And after tonight, he promised to include her in the planning and running of the Manor. She sighed, excitement and a smattering of annoyance carried on the exhale. Quint had insisted on surprising her with the rest of the public.

"So where'd the roses come from?" Evan's voice came to her from somewhere far away, bringing her back from her dream world of the Manor and kisses... Or more...

"I have no idea, there's no name on the card." She glanced at the roses before turning away from him to search for an appropriate place to display the treasured book still held in her grip. "You don't recognize the writing on the card, do you?"

Evan checked out the flowers before reading the card. "No, I don't think so, but they're pretty nice for someone not to sign their name. How mysterious. I think maybe you have a secret admirer. Otherwise, why would the flowers be sent *here* and not at the Manor where your husband might see them?" He batted his eyebrows at her in a teasing manner.

"Oh, thanks. That's what I need in my life right now." Sarcasm dripped from each of her words. "With this shop keeping me busy and my husband more gone than not, and his grand opening tonight...But then, maybe they're from my husband."

Evan pinned her with his gaze.

Meg couldn't shake off the cold sense of vulnerability that sent a shiver up her back. She didn't like an unknown admirer sending her flowers. Wasn't that what stalkers did in movies? It was easier to think the roses were from Quint.

She turned and moved down nearest different aisle, looking for the right place for the new book.

"You're nervous about tonight, aren't you?" Evan followed her.

"Yes, I am. Wouldn't you be?" She hated that he could read her like the many books in her shop.

"Probably."

"I'm nervous for Quint. He wants, so much, for this to be a success."

"I'm sure it will be great."

"The place is just so big."

"Yes, but that and the mystery and the idea of maybe seeing a ghost or two, as well as good food and lots to drink, will draw a crowd."

Meg set the book on the shelf. "True. You're coming tonight, aren't you?"

"I wouldn't miss it."

"I still can't believe Quint and I kept that huge old place. Can you believe it's got twenty-seven bedrooms and nine different sitting rooms? Who even needs twenty-seven bedrooms?"

"Joshua Montgomery, and Quint Falkner." Evan intoned.

"But Joshua Montgomery never used all of them. In fact, I think he only used one. And even though I know most of Quint's plans, despite the fact he won't let me see anything yet, I don't know if we'll ever get around to using all of them either."

"You don't think you'll have twenty-seven kids?"

Meg grinned at Evan's teasing tone. "I'm pretty sure I won't. And don't bring up ghosts anymore, either." She purposely changed the subject; the thought of kids touched an empty place in her heart. She and Quint were never alone long enough to *kiss* let alone try to start a family, and it never seemed to be the *right* time. Her clock continued to tick.

Evan shrugged. "Joshua Montgomery's wife was murdered in the cellar, you know?"

"Of course I know. Everyone down the Coast probably knows the story of her being stabbed to death and him hanging for her murder."

"Is Quint planning to incorporate anything about that or anything else about the house's history in his opening night?" Evan asked.

"Quint hasn't told me a thing. He's come home every night and all but fallen into bed. I'm hoping he can slow down after this grand opening. But, I think this has been really good for him. He's different."

"Different how, is he possessed by one of the ghosts that haunt that place?" Evan had his back to her, straightening a few books on a nearby shelf.

Meg thought, *he must be teasing again*, but there was little laughter in his voice. She pulled a book from a nearby shelf, thinking she needed to place it on the display counter. "Very funny," she tsked. "Seriously, in the little time I've seen him over the past months, he's just different. I don't know *how* exactly. There's something about his eyes, about the way he looks at things…the way he looks at me."

He turned and met her gaze. "How does he look at you?"

The chimes above the door rang to signal a customer's arrival. She looked up and stared at the man walking into her shop. It was Quint. At least she thought he was Quint.

"Like that," she said, more to herself than to Evan.

The man who entered her shop looked like Quint; he had the same dark hair, the same sharp features, the same fiery blue eyes, and the same six-foot muscular build that came from years of working construction. His deep, hard gaze never left her as he walked past the shelves of books toward her, his body moving with the same easy gait he'd always had. Yes, he was her husband.

Wasn't he?

His gaze caressed her, from the top of her head to the tips of her toes, undressing her with his eyes, seeing into the deep ocean of her soul. He looked like he wanted to devour her.

He held her bound with his unyielding look, and her heart pounded in her chest.

His expression was hungry, but his eyes said so much more. There was a look of excitement, as well as an anxious bearing of waiting, wanting, knowing. His dark twilight eyes lit with a savage, proud, inner fire that all but reached out and held her in place, a look that saw right into her, and read all her thoughts, her dreams, and her desires.

Meg forgot about the book in her hands.

She recognized that searching, intense, now-familiar look in his eyes. He might be exhausted when he came home late at night, but his fatigue never overshadowed the expression of need and hunger. Even though he was often too tired to act on it.

Now, in the light of the late morning, the look left her feeling naked and vulnerable, loved and desired and wanted and scared, all at the same time. Her heart felt as though it doubled in size, trying to choke her.

He'd come home each night with a strange, new look of desire. With her schedule at the shop, all her books to keep her busy, and Quint spending most of his time at the Manor, they weren't even together long enough to complain at one another. He rose with the sun and came home after dark, as she did.

She missed him.

Quint's intense focus never left her, and they could be alone in the world for all she knew, in a place just for the two of them.

Maybe Quint missed her, too. At least she hoped he had.

"Hello, Evan." Quint looked to Evan, but it was nothing more than a quick glance.

"How's it going, Quint? How are things up there at the Manor?" He and Quint shook hands.

"Good."

"Meg and I were just talking about that place. Have you seen any ghosts?"

Quint turned his attention back to Meg before answering, "Not lately."

She wanted to ask if that meant he *had* seen ghosts in the past. Also, she made a mental note to ask Evan if he noticed anything different about Quint, but not until the man in question had left. Quint was there, mere feet away, close enough to reach out and take her hand. If he wanted to. And she very much wanted him to. She wanted to touch him now more than ever. Her lips tingled with the need for a real kiss. She licked them, her memory of the taste of his lips fighting to resurface.

She felt her husband's allure, like the heat of a fire on a cold night. It bound her, immobilizing her, snatching the breath from her lungs. He was her *husband*, the same man she'd vowed to love, honor, and cherish for the rest of her life. The man who'd grown to be so familiar to her. He was the same man who had come home night after night and slid into bed beside her.

He'd changed, but she couldn't figure out why that caused her blood to rush through her as if she'd just met his gaze from across a crowded room.

She threw an inquisitive glance at Evan, but he didn't seem entranced by Quint as she was.

In fact, he reached out and took the book she still held. "I'll find a better place for this." He turned and glided out of sight.

She and Quint were alone.

She fought back a sigh and finally took the time to register what Quint was wearing. He wore black pleated slacks, a crisp white shirt, and a black jacket. He looked prepared, sharp, eager, and maybe even just a little dark and dangerous. He looked as far from the construction worker he usually embodied as he could be. And he didn't look anything like the man who came home exhausted and dusty and grubby night after night for the past two months.

For a long moment, uncertainty held her tongue. She ached to move closer to him, as something about him commanded her to do.

Or should she run in the other direction? She wanted to push aside Evan's outlandish idea that Quint was possessed by the ghost or a spirit that haunted the house they now owned.

Then, he grinned, and suddenly he was the Quint she'd known in college, the same man who smiled and asked her if she'd spend the rest of her life with him.

His smile cut through the haunted sensation that wavered through her, and she relaxed, but only a little. As if he commanded her without speaking, she stepped closer. He took her hand into his warm and dry and callused one.

It all but swallowed hers.

His grip was familiar and made her feel like he wasn't going to let her go any time soon.

"You must be swamped with last-minute things to do for tonight. What are you doing here?" Meg tried to make her question sound light and casual, even though Quint seldom came into her shop.

"I just had to see you. Are you excited about tonight, Meggie girl?"

She hesitated, then smiled. The nickname he'd given her when they were dating eased the tension. "Yes, I think so. And you look so nice."

It was a polite way to tell him she liked seeing him in something other dust-covered work clothes.

"Thanks. I wanted you to see me so you can tell me if you think this is appropriate for tonight. I wanted to look comfortable, but dressy at the same time. And I know this is a far cry from the work clothes I usually wear. But I thought if I was going to start playing host, I should look like a host, and not one of the hired help."

His hand in hers was so simple, nothing more than a familiar touch. And yet there was more, something close to an electrical current that flowed from Quint's hand and up her arm. A few short seconds beat out in unison with her heart.

She had to clear her throat before she could speak. "I think you look perfect."

"You're not just telling me that to boost my ego, are you?"

"Of course not. But I think you should've gotten a haircut."

Quint ran his fingers through his hair and grinned at her. "I kind of like it longer. It seems to fit in with the style of house."

Meg raised her brows. "Do you want to fit in with the style of the house?"

How odd.

"Perhaps." He shrugged. "However, whether I do or not, you're going to love it tonight, I promise. Everyone's going to love it. It's so much more than just a restaurant attached to a moldy old house." Meg loved hearing the excitement in his voice. It eased some of her fears she had about the huge project as well as the prospect of a ghost or two.

"You're certain?" She smiled. Why did this feel like a dream? Why did she feel like she was watching everything through someone else's eyes? She still couldn't believe that such a huge piece of property landed in their laps so…unexpectedly.

"Yes, really." His words were still full of exhilaration, that fire growing stronger in the sparkling depths of his eyes. He drew her close, "I'll let you in on some of the secret," he whispered into her ear. "Tonight's going to be a simple open house—lots of food, lots of drink, and tours of the new rooms we're opening. Then, everyone who attends will get the chance to sign up for a murder mystery dinner, as well as take a turn around the newly polished ballroom. Before long, we'll be booking that room. Won't that be great?"

Meg chuckled. "There's no one here. You don't need to whisper if you want to keep all this a secret. And all that sounds fun, but not really very simple."

"I just needed to hold you close," he continued to whisper before he kissed her throat.

Meg drew in a breath of his intoxicating aftershave mixed with the rich, familiar scent of man, and couldn't help but smile. "I always knew you were good with your hands and making brilliant plans, but I never knew you were this creative. I always knew, however you made it, it would be great. I've never known you to build anything that wasn't perfect. Put me down as the first to sign up for the mystery dinner."

"Wonderful. Thanks, Meggie."

She wanted to mention the roses then, and ask him if he had any idea who might have sent them, but his kiss captured her attention. His lips were hard and urgent, filled with need and longing, and she forgot all about the roses.

His mouth, warm and perfect, sent a burning tingle of longing through her. Had it been mere moments before when she'd longed for a kiss and had even considered taking Evan up on his offer of one? And if Quint had somehow known of that need, he was there to fulfill it. He could have just as easily reached in to her chest and squeezed her heart in the palm of his hand.

Her husband was back. There in her bookstore, where Evan could see them, where a customer could walk in at any moment, he teased her with the hot pressure of his mouth, the slight tickle of his tongue.

No, wait. This wasn't her husband. This could not be her husband. Her husband rarely came into her shop and never believed in public displays of affection.

She would have grinned had her lips not been busy.

If this was not her husband, she planned to keep him anyway.

Her senses whirled with the taste of mint and Quint, leaving her knees weak, and her soul uncertain.

Public or not, how long had it been since he'd kissed her with such overwhelming passion? She couldn't remember. She broke away. She fought to draw in a breath, but even that didn't ease the racing of her heart or the desire she felt in her lower belly.

She couldn't help but feel like she'd flown back in time, back to when she was in college and he in trade school, before they were caught in the easy familiarity of marriage and work and budgets and the hectic rat race that was life. Suddenly, she was younger, even though she wasn't all that old, young enough that the relationship was still new and exciting, when every kiss was meant to last an eternity.

When had those kisses ended? Meg couldn't remember, but she just knew they were lost beneath the business of everyday life and work.

Quint let her break the breath-stealing kiss, but he still held her hands, refusing to let them go. "I thought we could have lunch and celebrate before we get all caught up in the excitement of the evening."

Again, his words were warm in her ear. His breath, his touch, the feel of him down the entire length of her body, sent a shiver of anticipation through her.

She smiled again. Yet, a twinge of uncertainty slivered up her spine. "Celebrate? We're celebrating tonight."

Her lower stomach felt tight like taut bowstring. She couldn't remember the last time they were this close. She wasn't even sure if she knew this stranger of a husband. But she liked him. She wondered if he could feel the way her breasts pressed against his chest.

The sparkle in his eyes brightened. "First, I want to celebrate with you. Alone."

A shiver of anticipation ran through her with each word. And for a moment, she had the strange feeling he might lower her to the floor amongst the bookshelves and make love to her there.

"Where?" She forced out the single word, and forced in a breath.

"At home, in our bed." He whispered, his breath hot and sensual against her ear.

His invitation grabbed her and held her with the pull of an electrical current.

"I've missed you these past months. I've been working a lot, and I want to make it up to you. Besides, we've never had lunch in bed, have we, Meggie girl?"

That did it. The way he whispered, *"Meggie girl,"* was all it took to send her over the edge of desire and need. It had been so long since Quint had held her and touched her, so long since they'd devoted some time to one another and their marriage.

"Let me tell Evan I'm taking an early lunch." Her words were little more than whispered breaths.

"All right." He agreed, but it was only after another long moment that he released her. She turned from her husband to hunt down her assistant.

The chime of the bell on the door indicated the arrival of a customer, and Meg looked at the newcomer, uncertain if she was grateful for the interruption or not. Her legs were weak and shaky from Quint's kiss, and she needed to get control of herself until they were alone.

Melanie Wirthington walked to the counter with purposeful strides. "Melanie," Meg greeted her, hoping her smile didn't appear forced or that the fire Quint ignited in her wasn't evident in her expression. It felt like her cheeks were burning. "You're here for the Shakespeare."

"That's right," Melanie smiled and revealed a mouth full of perfect teeth.

Melanie looked at Quint then gave a double take. "Quint?"

His smile was relaxed. "I guess you're not used to seeing me dressed like this."

She chuckled. "I guess I'm not used to seeing you without dust in your hair."

Meg looked from Melanie to Quint. "You two know each other?"

"Melanie's an employee at the Manor," Quint explained.

That made her one of Quint's employees, but Meg noticed how he hadn't phrased it like that.

Melanie's smile grew. "Yes, and I didn't realize you two were—" she stopped, uncertainty marring her features.

"Married," Quint supplied. "Meg is my wife. I don't think you were there the day I brought her around to see the place."

Melanie looked at Meg, her face creased with a smile the size of the Grand Canyon. "I've been buying your books since you opened this shop, and I never knew your last name. Just wait until you see what he's done with the Manor. It's so much grander than before, and I can hardly wait for work tonight." Her face lit up.

Meg smiled. She hoped all Quint's employees enjoyed working for him as much as Melanie did. "Then I look forward to seeing you again tonight. I'll have my assistant, Evan, take care of getting your book for you, if that's all right."

"That will be fine."

Meg looked for Evan. She was pretty certain Melanie didn't mind having Evan's attention at all.

She searched the aisles quickly because she didn't want to leave Quint, not even for a moment. In fact, she was afraid to even take her eyes off of him for fear that he would change back to being the distant, overworked man he'd been the last few months. She was terrified that if she stopped watching him, he would change his mind about having lunch in bed. Or worse, that she would wake up and discover his kiss and his invitation were all nothing but a dream.

She found Evan in the third aisle. "I'm leaving for lunch. Can you come and help Melanie Wirthington?"

Evan quirked a brow at her, as though he knew where she would be spending lunch.

"Sure." He grinned. "You don't feel like bringing me back a sandwich, do you?"

Then again, perhaps he didn't know where she planned to have lunch.

Meg hesitated for a moment after she tossed a glance back at Quint. She might not survive the lunch hour, she thought. "I'll see what I can do."

She turned away before Evan could notice the slow burn on her cheeks. Quint had set a fire in her soul, and she had to leave with him before she spontaneously combusted and set all her prized books on fire. "See you in a while."

It was all she could promise.

She turned her attention to the counter where she'd left Quint. Even from across the room, he captured her with his gaze and made her feel naked, hot, vulnerable, and wanted—all at the same time. She looked down to make sure her blouse was still buttoned. "Ready?"

She walked to him, and he held out her sweater so she could slide into it. "Oh, most definitely."

If she didn't know better, she'd think he just set off a million sparklers inside her. She hadn't looked up at him when he spoke. She didn't need to look up at him. She didn't need to look to hear the passion deepening his voice or see the desire she knew would be in his eyes. Need touched her like misty fog on a cool night, only it was hot. His heat penetrated her like the warmth of the sun and turned her legs to water. She forced them to move as she headed to the door.

She no longer cared if the Montgomery Manor was haunted. If this was what fixing it and owning it did to her husband, she liked it. She liked him. Besides, she liked legends. She liked that the house, her house, *their* house, was filled with them.

The work somehow gave Quint more determination, more focus, moving this part of their marriage in a new direction—one she wanted to continue.

It was a direction that led her to lunch in bed.

The early spring air was cold on her cheeks, but Meg couldn't help but smile. The cool air didn't begin to touch the fire Quint had started inside her.

She looked up at the man who was her husband, and he smiled down at her.

She couldn't help but notice his smile held the confident look of a successful man.

CHAPTER THREE

Lost in the soft music and in the touch of Quint's hands, Meg floated in the clouds.

She looked into Quint's passion-filled gaze, terrified to question anything, afraid to even speak lest she wake from the dream and burst the bubble he'd placed around them.

Indeed, it had to be a dream. They'd been married almost five years, had been together two years before that, and never in that time had he made her feel as she did now.

Reflected candlelight flickered against the walls of the bedroom. The day was cloudy and had held the threat of rain over them all the way home. Whether the threat played out, she had no idea. Nor did she care.

The shades on the windows drawn against the afternoon light didn't keep it out entirely, but with candles, Meg felt lost. Lost in the touch of a lover she had never known till now.

Quint played her like a fine instrument; his hands caressed every inch of her flesh, setting it afire. Gentle and tender, warm and spiritually igniting, he all but touched every part of her being.

Yet, it wasn't just his hands that caressed her, warmed her, embraced her. The smooth firmness of his thighs brushed against hers. The light dusting of hair on his hard chest tickled her nipples. The roughness of the 5-o'clock shadow along his jaw on her skin left her filled with want.

With his hands, he caressed the inside of her arms. And he followed the action with a touch of his lips, teasing her with his tongue. Who knew the inside of her arms was so sensitive? She wanted his hands on her breasts, but she didn't move, couldn't move, could hardly do more than draw in one life-giving breath after another.

But even oxygen didn't seem so important then. Quint's touch was life giving. Every nerve ending in her body felt awake and filled with life of its own. He gripped her hands and moved his thumbs in a deliberate circle, slowly, as he massaged her palms.

He drove her mad, each touch luring her to the brink of insanity, where she would die if he didn't give her release. He straddled her, his muscular legs pressing against her hips. She felt his desire in every touch. It was skin against skin, warm against warm, fire against fire.

Yet, she wasn't sure if the fire was against her skin or deep in her soul.

"Come inside of me." Her words were breathy.

"Not yet." His voice was rough and raw. He sounded nothing like the man who'd muttered "have a good day" early that morning after downing a bowl of cereal five minutes before leaving for the Manor.

He clasped her hands in his, lacing his fingers through hers, his weight holding her in place. He leaned down and captured her mouth with his. Meg felt like his entire body held hers in its grip. She didn't fight against the sensation swirling through her. She forced in a deep breath and pressed her breasts against him. He groaned into her mouth before he moved to taste her throat.

"Please...." She quivered with need beneath him.

"Not yet."

"Why not?"

"I haven't touched and tasted every inch of you yet."

She sighed and closed her eyes. "I'm pretty positive you have. I think every inch of me is on fire."

The heat of his lips left her throat. She opened her eyes again and met his gaze through the candlelight.

The light reflected shimmers in his eyes as he grinned down at her. "You think so, do you?"

"I know so." She sighed.

He leaned down and kissed her flesh above her collarbone. "Have I already tasted you here?"

"Yes, I think so."

"And what about here?" The warmth of his lips never left her, and he held her hands as he moved up and nibbled on her earlobe.

She couldn't stop the shiver that passed through her. "I think you tasted there, too, more than once."

"Here?" He twirled his tongue at the soft hollow of her throat.

She replied with a soft moan that turned into something close to a giggle.

"You think you're ready for me?"

"More than ready..."

He shifted with a speed and grace that surprised her. He brought his lips back to hers and at the same moment thrust into her.

Meg gasped at the sudden invasion. She couldn't remember him ever filling her so completely, so perfectly.

He released her hands. "Touch me, Meggie, put your hands on me. I need to feel your touch."

She did as he asked, but it felt like so much more. It was as if she melted to him, unsure where she ended and he began.

He made slow, hot love to her, each motion, each caress filled with a desperation she'd never before felt from him, and she gasped again.

He made love to her with such raw abandon.

Again and again, he drove into her, as if trying to reach a part of her he'd never before reached, taking her to the edge of reason, but not allowing her to tumble over. His kiss muffled her cries of pleasure as she held on to him.

She did not simply tumble over that edge of reality. She soared over it. The room disappeared. Everything disappeared except for Quint and a bright flash of light before her eyes and the exhilarating feeling that he'd managed to send every atom of her body flying in different directions.

He halted his assault on her lips long enough to murmur, "Beautiful."

He didn't follow until he made sure her tumble was complete, but she didn't think about that until much later.

Later, blowing out the candles and leaving Quint was the hardest thing she'd ever done. She took her time dressing, not wanting to give up the afternoon just yet, but she couldn't put it off forever.

"Is something wrong?"

Meg stopped and looked at him. His voice was deeper, his words more precise and distinct. "No, it just feels like my skirt and blouse are too tight and rather uncomfortable. And it doesn't matter what I do with them, they feel like they're on crooked."

"Wear something else."

"That might raise questions I'd rather not answer." Meg pulled against her skirt again. She licked her lips and still tasted Quint. His familiar, masculine scent lingered on her, too. And she liked that.

"So?" He reached for his shirt.

Meg stared, noticing for the first time the claw marks she'd put on his shoulder blade. Had she done that?

Yes, she had.

He put on his shirt and buttoned it, his gaze never leaving her.

She ignored his question. "What time do you want me to come for the grand opening?" The way he watched her caused her to look down to make sure she hadn't missed a button hole.

"Can you be there by six?" He finished with his shirt and sat down on the edge of the bed to start on socks and shoes. His gaze still never left hers.

That look of desire was back in his eyes. He watched her so intently, she felt as if he were peering inside her.

She felt more exposed then than when she'd had her legs wrapped about his waist. How could he want her again so quickly? *That* had never happened before.

"I had planned to close early tonight and direct all my customers to the Manor." She avoided his gaze. Not that it did any good. His deep study of her burned into her hotter than the candle she'd just blown out.

"Can you do me a favor and wear that little black velvet number you've got?"

"Okay." She smiled. She was ready to go back to work, but she still didn't want to walk away from what he'd been so willing to share with her.

She looked at him just in time to see him slowly lick his lips.

Heat rushed her cheeks. Perhaps it was best she not linger, perhaps it was best if she headed out into the spring air to cool off before she burned up completely.

He stood and stepped to her. His warmth touched her even though none of the rest of him did. She couldn't escape his presence. She was caught, unable to move if her life depended on it. "One more thing—" He pulled her closer, and his hardness pressed against her.

"What?" She forced the one-word question from her lips. She half expected him to ask her to undress again.

"Can you pack a bag and spend the night there with me?"

She stilled. She'd wondered when this would come. The Manor was huge, plenty of bedrooms. Their house, the house they'd scraped together every penny they'd had for a down payment before they were married, was small. They had outgrown it almost before they ever moved in, and Meg always knew it wasn't the place where they would grow old together. Still, she wasn't so sure she was ready to give it up, either. Nor was she sure she wanted to make Montgomery Manor, a place with twenty-seven bedrooms and patrons coming to eat dinner, her permanent mailing address. But she could take things slow, one step at a time, and one night was something she could handle, given it was the grand opening. And with the way Quint looked at her...

Somehow, he'd managed to warm her up with his gaze, as if she were nothing more than putty he could mold into anything he desired.

"Sure, I'll stay there with you." She was lost in his gaze and could refuse him nothing.

"I fixed up the master suite just for us, Meggie. It's our own apartment, and it's just a bit bigger than this entire house, so it has plenty of space. And there are rooms in that wing we can add into it later if you want."

"Really?" She said, hope lacing her tone.

"Yes, really."

She stared at him for a long moment. "We could do that?"

"It's our house, Meggie. We can do whatever we want with it."

"I have to keep reminding myself. I knew about some of your plans, like adding more rooms for the Bed and Breakfast patrons, but I had no idea you planned anything like that for us. That's so sweet. I can't wait see it."

"And promise me you'll be honest. If you don't like it for any reason, I'm open to suggestions."

"I promise. And I hate to, but I'd better go. I doubt Evan was prepared for me to be gone so long. I hope we didn't have a busy lunch hour like we sometimes do."

He cradled her face in his hands and kissed her, taking his time. His lips were warm against hers, sending more of his heat into her. His taste was familiar but the rest of the kiss was new, exciting. She forced herself to pull away, otherwise poor Evan would have to spend the rest of the day trying to keep the shop afloat by himself, and Quint might miss his own grand opening.

"You're beautiful." Quint enunciated each word.

Meg let out a chuckle. "You act like you've never seen me before."

"Maybe it's just been a long time since I've looked."

Wasn't that what she'd thought, that he looked at her as if he'd never seen her before?

She contemplated the change in their marriage all the way back to her bookshop. Up until now, she'd always thought changes in a marriage were caused by both partners. Where did this change, this newness come from? Did it have anything to do with Quint's owning and working on Montgomery Manor? She knew Evan teased about him being possessed by a ghost. But she didn't—couldn't bring herself to—believe in ghosts. The idea made her laugh. Maybe working at the Manor gave Quint new enthusiasm and determination and purpose? She could believe that.

What she did know for certain was that her insides still quaked and burned from his touch. Making love with him completed her.

Just before she reached the book shop, she remembered Evan's sandwich and stopped at a drive thru to grab him a burger.

The shop welcomed her with its musty scent, and as she looked around, she thought of the candles Quint had lit before undressing her. She smiled. A few candles would add to the welcome of her shop, but she couldn't take the chance having flames so close to her books. Yet, she could get a few of those battery operated candles. Those would work.

The shop also needed more chairs, places for customers to sit and look at a book as they contemplated their purchases.

"I'm back." She didn't need to call out to Evan. The sound of the bells over the door was enough to draw him to the front of the store.

Evan held a stack of books in his arms. "Did you have a good afternoon?"

Meg felt heat come to her face, and she couldn't look him in the eye. To say she had a good afternoon would be the biggest understatement of the year. "Yes. Here's your sandwich." She handed him the paper sack.

Evan looked at her, studied her. "Gosh, Meg. Is this where he took you for lunch?" He looked at the name of the fast-food restaurant plastered all over the small sack.

"Why?" It was impossible to speak to Evan and not look at him at the same time. She had to bite her tongue to keep from telling him Quint took her to the moon.

"You look wonderful, that's why. I mean not that you usually don't, you just look," he paused as he searched for the right word. "I don't know, just different, like you're glowing, like you got some great news or something. I hope I feel and look like you do after I eat this."

She chuckled and tried to keep a poker face despite the heat that filled it, but kept to herself that while she didn't get any news, she did get something great. Hell, she just got the greatest sex of her life.

"And who was that guy that came and took you away, leaving me here to labor all alone?"

His question gave her pause. And she couldn't be sure if he was teasing or serious. "That was Quint, you know Quint?"

"I know Quint your husband. The one who was laid off and turned into somewhat of a couch potato in the past year before he talked you into keeping that huge haunted house. I know the Quint who wears construction clothes, and is most of the time covered with dust, and has lots of dirt under his finger nails. *That* guy was not the same man. I could find that guy in one of the men's magazines over on the rack."

"It was Quint. I told you he was different." Meg forced a grin. So someone else noticed a change, too. Not that it meant anything. People were allowed to change, to clean the dirt out from under their fingernails. "I think he just feels good about all the plans he has and everything he's done with the Manor. Also, having steady work and not having to depend on anyone else for it has helped him, too."

"Well, he sure does clean up nice. Good for him, and good for you, too. I know how hard the lack of construction work was on the both of you before he started working on that old haunted place."

"No, you don't."

"I think I do." Evan reached into the sack and pulled out his burger.

"Did you know I asked him more than once to come to the shop and help us, just to get him out of the house? I even told him I would talk to Mr. Jackson about Quint doing some construction repairs on this old place to give him something to do."

Evan stared at her for a long moment before unwrapping what would be his lunch. "I guess I didn't know."

"Not that it mattered. Quint refused. Giving that same excuse that he's not into books, you know. I think his pride was just in the way, though. It bothered him to take the handout, even if it did come from me."

Evan shrugged. "It's just as well that he didn't come, then. But I think it was more than just he's not into books."

"What do you mean?" The question slipped out before she could stop herself.

"I think it's more like he's jealous of your success here with something like books, something that wasn't hard, physical labor like his job requires."

Meg could never fault Evan for being so straightforward.

But his words stopped her in her tracks. "Quint's never been jealous," she defended him. "He doesn't have a jealous bone in his body, and not of me."

"Every man has a jealous bone somewhere in his body, whether it be jealous of other men or of kids getting all the wife's attention or even because of career success." Evan was straightforward, all right.

"Well, Quint doesn't, that's just your opinion."

He shrugged. "Whatever."

It was Evan's way of choosing not to argue the point.

"At least *I've* never seen it." Or had she? Because now, Evan's words, caused her to wonder. "Besides, it doesn't matter."

Was she trying to convince Evan or herself? "It seems things are looking up, anyway. This shop is doing great, and Montgomery Manor has done wonders for Quint, too. And I told you that we'd be closing early today, didn't I?"

"Yes, and you sure picked the right afternoon to skip out. We've had a whole two customers."

"That's all?"

"That's all, but Melanie Wirthington bought all the Shakespeare we had in stock, and the other was an excellent sale, too."

"That's great."

Evan went on to tell her about the second sale of the day, and Meg couldn't be unhappy. "So since it's been so slow, I've been taking the time to go through some of those boxes of books you've been holding in the back for the past week. I've got a lot of them logged into the computer, and now all I have to do is get them in the proper places on the shelves."

Meg reached over the counter to the stack of mail resting there. When she saw a letter from her landlord, she tore it open. "It may be a good idea to leave them in the boxes. With that greedy Jackson raising the rent on this old place, I don't know how much longer we can afford to stay here."

She pulled out the folded paper and glanced over the words of the notice, letting out a huff of frustration at the unjust amount of money Mr. Jackson wanted for the old building that definitely required some of Quint's handy work.

"Still, I'll bet you didn't even know what treasures you had back there."

Evan stopped, and stared at her neck with an intensity that made her uncomfortable.

"What?" she asked. She put the note back in its envelope and dropped it back onto the stack of mail.

"Nothing." Then he blinked and went on. "There were quite a few books of poetry and inside one was a whole bunch of old interesting newspaper clippings."

"What did you do with them?"

"Recorded them in the log and put them in the glass case with the other relics. They're on the second shelf if you want to read them."

"Thanks." Meg saw the way he fought to keep his gaze on her face, into her eyes, and away from her throat. Wondering what held him so spellbound brought more heat into her face. She couldn't wait to get to a mirror and take a look for herself.

"Great. What do you think about putting a few more antiques in this place?"

"Like what?"

"I don't know, maybe some chairs that people could sit in or buy, something like that. Or perhaps some old book cases or an old secretary or two. I think they'd look nice near the front."

"Sounds good to me," he agreed. "But I don't know how much work you want to put into things here if the rent is going to go up."

"Oh, yeah, right."

Now she felt she was the jealous spouse. Quint owned the building where he worked his business. He might have to pay expenses, but rent wasn't one of them. And hard telling how many antiques were at his disposal.

The bells warned them of a customer, and Evan dashed off to see about the new arrival. Meg made her way to an antique mirror at the back of the store.

Who was the woman starring back at her? Meg hardly recognized the shine in her own eyes, the high color accenting and sharpening her cheeks. She glanced at her neck and gasped.

When was the last time she had a love bite in plain view?

She couldn't remember. Maybe never. She rubbed at it, but it didn't come off. Not that it would.

"Wow," she whispered to her own reflection. Then she smiled. Quint left her feeling young and more alive than she had in a long time. She wanted to live every second of this newness of her marriage to the fullest. And despite the cloudy sky, she spent the rest of the day torn between anticipating the evening and spending the night at the Manor, and wanting to sing at the top of her lungs. And she couldn't stop thinking about her afternoon with Quint.

Quint had awakened her senses in every way. The rest of the afternoon, every book she touched left her relishing in its feel. She was aware of every soft, leather binding, every musty smell, and every delicate touch of parchment.

She fought the urge to call Montgomery Manor or Quint's cell just to talk to him, to hear his husky voice, and she told herself not to be let down when he didn't call her. He was bound to be busy with last minute details, just as she tried to finish her day and get to the Manor. She hoped this night was a perfect beginning for his—their—new business.

The afternoon dragged by. The unusual lack of customers in the shop didn't help.

Evan left at four, an hour earlier than his usual time.

The phone rang five minutes later.

Meg picked it up on the second ring. "Treasure Hunters." She half expected to hear Quint's voice asking her when she planned to leave. That was why the heavy breathing was such a surprise.

"Hello?"

The heavy breathing continued.

Heavy breathers didn't scare her; not now when she had so many other positive things on her mind. Besides, her phone number was very close to the number of the First National Bank. This was perhaps someone who dialed the wrong number and was afraid to say anything.

She tensed to hang up but a deep, whispered voice stopped her.

"Did you like the roses, Megan?" The way the caller whispered her full name sent chills snaking up her spine.

She'd been so caught up in her afternoon with Quint, she hadn't thought about the roses since she'd returned to the shop. "Who is this?"

"Have a good time at the grand opening of the Manor, Megan. I'll see you there. I'll be watching you."

The voice was rough and harsh, and the hushed whisper telegraphed threat. The phone went dead, leaving her heart pounding in its wake. She wondered who that was and why they called her.

Five minutes later, Meg taped a Montgomery Manor Grand Opening poster on the door to the shop. The call left her uneasy, and her hands trembled as she held up the poster. She wondered if she should tell Quint about it. The last thing she wanted to do was rain on his parade, he didn't need anything else to worry about tonight.

She turned down the shop lights and took her cash bag so she could make a late deposit on her way home. At the door, she looked back at the dark shop. This was the only time she didn't like the place, and the eerie feeling lingering in her from the phone call didn't help. In the dusk, when there was not yet complete darkness, the books seemed to grow in size and cast an array of unaccountable shadows. Her imagination could run amok in the shop in this light—or lack of it—if she let it. She took a deep breath, set the alarm, then stepped outside, pulling the door closed behind her. She slipped her key into the lock.

The rain that had threatened all day still hadn't come, but the wind blew up her skirt, and there was a crisp, moist smell to the air. Bits of fog slithered about like slow-moving snakes trying to swallow her feet up to her ankles. Somewhere close by, the wind scattered a few remaining stiff, dead leaves, and she recognized the sound as they scraped across the sidewalk. But though the streetlights were flickering on, she couldn't see the scattering leaves through the mist.

With the promise of things new and fresh, spring was her favorite time of year. But so far, winter's dreariness refused to let go. For the last few weeks, the days were blustery and rainy with bits of thunder and lightning tossed in. At least she'd been able to give up her winter coat for something lighter, but she always had to have an umbrella in her hand.

Tonight there was something heavy in the air, something she couldn't quite put her finger on. It was more than the hint of rain or fog or a storm or the chance of a temperature drop. She looked down the street again. Most of the other shops—the post office, the bakery, the dentist office, were already closed. Dim, eerie lights poured from their windows. A neglected newspaper blew its way up the gutter behind her, pulled by some unseen guide. The wind whistled through the rain gutter above her head, and she jumped.

She took a deep breath and told herself to get a grip, but the unspoken command didn't help. She felt like her insides were trying to shake loose from the rest of her body.

The small grocery store and the liquor store two blocks down were still open, but between here and there, the walk was empty. There was nothing but that scraping sound of leaves against the sidewalk, a sound reminiscent of nails on a chalkboard.

Meg tried to ignore it. It was natural, just leaves in the wind, right? Her hot sex with Quint had left her emotions on high alert all day, and now they joined the over-active imagination spurred by the strange phone call. The scratchy echo of the leaves scraping against the ground seeped to her, sending a shiver through her, and causing the hairs on the back of her neck to stand up, and her stomach to clench tight.

It had been a great afternoon, don't get jumpy now, just because it's growing dark and some creep is trying to scare you on the phone, she thought to herself. Meg hated the dark.

Her attempt at positive thoughts didn't help.

There was something else in the wind, something besides newspapers and gutters and leaves.

Or maybe someone.

The street was empty of people, at least as the part of the street she could see in the scraps of overhead light. She looked over at the other side of the street. No one there, either.

It didn't matter that no one was there, what mattered was what she *felt*.

And what she felt was the heavy gaze of someone studying her. Someone was watching her. She was certain of it. She felt it just as sure as she felt the wind caressing her legs.

Hadn't the voice on the phone said he would be watching her?

Perhaps he already was.

She tried laughing it off, but her false laughter was lost to the wind and failed to ease her mind in the least. "It's just because Quint watched me so weird earlier, like he sees right into my soul," she said out loud. But her words brought little comfort.

Fine, I'll be just fine. All I have to do is get to the car. Just get home.

What she needed was a quick hot bath before donning the softness of the black velvet dress Quint requested she wear to the grand opening...and the first night of her and Quint's new beginning.

She just needed to think about the afternoon, when she'd felt so secure and wild, so loved and wanted, in Quint's arms. Thoughts of Quint's kisses had her licking her lips longing for another kiss. But the cold sense of dread allowed for no sense of safety.

Feeling like a bird trying to fly against the wind, she dashed toward her car, one lonesome vehicle parked across the street and a half a block away. In the dark, eerie town, the distance seemed more like ten miles. She seemed to move slow motion despite her effort to run.

Something hit the concrete sidewalk behind her.

Was it a footstep?

Meg's heart raced quicker than her legs. She didn't venture a look back, terrified at what she might see if she did.

She reached her car. There was another sound along the pavement. Or at least she thought there was.

She was smart enough to have her keys out and ready, but when she moved to press the unlock button on her key fob, she dropped the key ring. They clattered to the pavement, the sound loud in the combination of wind and stillness surrounding her. Her heart skipped a beat before continuing to slam against her chest.

She held her breath and looked behind her.

Was that a movement she saw in the shadows of the alley beside her shop? Was there someone in the mist watching her?

She couldn't breathe. With stiff fingers that refused to obey her commands, she managed to grasp her keys and hit the right button.

Her cold and clammy palms almost slipped on the door handle, but she held her grip and pulled it open. She tossed her purse onto the seat and jumped in behind it. She didn't care in the least that she hadn't thrown her purse far enough, and was now sitting on it. Nor did she care that she'd caught her skirt in the door. She locked the door behind her.

She sat in the stillness of the car and willed her racing heart to slow. Damn, she could hear its pounding beat in the silence as blood rushed through her ears. She didn't even try to calm her breathing, it was useless. She had no choice but to sit in the quiet for a few long moments as her body calmed.

She stared out the windshield, but still saw no one. Despite the lack of people, she was positive she'd heard and seen something or someone in the alley beside her shop a moment ago.

And even now, she felt the presence of someone watching, someone waiting. But for what?

And why?

She had no answers, just as there had been no reason for that phone call.

"This is silly. There's no one there." Her voice was loud, and her words were breathless in the quiet car. "There's no reason for anyone to be there. And even if there was, what could they possibly want with me? It's just my imagination after that stupid call. I've just been reading too many classic horror stories, and my afternoon with Quint has left me feeling weird and tightly strung." She paused, then chuckled. "And now I'm talking to myself, too."

Her words did little to calm her nerves.

She had things to do before she could get to the Manor where Quint waited. And she wouldn't get any of it done sitting in the deserted street letting her imagination run wild. She slid the key into the ignition and started the car. The few drops of rain hitting her windshield told her the threatening storm was about to make good on its threats.

She put the car in gear and sped off for home. There was so much she had to do, and very little time in which to do it. She refused to look back, putting energy into calming herself before her night with Quint.

If Meg had looked back, she might have seen the dark figure that took two steps out of the dark alley and onto the sidewalk. A dark figure who's features were still hidden in the shadows, fog swirling about his legs, giving anyone who might see him cause to wonder if he were anything more than smoke.

She had known, he thought. She had known he was there watching. She had felt him. She was, indeed, smart. Smart, clever, quick and cunning, and, of course, beautiful. And she was in tune to him. He liked that.

He wondered if he would have been able to touch her. He wanted more than just to touch her, he realized. He wanted her, all of her. Just as he'd wanted her the first time he'd seen her. Just as there were so many other things he wanted, so many other things he planned to get his hands on. But he'd let her go now. Now was not the right time. Not yet.

But he didn't plan to let her slip away forever.

He wasn't quite ready to reach for her, that's all, he told himself. He wanted things to be perfect when he made her his. For now, he wanted only to watch her, to learn from her, to let her discover for herself that she belonged at Montgomery Manor. Now, he must practice patience, for his plan had already been set in motion. He would play it out so there'd be no mistake, so that all that should be his would be. Yet, when it came to Meg, he found patience impossible. Perhaps it was because he could not explain his want of her. To him, Meg was a life-giving need like food, water, or air. This desire for her was an odd sensation, one he had never felt before, one he wanted to explore.

He looked up at the sliver of the moon that trying to push past the clouds threatening it. And for the first time, his eyes caught the small twinkle of light.

No, as close as she'd been to him, tonight was not the right night for him to take her or to touch her. She wouldn't understand him, wouldn't want him.

He watched her drive away, watched until her taillights were small specks, soon disappearing altogether. And he smiled. His plan would work. Soon she would be his.

For now, he had a grand opening to attend. The bone-chilling rain that had finally made its appearance had no effect on him as he turned and allowed the fog to swallow him.

His trip to Montgomery Manor was uneventful.

He had waited for this night for so long.

Tonight was only the beginning.

He smiled as he looked up at the house in all its grandeur, lit with welcoming lights.

CHAPTER FOUR

Quint entered the old house through the front doors, relishing the feel of the door handle under his palm, as well as the different aromas touching him like warm fingers. There was the smell of polished wood, new linens, fresh paint, new furniture, spices from the kitchen—oregano, sage and garlic, and the scent of newness he couldn't quite define. Excitement rallied through him, sending waves of sensation all the way to his toes.

This house was his—and Meg's—and tonight was just the beginning. He was excited about showing it off and making the whole of it something wonderful. The thrill of being under its roof and sharing his accomplishment accelerated his heart rate. He looked around. The house had so much potential, so much character. Why Mitchell Greensburg had not done more with the house than open a few rooms and keep the restaurant running, he had no idea. Brad, the manager who'd worked for Greensburg for years, was an asset with many ideas, but Greensburg never put any of them into plan. Maybe Brad just never voiced them.

Brad Mills stood near the podium in the grand foyer. "Hey, you're back."

"I didn't want to leave in the first place, but you forced me to take a break and get out of here for a while, remember?"

Brad grinned. "Yeah, well I was worried if you didn't take a break your eyes would pop out and your head would shake from side to side a thousand times a minute like one of those cartoon characters."

Quint chuckled. "And did you get a break, too? You deserve one just as much as I do."

"Sure, but mine was just a cigarette break. You sure you don't want something to eat?" Brad glanced down at the list of people who'd RSVP'd to the night's gala. "You'll be greeting about two hundred people in the next—" he glanced down at his watch, "four or five hours. I'd hate to see the new, proud owner of this place pass out in front of all his patrons when his sugar hits the rocks."

"I'm fine," Quint gave the room a quick glance, noting that everything was in order according to his specifications. "I hope to meet that many people, if not more. I'm just eager to get this going. Is everything in the dining room ready?" He wondered if he would ever feel ready. He knew the more he looked around, the more he'd find to fix before his guests arrived.

"As ready as it can be, unless of course you want to try and finish off one more room and have it ready for the tour before people arrive."

Quint chuckled. "Not tonight, we'll save the north wing for next week." He stiffened and the smile left his face. "Oh, by the way, I appreciate your staying on as my manager."

Even though Quint appreciated Brad's expertise regarding the Manor, he couldn't figure out what the guy was doing there. With his dark hair and dark eyes, women seemed to be drawn to him. Even Quint's other female employees always worked their way around to Brad. He had an easy smile and charisma, and yet, he wasn't interested in one woman. He was polite, but he didn't flirt. Maybe he didn't like women. It wasn't Quint's business, so he pushed it from his mind and utilized Brad's talents where they mattered most—upgrading the Manor.

Brad gave him a nonchalant shrug. "I like this old place, it feels like home. Now if you don't mind, I think I'll grab a cup of coffee and head to the office to finish up paperwork before the crowd shows up."

Quint nodded. "Of course. I'm going to make a last-minute look around. I want to make sure the game room is in order, and all the old wooden games are ready for play. One more thing," he snagged Brad's attention before he was able to duck into the office. "Did you have someone lock up all the rooms that aren't on the tour?"

"Yes, of course. I checked them myself."

"Good thinking. Thank you."

A few moments later, Quint entered the dining room. He wanted to walk through the rooms his patrons would later tour and make sure everything was as it should be. This was his dream   his own business, a business with class and character, in a legendary house known throughout the east coast, if not the country. Why shouldn't it be perfect?

It might be nothing more than a big party, but it was *his* party, and he wouldn't get a second chance to make a great first impression. There was more than enough food to feed those expected to attend. The rich aroma of professionally crafted cuisine filled the entire first floor. There were musicians—not just a DJ—scheduled to start at nine and play until one in the morning, which would also be the same time the cash bar locked up the liquor.

Quint looked around the dining room lit by candles on each table and sconces on the wall. The flickering flames created the warm, romantic mood he wanted while maintaining the nostalgic atmosphere of the house. Who wouldn't be comfortable here? No one.

Everything was in place. For the remainder of the evening, all he had to do was smile, be polite, show the house, and let everyone know his plans for the future of Montgomery Manor. Everyone would marvel at the taste of the great food. The music would keep people dancing. The atmosphere would add a sense of welcome as well as mystery, inviting everyone to explore. The house was well on its way back to its original grandeur.

Then Quint would be home.

He smiled and thought of Meg. He imagined sharing this house with her and their future children.

It would be *their* home.

And it would be home for anyone who stayed there. Why wouldn't it feel like home? The rooms were warm and comfortable, and the brand new beds were covered with new sheets and pretty, homey quilts—not heavy, ugly spreads that were found on the beds in most hotels.

Quint left the dining room and reentered the foyer, moving his attention to the front doors. Soon Meg would walk through them. So much about the house had been changed, redone. But not the doors. He loved those double front doors. They were nothing less than a work of art. Complete with huge knockers resembling the faces of lions, the doors stood several feet over Quint's head, so he guessed they had to be eight or nine feet, considering he was right at six. Made of thick planks of oak, they looked to weigh a thousand pounds, but they opened without much effort. They were marked with age but they still fit the archway perfectly. Every time he looked at them, he couldn't help but wonder at the tales they could tell if only they could speak. They could probably tell countless stories of all those who had passed through them. He wondered if the doors could feel the anger or pain or fear or happiness left by those who had touched them. He wondered to whom they had barred entrance or refused escape.

He knew Vivian Leigh had passed through the doors and that she had slept the night in what was now the Sunflower room. It was one of many things he knew without knowing how he knew it. He dreamed of this place and he just *knew*. Now, as he looked at those doors, he admired them. They were one of many things that gave the house its character. So he didn't change them, he left them as they were; sentinels of oak, watching over Montgomery Manor.

Quint couldn't wait to share this with Meg. More than once, he thought of taking a break and calling her. But he didn't. Oh, how he wanted to hear her deep, sexy voice. What he didn't need was his own reaction to it. A hard on was the last thing he needed when he shook the mayor's hand. More than once over the past three months, he considered sharing the whole design and remodeling process with her, rather than try and surprise her on opening night.

Not that it made any difference now. She'd be there soon; he'd share it with her then. What if she didn't like it? What if she didn't like the suite he'd furnished for them? What would he do if she didn't like even a single thing about it? He'd let her change it and fix it anyway she wanted, that's what.

He tried to push thoughts of Meg from his mind, working to concentrate on the night ahead, on this being the start and the first impression of his business. But to forget about Meg and the afternoon they shared was an impossible task. He still tasted Meg on his lips, and his groin tightened, his cock hardened. Her passion was a wild fire in his soul, and it took every ounce of will power he had to not claw at the top button of his shirt and the tie at his throat.

He grinned. This afternoon had been the wildest afternoon of his life. The memory of it played over and over in his mind. At one point in their intimate moment, he thought he managed to escape his own body and watch himself making passionate love to his own wife.

This afternoon was only the beginning of what he wanted to share with Meg. There would no more going weeks without making love. In fact there would be no going twenty-four hours.

He took a deep breath in an effort to curb his need for Meg. It didn't help.

Brad was right, Quint needed another quick break. He wanted to calm his nerves with a glass of brandy and a cigar, but he settled, instead, for a glass of ice water. He forced himself to drink it, instead of pouring it down the front of his pants as he needed to.

Meg inched the car up to the gatehouse.

Light poured from its small windows, exuding warmth and welcome. Quint had given it a layer of new paint and new, small shutters graced its tiny windows. Dark green, leafy ivy climbed up one side. A man stepped out the arched wooden door and watched her approach, but he remained under the eaves, sheltered from the mist until Meg stopped and rolled down her window.

"Good evening, Mrs. Falkner." His words were slow and precise, and "evening" was slightly accented. He stood straight and distinguished, reminding her of a butler answering a front door. He wore a dark cape over his gray, buttoned up coat. He fit in well with a presumably haunted house.

Meg smiled hesitantly. "And you are?"

"I'm Theo, the gatekeeper." His gray hair blew in the wind, and the small grin he offered her revealed a dimple in his left cheek. "Of course my job isn't the same as the gatekeeper back in the day when the house was built. Now I have a computer and intercom linked to the restaurant or the front desk so I can let them know who's arriving."

"That sounds easy."

"So far it's working out very well. Your husband told me to be expecting you about this time. He said to direct you to park in the old carriage house. Just follow the drive, and it will be on your left before you reach the house. The doors are open."

"Thank you." She rolled up her window to keep out the heavy mist in the air. The huge double doors of the carriage house were open, just as Theo said they'd be. Meg drove in and parked next to Quint's truck. The room was about the size of a gymnasium, and soft lantern-like lights hung from the walls, casting an eerie glow in the large space. She stepped out of her car and stared around at the old building.

"I guess I don't have to worry about busting the mirror off the car in here like I do the garage at the house." Her words echoed in the shadows.

Two old carriages masquerading as dark forms were parked at the far end of the building. The sweet, musty smell in the air wasn't unpleasant. The carriage house was appropriately named, and she couldn't help but think she'd somehow traveled back in time. Her car seemed out of place.

Her heart pounded in her chest.

My husband and I own this—all of this. She fought the urge to giggle.

She was afraid she'd wake up and find this was all a dream. She looked around again. This was just the carriage house, and it was *so big*. Truth be told, it still scared her.

She stepped out of the carriage house and looked up at the massive Manor before her. The shutters hugging the windows looked new and were larger versions of those gracing the gatehouse. A welcoming candle-like light glowed in every window at the front of the house. The stone appeared new, too, although Meg knew those stones were from a previous century. The gables that, in the past, appeared weathered and beaten, were now strong and standing proud in the falling darkness. The two gargoyles perched on the north and south corner towers stared down at her through the dark.

Meg studied the house wondering how she ever thought it menacing. On the contrary, it was, "Beautiful..." she whispered into the gathering mist. She didn't waste any more time heading toward the door. The rain had been in at her shop when she left, so she knew it wouldn't be long before it reached the Manor. She inhaled and couldn't mistake the subtle smell of oregano mixed with the approaching rain and the salty scent of the nearby ocean that she heard crash upon the cliff rocks.

Her heart fluttered with anticipation as she moved up the front steps. She smiled at the change in the front walk with the addition of a handicap ramp. She knew it was new, and yet it graced the front of the house in a half circle matching the design in such a way it showed no contrast of modern. She made her way to the massive front doors. A man wearing a uniform that matched the gatekeeper greeted her with, "Welcome, Mrs. Falkner," as he opened the door for her.

"Thank you."

She stepped into the welcoming lit foyer and slid her shawl from her shoulders. Her black heels made little sound on the wood floor. No one stood near the podium but to the left of the foyer was a small registration desk. The girl behind it had a pencil perched behind her left ear and was busy at the computer terminal. She looked up at Meg's approach. "Good evening, Mrs. Falkner."

Meg was surprised Quint's employers knew her. "I'm afraid I'm at a disadvantage. Everyone seems to know me, but I don't know anyone else."

The girl smiled and popped the gum she chewed. Her blonde ponytail bobbed behind her head as she moved and her bangs crowned her thin face. "I'm Molly."

"It's nice to meet you." Meg looked around, taking in people, lights, decorations. Do you know where my husband is?" She didn't want to search the house own for him on her own. The thought only gave her shivers. She envisioned herself wandering around for hours, lost, and never finding Quint *or* the way out.

"I saw him about twenty minutes ago. He might be in the dining room. I know they're setting up food in there. He's got his cell phone. Do you want me to call him?"

"No, thanks." Meg smiled and shifted her over-night bag from one hand to the other. "I'll take my chances of finding him in the dining room." *I can always call him on my cell.*

She didn't want to have to call him, though. She didn't want to pull out her cell phone at all. With the Victorian furniture and the old-fashioned woodwork and the soft lighting, modern technology seemed out of place.

She turned from the registration desk and moved a few steps before stopping. A small bar was tucked into the corner. The bartender wore a crisp white shirt with garters on his arms and black slacks with suspenders. He grinned at her.

"Don't tell me you know who I am, too." Meg let out a breath and hoped she didn't sound annoyed.

"It's nice ta see ye in person, Mrs. Falkner, and I'm glad ye finally get ta see the marvelous work yer husband has done wi' the place. I hope ye like it." His words were thick with an Irish accent. He tipped an imaginary hat to her. "Can I offer ye a drink, something ta warm ye on this wet night?"

Meg was, indeed, feeling the need for a drink. The house could be so overwhelming if she let it. Unfortunately, the last thing she needed for Quint's opening night was to be tipsy in front of all his patrons. She settled for a club soda with a twist of lime. The bartender made it in a tall, beautiful glass, and set down on the bar.

"You haven't seen my husband, have you?"

"I believe he's in the dining room."

"Is it in the same place it was before?" She should have asked Quint for a map.

He grinned at her again, his green eyes sparkling. She had no doubt he'd have little trouble serving the ladies tonight or any other night.

"Yea, but things look different getting there now. Yer husband has done a remarkable job restoring many of these rooms ta their original grandeur." He wiped the bar with a white towel but never took his attention from her.

"I can hardly wait to see it."

"Anyway, take that doorway there and walk straight across what's known as the fountain court. Now, there're two doorways in there, and you'll want ta go through the one straight across. That one leads ta the dining room."

"Thanks." She took her drink and headed off to follow his directions. A short jaunt later, she turned the corner and stopped just inside a doorway. The fountain court took her breath away. Beautiful lights accented with antique brass hung from the ceiling, casting a soft glow on the many plants. Large ferns and small potted trees surrounded a fountain of a beautiful woman pouring water from a pitcher. Meg ran her palm along the marble rail surrounding the fountain. It was smooth and cool and damp beneath her touch. Several of the larger trees were lit with strands of small white lights. The soft sound of flowing water was tranquil and inviting. The benches surrounding the fountain would fill with people enjoying the beauty of the room.

It will be a wonderful place for patrons to wait for open tables.

"Just think how we could decorate this for the holidays." Meg didn't mean to speak out loud as she stood imagining how gold and silver ornaments would look in the many trees.

She tried to take in every detail of the room as she moved through it, but she failed. It would take much longer than a few stolen moments. She moved through the door the bartender indicated. The rich smells of spices and bread and coffee grew stronger.

She passed through another arched doorway, and stopped to take in the lavish dining room. It was nothing like the dining room she'd eaten in those so many months ago. Gone were the plain square tables covered with vinyl red and white checkered tablecloths. Now, in a perfect display of balance, the monstrous room was set with beautiful oak tables of various sizes and shapes. There were small tables for two, big oval tables that could seat eight, and booths hugging the far wall. Each table held an array of candles, adding a hint of romance to the soft lighting trickling down from the three large chandeliers hanging from the ceiling and the sconces on the walls. Fire crackled in the two fireplaces, one at each end of the room. She noticed there were gas logs in the fireplaces, which made them easier to maintain while still adding warmth to the large room.

She pivoted to take in the room.

From across the room, she met Quint's gaze.

It was impossible for her to look away.

Never looking away, he drew closer.

My God, he looks dangerous. Perfect, wonderful, mysterious, handsome. And dangerous.

"You look like a dream dressed in black velvet," he said when he reached her. His gaze lingered over every inch of her body, from her toes in her heels to the crown of hair on her head.

How he managed to heat her up with nothing more than a look, she didn't know.

He leaned in, his lips sliding over the tip of her ear. "I love that dress on you. It reveals every perfect curve." His whisper, like the velvet of her dress, slid over her skin and burned her insides. "Later, when we're alone, that scooped neckline will give me easy access."

She meant to set the over-night bag down, but it dropped from her hand, plopping onto the floor. He took her drink and set it down on a nearby table before she spilled it. His nearness and his hot whisper turned her to jelly. He kissed her softly.

Two kisses in public in one day. When he allowed the kiss to end, he left her legs feeling weak. She sucked in a breath.

"I can't believe what you've done with this place." Her words were breathy. "It's beautiful."

"*You're* beautiful." He squeezed her hands in his.

The hungry look in his gaze drew heat into her face. She felt like an untried schoolgirl. "Thank you."

She took another deep breath and noticed the way the dress hugged her breasts. She also noticed the way Quint watched the fabric tighten over her chest. Fire exploded within her.

She licked her lips, but it didn't help cool her. "It smells wonderful in here. When do we have dinner?" She didn't really want dinner. She wanted him alone.

"Let me show you to our room, then I'll see that you have something to eat. By the way, where'd you get the drink?" Quint bent and picked up her over-night bag.

With his reminder, she reached out and took her glass again. "From the bar just past the front desk." She took a sip.

Quint looked at her. "What, did you pour it yourself?"

Meg let out short laugh. "Of course not. Your handsome bartender poured it for me. He's very nice. I'm sure he'll be busy all night flirting with the ladies. And they'll be falling all over themselves to hear his accent."

"I don't have a bartender assigned to work there until closer to dinner service. I didn't want people drinking until after they've had a chance to eat. And I want everyone to get past the foyer and see the place before they get drunk."

"Well, there *was* a bartender, and he spoke with an Irish brogue." A cold chill skittered up her spine, like a hundred tiny spiders were working their way up to her neck. "I talked to him. He knew you. He complimented everything you've done with the house so far. And he knew who I was."

"I don't even have an Irish bartender."

A mixture of terror and anger sliced through her, making her shiver and leaving her hot at the same time. The last thing she wanted was to ruin the night for Quint, but when she'd finally recognized the beauty of this house and gotten over her fear, she didn't need to think about any ghosts. "So what are you saying, I was served by a ghost? And Molly, at the front desk, is she a ghost, too?"

"Maybe."

Meg let out a huff and fought down both the anger and the fear. She didn't need either, not now. She forced a laugh, trying to see a positive side of this. It wasn't really too hard to do, considering she was drinking a *real* drink.

"Oh, I see what you're doing here, trying to make the house really seem haunted. That would be a great way to draw a crowd." She forced another laugh, but goose flesh rose on her arms. "This drink is very real and tastes good, just like I like it." To prove her point, she finished off the last few swallows and set down the empty glass. "It might work on everyone here tonight, but don't try it any more on me. Besides, did it ever occur to you Brad might have hired someone?"

"I'm not trying anything," Quint said, getting back to the topic of the unknown bartender, "except that I have no idea who served your drink. Not that it matters. All that matters is that you drink and eat hearty." He leaned close and whispered in her ear, "You'll need your energy for later."

How was it possible that more heat rose into her face?

"I'm glad you don't mind staying overnight."

More warmth swirled through her middle. "I figured since I own half this place, I can stay whenever I want. And if you and I have a fight, I have plenty of rooms to pick from."

"That's true, but we are not going to do any fighting." Then, right there, in public, in the midst of the restaurant and Quint's many employees attempting to get ready for the public due to arrive any moment, he kissed her again.

Not just a simple kiss like his greeting a few minutes earlier, either. It was a scorching, passionate kiss. The last time he'd done anything so personal in public was when the reverend had pronounced them man and wife and instructed him to kiss his wife. But then, he'd kissed her in her store earlier, too. Three public kisses, two being very passionate, in one day? Not to mention with the many kisses and…more…they'd had at lunch in bed. She wasn't certain who this man kissing her now was, but she liked him. Just thinking about their afternoon together and the way he held her now caused her heart to slam against the wall of her chest. Her nipples tingled. She was hot, but shivering at the same time.

He teased her with his tongue.

Meg pulled away before she could melt to the floor. She stared into his eyes, trying to see if the man he used to be still existed in there. "Careful, there," she warned.

"Or what? I have lay you down on one of the tables and make love to you right here in the dining room?"

The warmth of his kiss, the taste of him on her lips, lingered in her soul. She swallowed hard. Was he serious? What she saw in his eyes was Quint, her husband, her lover. He was familiar and new at the same time, just like the house. Yet, there was something else about him—he was dressed as she'd seen him earlier that day, only now his long, dark hair was tied back in a que, it's length reaching just the middle of his collar—he *belonged* here. He was, beyond the shadow of a doubt, a perfect host and owner for the place.

At the same time, he wasn't her husband. He was not the same man who sat on the sofa watching talk shows all last winter. He was not the same man who refused to help in her store.

He was, well, *different*. There was a fire in his eyes and a determination in his stance she'd never seen before.

And there was a hunger, the way he looked at her, that had never been there. She'd experienced the new hunger first hand during their intimate lunch that afternoon. They'd been married five years. They'd shared a terrific honeymoon and slept together in the same bed every night. And while their sex wasn't bad, she'd never known the hunger she saw in him now. Nor had she ever felt what he'd given her at lunch.

"Who are you and what did you do with my husband?" She tried to make light of his sensual invitation.

"I traded him in on a new model." Quint stared down at her. His gaze boring into her, heating her, stealing her breath.

Is he serious?

"Would you like for me to make love to you on this table over here or that bigger one over there?" He pointed first to a small table for two right behind Meg before he indicated the round table for eight several feet away.

He really was serious.

Meg's cheeks burned. Her stomach clenched and unclenched in her belly. "Do you think anyone would notice?" She forced a weak laugh, praying he was just joking with her.

"All I have to do is tell them to leave, and they will."

Damn, he really was serious. Meg trembled.

"Do you kiss all the customers?" a voice behind Quint asked before Meg could reply.

Quint turned and the moment was swept away, although he kept one arm around Meg's waist as if he couldn't bear to let her go. Not only was his smile was more charming than Meg had ever seen, but something else was different about it, too. It was a little crooked. "Meg, you remember my manager, Brad Mills. Brad, my wife, Meg."

"It's a pleasure to meet you again." Brad shook her hand warmly. "I can't believe Quint has managed to keep this a surprise from you all these months. Weren't you the least bit curious?"

Meg had forgotten how easily a woman could get lost in Brad's endless, dark eyes. She wasn't the least bit attracted to him, but she could see how other women would be. And she bet he, alone, could draw a lunch crowd of women just wanting to see the host who might show them to their tables. "Oh, I was way beyond curious, but he made me promise to stay away. Although you'll never believe how hard it was not to sneak a peek during the day to check things out. Seeing it now, I am glad I did stay away. This is a wonderful surprise, probably one of the best I've ever had. I love the fountain room." She glanced around at the polished woodwork and the fresh paint. "Everything looks beautiful, but still fits with the décor of the house."

"Well, you've certainly got quite a worker for a husband, and he's full of fantastic ideas. Not to mention, he was kind enough to keep all of the employees on as well as add a few new ones."

Quint gave her small squeeze, tucking her closer against him. "There was no reason not to. And if you see any changes you think might work better, just let me know. I'm always open to suggestions."

Brad smiled at Meg. "Well, I'm glad you're here." He turned his attention to Quint. "I'm going to have Susan start setting out the food."

"That's a great idea. I'm going to show Meg our room, then I'll bring her back down to sample some of it."

"See you later, Meg." Brad moved toward what must have been the kitchen.

They passed the fountain to reach the huge grand staircase. Meg glanced into the foyer, catching just a glimpse of the bar. No bartender. In fact, the lights above it were off, and it was devoid of life.

"What are you looking for?" He asked, noticing her glance at the darkened bar.

She grinned. "Maybe I did get my drink from a ghost."

He chuckled then took her hand and led her up the stairs.

The second floor was wonderful, with bright, flowered wallpaper. Wall sconces lit the way. There were velvet chairs and narrow hall tables placed about, decorated with doilies, various plants, and vases of fresh flowers. The ceiling was high and white, with sparkling swirls in the plaster that reflected the soft light from the sconces. Three still life paintings adorned the landing.

Meg studied each one. After the third, she stopped and turned her attention to her husband. "You are clearly a miracle worker. You took this old, broken house and made it new again. Everything's so beautiful. I can hardly wait to see our room."

"I'm glad you like it."

Meg felt like a child at Christmas who discovered a hundred presents under the tree. "I still can't believe all you've done in such a short time. This is wonderful. I'm sorry I couldn't have helped you with it."

"You can help from here on out, but I'm glad I could surprise you."

"It was a wonderful surprise. Thank you. Which room is ours?"

"Ours is what was once Joshua Montgomery's master suite." Quint strode down the hall, still holding Meg's hand as he carried her bag in his other hand. They passed five doors, all of which stood ajar, revealing bedrooms decorated to coordinate with each other. Quint stopped in front of a closed door at the end of the long, empty hallway.

"The master suite?" Meg's words were nothing more than a whisper as she took in the ornate handle and the handcrafted arched door.

He smiled down at her, his eyes still filled with their unique dark blue sparkle. He paused, his hand on the crystal knob. "I know you might not be ready for a move to this place, but I worked on this room just for you. If you don't like it or want something different, just say so." He turned the knob and pushed open the door, inching the opening wider heartbeats at a time, until the secrets of the room revealed themselves to her.

The entire apartment took Meg's breath away. Decorated in shades of soft yellow, the bedroom held unmistakable energy, like the sun. The bed was large, covered with a patchwork quilt—each block a different pattern with yellow or gold—and a soft yellow crocheted canopy. The woodwork was dark and elegantly carved to match the house's late nineteenth-century roots. A mirror hung over an elaborate, large dresser. A washstand, complete with a ceramic bowl and pitcher and yellow hand towels occupied one corner. The wall at the far end was rounded, it must've been part of the tower that made up the northeast corner of the house. It created a nook that was a complete room. Two chairs and a small table filled the space beneath a large window. Two glasses, a bottle of champagne in a silver ice bucket, and a large clear glass bowl filled with perfect red strawberries covered the table.

Quint led her to the window. "I know it's too dark to see, but there's a magnificent view out this window. Wait until you see the sunrise from here."

Meg let out a breath of awe. "Saying this room is beautiful is a bit of an understatement."

"I'm glad you like it."

"What's through there?" Meg pointed to a nearby door.

"A kitchen and a sitting area for if you ever want to live here. There's also a bedroom on the other side that would be easily accessible, too, as well as the several rooms further down that we passed."

All in all, the apartment was beautiful and welcoming.

"I love it. I can't get over how this apartment alone is about the same size as our house." Meg let go of his hand and moved about the large room. She looked around, gently ran her hand across the softness of the quilt on the bed. "I was just thinking this morning of adding more furniture to my bookstore and these pieces are just what I had in mind. These, however, aren't old, and I was looking to put in a few genuine antiques to go with my books."

She looked at Quint. He was gazing down at her, his blue eyes darker and more mysterious than ever. Without looking away, he set her over-night bag down.

"I knew you'd like it." His voice was deeper than usual, sounding a great deal like his whispers of earlier that afternoon when they were in bed. She wasn't so certain he was talking about the bedroom set or the color as he talked about knowing she'd like it. She had the idea he was referring to the way he held her and kissed her and made love to her.

She had to clear her throat before she could ask, "You did?" She raised a questioning brow. "How?"

He shrugged as if it was no big deal, but he never took his gaze from hers. "I haven't lived with you for five years and not learned of a few of your likes. We've even got our own bathroom, a nice large one, as a matter of fact." He nodded toward another door. "Right through there. Not every room in the house has that."

"So do you want to move in here, I mean for good?" She should have expected as much.

"You sound uncertain."

She didn't point out that he hadn't answered her question. "Well, I have to admit, this is all wonderful, but it's almost like a dream, too. Sometimes, I can't help but wonder if it isn't all too good to be true. I mean who leaves a house like this to virtual strangers? It still scares me."

He looked at her squarely. "Yes, it is wonderful, and yes, it is true. I'd be lying if I said I didn't want to live here." He moved closer and pulled her into his arms. "But only with you, Meggie girl. And I want you to know, the week before we closed for the major remodeling, I watched the people here. Everyone enjoys this house. Even without all the work that we've done in the last months, and even with the idea that the place might very well be haunted, people love to come here; and they enjoy themselves when they're here. They want to look around and explore and take a good look at the past by seeing it in this place."

He held her closer and Meg felt his words rumble through his chest as she pressed her face against him. "I'd be lying if I said I didn't enjoy being here, too." His voice was softer, gentle. Calming. "But I want you share it with me. Of course if you're not certain about the idea of living here, you can just take your time thinking about it."

A rumble of distant thunder rolled through the room as if in reply.

"I'm just afraid I might get lost in this place." Meg breathed in the alluring, familiar scent of his aftershave. "But I'll think about it."

"Good. Besides, I'm still learning the layout of this place, too. We can take our time and study it together. Draw a few maps if need be." Still holding her within his arms, he reached up with his hand and cupped her cheek. "Have I told you how incredibly beautiful you look tonight?"

Her heart pounded in her chest, and again she felt like that untried schoolgirl on a date. Before today she couldn't remember the last time he'd told her she was beautiful. "Yes, you did, but thank you again."

"I love your hair like this, pulled back from your face but still flowing down your shoulders and back." He slid his fingers through it. "It looks like dark fire."

Dark fire? His *eyes* sparkled with dark blue fire.

"You should wear it like this all the time." He gathered her hair and held it in his fist, holding her in place.

"I will when I'm with you," she promised. "But at work, it's easier to have it up or tied back out of the way."

He studied her for a long moment, gazing at her intently with a look of utter contentment on his face. Then he bent and captured her lips with his. His kiss was slow and warm as he tasted and explored her mouth. She couldn't move away, even if he wasn't still holding her hair.

His kiss lingered over her mouth, then slid down her jaw to her throat, below her ear—she shivered beneath the million butterflies she felt fluttering in her belly, along her skin, into her chest.

"And I never noticed how much this dress makes the gray of your eyes look so deep and wild, like a thunderstorm."

She grinned at his whispered words. "All right, stop it, you're embarrassing me talking like this. All day, you've looked at me like you've never seen me before."

"Okay, I'll stop talking." He let go of her hair and moved his hand to her chin. Gently ever so gently, he tilted her chin up and brought his lips back to hers.

Though his touch had been gentle, this kiss was not, far from it. Hard and searching and filled with need, he ravished her mouth with his, setting her soul on fire.

A flash of lightning lit up the room for an instant as the building storm worked to take hold. A much louder clap of thunder followed in its wake. The storm was getting closer.

For the life of her, Meg couldn't determine if the storm was real or if Quint had somehow set off a maelstrom inside her.

His mouth covered hers, deepening their kiss; the pressure of his lips sending electricity into her blood.

He was delicious. He tasted of Quint and…mint.

The emotion and sensations awakened in his simple kiss were stronger than anything he'd made her feel in the past five years except for what he'd shared with her that afternoon. She wanted to melt right into him, somehow become a part of him. His kiss was hot and wanting. With the mere touch of his lips, the slight tickle of his tongue, he somehow touched her heart with more mastery than he had in the dining room. He released her, leaving her lips tingling, and her body craving more.

It took her several seconds to catch her breath. True, they weren't in the dining room where she had her choice of tables to make love on, but there was a bed two strides away. All Quint had to do was lean her back, lift the skirt of her dress, and pull down her panties.

"As much as I'd love to make love to you right now, Meg," he remarked, as if he read her mind, "I want to save it for later, when I can savor every touch and not rush down to my guests."

He rubbed his thumb along the side of her lip, cleaning a smear of lipstick. The touch was as erotic as his kiss.

I'd better step away, or he won't have to lift my skirt. She'd do it for him.

It took a moment before she could think enough to form a coherent sentence. "Do you think the weather will keep anyone away?"

"I think a storm with a house like this would be very fitting, it'll add to the decor. Maybe more people will book rooms and stay the night if it storms, which will be great since I have a breakfast buffet planned. I'll announce it to everyone later." He pulled away, but not too far. "Would you care to see the rest of the house now, or wait until other guests arrive and have something to eat first?"

At that moment, she didn't care about seeing the house or eating. She wanted to melt to the floor and make love with him, but something about the way he asked told her he wanted her to see the house. He wanted to show it to her.

"I'd like to see the house, with you as my personal tour guide. I can always nibble later."

He held her gaze locked in his own, knowing full well that the word nibble had nothing to do with eating in the dining room with the other patrons. "Oh, Meg, I plan to do a bit of nibbling, too."

She raised her brows and let a seductive "Mmmm... Sounds wonderful. I can't wait." The mood lightened. The passion, however, remained, joining the energy of the approaching storm.

His hand on the small of her back directed her as she preceded him out of the room.

CHAPTER FIVE

Quint leaned in close behind Meg and breathed in the fragrant, flowery scent of her hair. He felt her heat through her black velvet dress. Everything about her was soft and inviting. He fought against the need to pull her back into the room, press her to their bed, and make her his. Completely. But he had to take things step by step.

Yes, he planned to make love to her.

He planned to do *more* than make love to her.

In fact, he planned for so much more. Making love to Meg and moving her into the house was just the beginning.

But now, his guests were waiting.

CHAPTER SIX

"This dining area was what used to be Joshua Montgomery's dining room, built to seat up to a hundred people at one long table." Quint explained something about every room he showed her.

"Gosh." Meg looked around and worked to absorb everything. "What about all the paintings? Any of them originals?"

"Not down here, but there are a few up in the Bed and Breakfast rooms that were locked in the attic and hidden between the floor joists."

"How do you know so much about everything?"

Quint shrugged. "Just what I've heard. Everyone who comes in here seems to know a little bit and always has a story to tell. Brad has been a great help, too. He has studied this house. Besides, there are also a couple books about the house on sale here in the small gift shop on the other side of the restaurant, and I spent some time reading through them before I started the work. I wanted to get the house as close to its original grandeur as possible."

"I thought you didn't like books."

He had made that clear when it came to stepping into her shop. Evan's words about Quint being jealous tumbled through her mind before she could stop them.

"Maybe I just never read the right ones." Quint took a moment to study the carving in the wood paneling decorating the room. "Besides, before I had a business of my own, I didn't understand how important something could be. Now I know how your shop must be for you."

He reached out and took her hand, and she noticed the strength in his grasp. His palm was covered in fresh calluses.

She knew from experience that people changed; they didn't need to be possessed by ghosts to transform or think differently. She knew she wasn't the same person she was when she and Quint got married, just as she wasn't the same person she was when she started her book business years before. Her business changed her in some subtle way each and every day, just as owning and working on this house was doing for Quint. She leaned against him for a moment and sighed contently.

"I can't believe how much this place as changed you. Evan even suggested you might be possessed by one of the ghosts here, are you?"

He stopped suddenly and turned to her. "Yes, however did you guess?" His voice was deeper than usual. That new crooked grin was firmly in place. "I'm possessed by the ghost of Joshua Montgomery, but don't let that secret out of the bag until we have a long list of loyal patrons."

He took her in his arms and leaned her back in a deep dip as if they were dancing. His kiss was hard and quick. Then he pulled her upright so fast, it left her dizzy. She giggled. He chuckled with her, his eyes twinkling with laughter as he took her hand.

"Come on, guests have started to arrive, and there's more I want to show you before I'm forced to give the tour to everyone else."

More thunder tried to work its way into the old house. Rain clattered and poured down the windows. The storm had arrived.

"Do you think what they say about Joshua Montgomery is true?" She held his hand and paid little attention to the direction he led her.

"What? Do I think he killed his wife?"

"The world believed he did enough to hang him," she pointed out.

He stared at her. "No, I don't."

"You say that with so much certainty. Gosh, you didn't even have to think about it."

"A man with the connections and the brains Joshua Montgomery possessed could have gotten rid of his wife without incriminating himself if that was what he wanted, which I doubt." Quint gripped her hand tighter and led her across the room. "Not to mention, he didn't have to kill her if he just wanted to get rid of her. With his money, he could've set her up in a house on the West Coast where he never had to see her again. But I think he loved her."

Quint stopped and looked at her.

"I thought perhaps with all the excavation and redoing you might've unearthed the answer to the great mystery as to who killed Ellen Montgomery." Meg searched his eyes for answers, and thought she saw a hint of something there.

Quint didn't speak for another long moment. "I'm not certain I need to know or that I need to unearth anything. I look around and see other things that are so much more important."

"You don't think that his standing over her with a bloody knife in his hand was evidence enough to hang him?" Meg matched his steps as they toured the house.

Quint grinned. "Meggie, we've seen enough movies where some poor innocent sap pulls the knife out trying to save the victim."

Meg grinned back. "I think the bartender who served me the drink is actually a ghost, and maybe if I see him again, I can ask him to tell me what happened."

"You might draw a bigger crowd if you just put out the story that we have a ghost for a bartender," Quint suggested. "But if you do see him and decide to say anything to him, remind him not to serve any more drinks until people have had a chance to sample the food."

This time when they walked past that bar on their way down, Melanie Wirthington manned it. Again, Meg's Irish friend was nowhere to be seen. There was, however, a vase of roses now sitting on the bar, a vase of roses like those Meg had received earlier that day.

Melanie greeted them with a wide smile. "Meg, these roses were delivered for you."

CHAPTER SEVEN

Quint fingered one velvet rose. "So who's the secret admirer?"

"I have no idea." Meg stared at the flowers, but didn't touch them. "There were roses delivered to me at the book shop today, too."

She wanted to tell him about the mysterious phone call, but now just didn't seem like the right time. He was too excited, too eager for this night to begin. The last thing she wanted was to put a dark cloud over his evening—despite the real storm raging outside.

She pulled the card from the clip in the center of the bouquet, and read it. "Enjoy the evening."

"That's all it says?" Quint leaned down and inhaled the scent of roses.

"That's it. The roses at the shop were just as mysterious. Maybe the ghost bartender sent them." Meg tried to make a joke of the situation.

Quint didn't laugh. She could tell by his silence and pursed lips that he was bothered by the unsigned card, and they had no idea who'd send roses to her. Quint took the card and read it a second time. "Let me know if you receive anything else."

Again, she debated telling him about the phone call, but she was determined not to ruin the evening for him. In fact, she didn't want to think about the roses or the phone call at all—or the mystery person behind them. This night was already so magical, and it was just beginning. This night belonged to her and Quint. No outside issues should be allowed to interfere and ruin their enchanted night.

She smiled at him and squeezed his hand. "Let's just leave these here on the bar for everyone to see and enjoy, and you can show me more of the house."

He smiled back, but his grin was hesitant, some of the charm dimmed. The look in his eyes reached out and grabbed her, his gaze was intense, imploring, almost angry—he didn't look like her husband at all. It held her spellbound for long moments. She managed to tear her gaze away and let out the breath she discovered she'd been holding. Fighting to keep her hand from shaking, Meg slid the vase to the center of the bar. "There, that's a good spot."

She moved away. "Come on, forget the flowers and show me some more of the house before you have to show it to everyone."

"All right." He gave the vase of roses one last glare. "The original kitchen was in the basement, and the kitchen for the restaurant before wasn't in too bad of shape. I only had to replace a few appliances. Which one would you like to see?"

She took his hand. "The original one."

Quint's true smile returned. "That's what I thought. You'll like it."

Meg forced an answering grin, wondering how he knew when she wasn't sure why it even made a difference. Kitchens were kitchens, right? The truth was, though, that she didn't want to see the new stuff, she wanted to see the old parts of the house. "Show me the history of the house, the way Joshua Montgomery built it. Unless, of course, you'd rather take me back upstairs to our room and make love to me." She didn't think he'd take her up on her offer, but she wanted to erase the worried look that still lingered in his eyes after reading the card that accompanied the flowers.

"Hmm...Temping. Very temping," he muttered. "But I'd better stick to the tour."

Quint led her down a narrow and bare wood staircase. The musty, almost-moldy scent in the air filled Meg with a strange sense of loss. All this space, all empty now, used only by spiders building webs.

"These were servants' stairs. Be careful. The stairs themselves don't need any work, but I do plan to install a better banister." Quint held her arm to steady her as they descended.

She felt the heat of his hand on her arm. "Are they safe?"

He offered her a reassuring smile. "The first thing I checked was every set of stairs in this house. I didn't need something to collapse and someone get hurt. And rest assured, Meggie, Joshua Montgomery built this house to last more than one century. The stairs are all safe and sound."

Meg looked down. "Do the dumbwaiters lead down here?" The emptiness in the narrow stairway echoed back her hollow words.

"Yes, three. And they still work. I'll show you. Montgomery and his wife loved to entertain, and he made sure the house was equipped with every necessity—four ovens, two stoves, work space for a few dozen servants, and cabinets to shelve several sets of China. He never skimped on a thing."

She paused and looked at him. "Just how many books about this house did you read?"

Quint met her gaze. "All of them."

Was he the same man who refused to come into her shop or crack open a single book?

No doubt he noticed her surprised expression. He grinned. "Did you think I didn't know how to read, Meggie?"

"I just didn't think you liked to." It wasn't a direct answer to his question, but it was the truth. "Since you continued to tell me that every time I asked you to come to the shop."

"Like I said, it all comes down the material, *mon coeur.*"
What did he call me?

Before she could form a reply or question him about what he'd just called her, they reached the bottom of the stairs. "Did you know Montgomery entertained a French ambassador more than once?" Quint reached out and took her hand again.

"Really?" She was still reeling from the name he'd called her, now he's talking about entertaining French ambassadors? Meg didn't know which to question more.

"Yes, he set up a buffet table that ran the length of the dining room, and he hired five separate groups of musicians to keep music playing for three days straight."

"That's interesting." She returned to the question burning a hole in her brain. "Did you just call me something in French?" Meg looked around the kitchen and hoped her question sounded like no big deal.

"Did you like it?" He walked ahead of her but glanced back over his shoulder.

"I didn't know you knew French."

"I know those two words. It means *my heart.*"

"Really?" Funny how his two words had the power to send her heart racing for what must have been a whole minute. "And how did you know about entertaining the French ambassador? Was that in one of the books of you read?" She'd read one or two books on Montgomery Manor, and even had a few in her own shop. Yet, she couldn't remember ever reading about that particular fact.

He just shrugged without replying then flipped a switch and lit up the room. His words and her questions were forgotten as she took in the old kitchen before her.

"After tonight, patrons can pay to see a tour of this room, so it's made to look a great deal like it did in Montgomery's time." There was unmistakable pride in his voice. He was quiet for a long moment as Meg looked around.

"I was thinking, too, about having it as more than just a tour. I thought I'd open it up for groups who would like to come and actually cook in it, like Scouts learning history hands-on, or the Ladies' Auxiliary, and things like that."

The large room was far from the breeding ground for spiders or wasted space she feared it would be.

Old utensils hung from a ceiling rack, several butcher-block tables made up the workspaces about the large area, and the stove at the far end of the kitchen was a cast iron monster that looked as if it might come to life at any moment and walk away on its peg legs.

Meg swallowed and let out a breathy, "Wow." She calmed her nerves and continued. "Just think of the many culinary works of art were made in this kitchen. Does the stove work?"

"Yes, everything works. And over there in the corner, that's where the pastry chefs worked."

Meg's gaze followed Quint's and took in a large table. She smiled. "I'll bet men in tall white hats iced cakes or *petit fours*, and filled cream puffs."

"You're right. There's a picture of them in one of the books upstairs." He tapped one of the ladles hanging from the ceiling, sending it swinging to and fro.

"I wonder what creations were made there for the French ambassador." Meg felt lost in another world, her voice filled with wonder.

Quint sighed. "Wonderful things, I'm sure. In one of the old boxes I went through, I found a menu for a dinner party. Imagine making up a menu for a dinner party!" He said, excitement lacing his tone. "One of the things listed was something called strawberry dream cake."

His smile was easy, but it didn't quite reach the mysterious darkness in his eyes. "Here, let me show you the dumbwaiters."

They were magnificent, complete with ropes and pulleys. Both were big enough to hold Meg. She watched as Quint maneuvered the rope and moved them. "I don't think we should move here," Meg said playfully.

"Oh?"

He couldn't look more stricken had she stabbed him in the chest with one of the knives from the block on the counter. She smiled to put him at ease. "Our kids would have a field day in these things."

Quint visibly relaxed and cracked a slight smile as he slid the door to the dumbwaiter closed. "Thinking about kids, are you?"

The question threw her for a moment. "Yes, I suppose I've been thinking about them a lot," she admitted.

He turned and met her gaze. "Is that why you were so afraid of this huge project?"

"I don't know, maybe."

He appeared in deep thought and was quiet for a long moment. "We'll talk more about it later," he said slowly.

With her hand once again tucked into his, she followed him up another narrow staircase. "There are several sets of servants' stairs. They give access to every part of the house." They ascended past the main dining floor to the second, yet they were in a separate section of the house from the bed and breakfast rooms. He showed her the huge, beautiful ballroom, where the band's instruments rested on the platform at one end, and many wonderful paintings graced the walls. One painting depicted dancers in formal dress—men in black jackets with tails, ladies in long dresses. It was entitled *Night of the Ball*. Another showed a beautiful woman in a long deep blue dress. The woman in the painting was looking away from the artist and the fan she held hid the lower part of her face. The artist had done a remarkable job capturing her beauty and adding a flare of mystery.

Meg studied the mystery woman for a long moment.

"She's Ellen Montgomery; painted a short time before her death." Quint's spoke softly, but his words still seemed to echo in the huge, empty room.

"She's beautiful." Meg breathed the words.

"Yes, she is."

Meg stepped further into the room, her gaze lingering here and there, taking in everything her greedy eyes could. The wood planks of the floor glistened with a new shine, strands of lights wound up around four columns, deep red velvet circular sofas surrounded each column, and the hanging lights cast a soft glow. She could hardly wait for the dancing to begin.

"I doubt you'll have trouble renting this room out for banquets and receptions."

"I thought so, too." Quint looked at his watch. "I have just a few minutes left. Let me show you some of the new Bed and Breakfast rooms and the bath at the end of the hall. You'll love the fixtures. The shower is the neatest thing."

He was right.

The bathroom was as big as some of the bedrooms. The sink resembled an old-fashioned washstand. The plumbing was modern—turn on the faucet and hot and cold water flowed. But the fixtures themselves arced out over the bowl; the faucet handles were made of wood and made to look like something from the early twentieth century.

The shower, a small room, was set in the corner. It was encased with stones, and potted plants dotted the built-in rock shelves—stepping into the enclosure was a bit like walking into a cave. Showering in there would be an experience—rinsing away the cares of the day while surrounded by nature.

Meg half expected to find a large water filled bucket suspended with a pull rope, just waiting to rain water down on her head. But the fixture was modern, complete with a two showerheads to spray in several directions, hitting the body everywhere at once.

She touched the stone wall. The stones were cool, smooth, and felt real. "I might take my shower here instead of our bathroom."

"We could take a shower here together if you like." His deep, seductive tone told her he'd like to also.

She felt heat rise into her cheeks. Amazed that he was her husband and yet this felt so new. She thought for a moment he might kiss her as he had previously. Instead, he gently touched her cheek with his fingertips as he looked into her eyes.

"As much as I'd like to stay here and show you just how well the shower works, we have guests." He sounded as if the words were not easy to say.

They returned to the hallway and heard voices drifting up from the foyer. Quint led her to the balcony, and they looked down at the growing crowd. He tightened his grip on her hand.

"Are you ready to meet our guests?"

She smiled at him. "I guess, but they're really *your* guests."

He gazed into her eyes, shaking his head. "No, they're *ours*. We are in this together. Always, *mon coeur*."

He gave her a quick, easy kiss. "And later, I promise I'll show you the basement on the other side. There's a swimming pool down there."

She looked at him, astonished. Quint didn't know how to swim, had never liked the water. Their vacations were never to the beach. "Really? Are you teasing me?"

"Really. Montgomery used to have parties where the guests would swim all night. It'll be a while before we're ready for that. Once it's operational, I want to spend a few nights swimming with you. Alone." He paused, looked back down at the crowd. "And later I do plan to tease you. A lot."

His words sent fire to her blood. For a moment, she couldn't draw in a breath. Before she could think of a single word to reply, he asked, "Are you ready to go down?"

Meg was still speechless. She nodded.

He squeezed her hand, and they descended the stairs together. Quint brought her hand to his lips, kissing it before reaching the bottom of the stairs. The subtle touch sent the fire he'd already put in her blood pooling to the pit of her stomach.

How dare he put a spark in her soul, toss on a can of kerosene, and then move on to greet his guests?

Meg had no idea. She plastered a smile on her face until she thought her face would freeze.

The party started.

Aside from the mayor, the guest list included the governor and two senators. The governor deigned to make a quick appearance, and the two senators declined having made previous commitments. Everyone who did show up, including the mayor, was excited to see all the wonderful things Quint had done to Montgomery Manor.

The press was there and, for a long moment, Meg thought she might go blind from the flashes as pictures were taken. Her jaw hurt and she held tight to Quint's hand. He gave a quick interview and explained, in a nutshell, all the work and changes he'd made over the past two months.

The tour was a success, and Meg discovered that tour was only the first of many planned for that night. Patrons were awed by the kitchen and the many other refurbished rooms, just as she'd been.

The wine cellar was, by far, the most praised room on the tour. It was an awesome place, tunnel like, with cobblestone floors, stone walls, arched doorways, and iron gates guarded stacks of old barrels and wine racks. A musty smell wove with the sweet aroma of fruit. Small lights along the walls gave the tunnels a haunting and mysterious atmosphere.

According to historical record, the wine cellar was the very place Joshua Montgomery killed his wife, Ellen. It was there that witnesses discovered him standing over her, holding a bloody knife, his hands covered with her blood.

Meg noticed how the tour members lingered in the cellar, the question of whether Joshua Montgomery killed his own wife lingering in the air like the tangy scent of grapes. She knew the press would feed on the old mystery for weeks to come.

"And where exactly was Mrs. Montgomery found?" someone asked.

"Just about right where you're standing." Quint grinned his now familiar crooked grin. It was obvious he loved the attention.

A camera flashed. "Is it true Joshua Montgomery was standing over her with a bloody knife in his hand?"

"That's what the books say." Quint met Meg's gaze from several feet away, and winked at her.

Meg watched, enjoying this time for him.

"And what was she wearing?" another patron asked.

Meg caught the sadness in Quint's eyes. It was a mere flash, and no one else seemed to notice it, but she saw it before he forced another smile.

"A deep blue silk dress. They were having a party."

"What about his treasure? Did you find any hidden vaults?"

Quint blinked as another flash of a camera brightened the room. "Not yet, but I'll be sure to call the press as soon as I do."

Laughter rippled through the cave-like room.

The group moved through the tunnel, and Quint led the way. Meg stepped in beside him. "You seem eager to get out of the cellar." She whispered so none of the reporters could hear.

"Knowing this was where Ellen Montgomery was murdered gives me nightmares. How are you holding up?"

"I feel like I've met a million people, and my jaw hurts from smiling. I hope there's not a quiz at the end of this because I can't remember any names."

He leaned close. "Well, you are the perfect hostess. Thank you." He gave her cheek a peck.

"With you beside me, it's not too hard. I admit this place was really scary at first, but now…" She looked around as she spoke. "It feels like home, especially when you're beside me holding my hand."

He released her hand and placed an arm about her shoulders and squeezed her to him.

The tour group stopped again. "And as you can see, this room is where the wine was stored before it was bottled…"

Meg glanced at the stacked barrels, but she could ignore her growling belly no longer, besides, she'd heard this part of the tour three times already. As Quint continued his speech, talking about the history of this room and more changes he planned to make, she broke away from the tour to find the dining room and grab a bite.

She followed three tunnels before finding the steps leading to the main floor. They were simple spiral stairs twisting around a single large pole, with a single wood banister to keep one from falling over the edge and onto the stone floor below. There wasn't much light, and each step creaked beneath her weight as she ascended.

Her shoe heel caught on the uneven, top step, and she stumbled. She had a grip on the banister, but it wasn't tight and her hand slipped. She was saved from falling to the stones below by a pair of strong arms that grabbed her.

From her angle, she saw a man's legs wrapped in black slacks, then she saw the white shirt. For a brief moment, only a moment, she thought she'd be caught by her mysterious bartender. She regained her footing and looked up. It wasn't the Irish bartender who had saved her.

Brad.

He held her a few inches from him, but he looked down at her with a strange twinkle in his eyes, the bright light of the room was behind him and did nothing to light up his shadowed face. She blinked, trying to make out his expression in the dim interior of the stairwell.

"Brad?" She breathed the single word, a mixture of relief and anxiety—she didn't like the way his hands lingered on her arms.

"Are you all right?" He seemed surprised to find her here. His words were hesitant as if he didn't quite know what to say to her.

He gazed down at her intently, laser focused on her face. She felt like an actor under a spotlight, the unseen crowd devouring her with its eyes. "Yes, I'm fine, thank you, and thank you for grabbing me. I hate to think what might have happened if you hadn't."

"It's a good thing I was here to…keep you from falling."

His words were still uncertain and left her wondering what he was doing. "What are you doing here?" she asked.

His hands still gripped her arms, and his gaze still probed her face. She felt naked and vulnerable.

A disturbing thought darkened her mind. *All he has to do is shove me backwards, and I'll go tumbling down the stairs.*

She fought back a shudder. Why would she even imagine he'd do something so terrible, when he saved her from doing just that? He had, hadn't he?

Yes, he had. And he still held her, like he enjoyed holding her. She didn't enjoy him holding her. She shrugged to send him the unspoken message to let her go. His grip on her arms softened, but his palms slid to her shoulders, then down to her elbows, an unwelcomed and inappropriate caress. She stepped from his grasp, and holding tightly to the banister, took the last step up to the next floor. She didn't stop there, though, she moved a few steps further than that, clearing the stairway.

His smile didn't reach his eyes. In fact, it looked really forced. He licked his lips, slowly running his tongue over them, almost as if he was hungry to taste something delicious. He now reminded her of the big, bad wolf who wanted to eat her up. "Just walking around making certain everything is order and the guests have everything they need. Are you enjoying your evening?"

"Yes, thank you." At the beginning of the evening, when Quint had introduced them, she liked Brad, but now, after their uncomfortable encounter on the stairs, she found her like had turned to disdain. She didn't like the way he watched her, like a cat watching a mouse before devouring it. When she's first met Brad, Quint was with her; and Brad had shaken her hand. He hadn't looked at her then as if he'd like to have her for his next meal. He hadn't put his hands down her arms. Perhaps it was just the light coming from behind him casting a shadow that transformed his face into an unsettling and untrustworthy mien. Or maybe it was the way he'd held her too long. It didn't matter. All that mattered was not being alone with him any longer.

"You seem a bit shaky, off balance. Quint's been keeping you busy with tours and holding his hand. You just need a bite to eat."

She almost asked him how he could know that, unless he'd been following her and Quint around.

He didn't give her the chance to ask. "The dining room is this way."

Without hesitation, he led the way to the dining room. It was filled with people, some standing and talking and eating and drinking, some sitting at the many tables, doing the same, some moving about the large room admiring the art and the décor.

Meg looked around the large room, amazed. "Wow, I hadn't realized so many people arrived while we were down in the cellar."

She turned back to Brad, determined to ask him a few questions of her own, but he was gone.

"Maybe *he's* a ghost," she let out, hoping it wasn't true. If it were, they may never get rid of him. She moved to introduce herself to a group of guests gathered near the door.

A short time later, the party was getting to her. Her face hurt. Her eyes were tired. She needed to sit for a while, but all the seats in the dining room were taken.

Meg let out a heavy breath and took another drink of her diet cola. She wanted something stronger, much stronger, but she didn't dare in case the alcohol went to her head, causing her to lose her inhibitions, and making her into the laughing stock of her own husband's big night. That's the last thing she wanted. She couldn't envision herself dancing on one of the many tables, pulling off her velvet dress, and tossing it to the crowd, but she thought she better not take the chance.

The party moved along like well-written music. She shouldn't complain about the festivities, but the strappy heels she wore hurt her feet. It seemed like hours had passed since she'd enjoyed the small plate of meatballs, toasted ravioli, and hard, Italian bread. She couldn't remember the last time she'd done anything more than meet Quint's gaze from across the crowded room.

She watched him now as he returned with yet another group. He came close and whispered to her. "We've booked six rooms for the night."

"That's great." She felt her happy enthusiasm was forced. She was too tired to feel happy or enthusiastic.

"I'll be back."

Before she could respond, he was off again, talking or sharing more history on the house.

She was happy for him, and for the successful evening, truly she was. But she couldn't stop thinking about the whirlpool in their room, and how wonderful it would feel once she could climb into it.

Another nameless person came to her, shook her hand, and told her how wonderful everything was. She groaned and moved her jaw around when he moved on.

Though she wanted to with all her being, she couldn't go up to their room; besides, she didn't want to climb into that whirlpool tub alone. Maybe she'd just take her own little tour and get away from the crowd for a while.

Why not?

After all, she did own the house, or at least half of it. Just as she could stay here whenever she wanted, she could also look wherever she wanted.

She gave one last quick glance about the large room but didn't see Quint anywhere, otherwise she would have told him she needed to find a quiet place to get some air. Instead she wandered away from the party. It wasn't difficult. Other partiers were either caught up in their own conversations or busy studying the décor. She headed toward the kitchen, but once there, she bypassed it, found another small stairway, and ascended. After walking a long, dark, dusty hallway filled with tools and ladders, Meg realized she was in the part of the house Quint continued calling the North Wing. It was the part of the house he hadn't refurbished or remodeled yet. It was quiet and dark and a bit colder than the rooms she just left, suffering from years without heat or cleaning or maintenance. She welcomed the cooler air.

Though echoes of the party drifted up to her through the darkness, for the moment, this place was what Meg needed. Quiet from the storm of the party downstairs, and the emotions pinging through her. She made her way to the windows at the end of the long hallway, and slipped off her shoes, allowing the bare floor to soothe her aching feet.

The view from the window captured her gaze. Through the steady rain and lightning of the storm, she saw the neglected gardens filled with weeds and trees and shadows. She heard the surf crashing against the nearby rocks and knew, without a doubt, that on a clear day, this window would offer a magnificent view. For now, she could only see the part of the parking lot lit by the streetlight.

She took a deep breath and inhaled the heavy scent of must and the lumber stacked nearby.

She closed her eyes and pressed her head against the chilly glass.

A slight frigid breeze flowed through the hall. Had someone opened a door? She didn't open her eyes. The chance to rest against the chill of the glass was simply too good. What did she care if someone else snuck up here for a moment alone?

He moved her hair slightly. She could have sworn she felt Quint's familiar touch. There was a soft touch to her neck; hardly more than the touch of a feather. It could have been fingertips. It could have been lips.

She sighed. So Quint had followed her to steal a moment alone. Wonderful...

She waited a few heartbeats, but the soft touches didn't continue. Meg opened her eyes and looked over her shoulder.

She was alone in that dark, cold, musty hall.

How? Who touched me... She turned, straining to see through the mirk of the darkened hall. No one. Her hand flew to her neck where she knew she'd felt someone touch her. She forced in a ragged breath.

She scratched at her neck and swallowed to moisten her suddenly dry throat. She couldn't help but remember her earlier sensation of being watched. The same sensation clamored through her now.

"Who's there?" she called out, her voice barely audible over the rumbling storm outside the window.

No reply.

Maybe I'm so hungry for Quint's lips, I just imagined it.

"Right, maybe." Though whispered, her sarcasm sounded loud and out of place.

She hurried to put her shoes back on and then turned away from the windows.

She didn't want to be in that dark hall, but she wasn't quite ready to return to the party, either. She'd wander around a bit more, see another small part of this house on her own, but not linger at any more windows where she'd feel phantom touches. Once she'd wandered her fill, she could return to the party and do her best to ignore her aching feet while standing beside her husband.

She picked the closest door and opened it wide enough to allow the small amount of light from the windows to filter in. She expected an empty, neglected bedroom. Finding that the room was no larger than a closet was another wooden spiral staircase surprised her.

"I know Quint said there were servants' stairs leading to every part of the house, but I wonder just how many there are in this place." She'd ask Quint as soon as she found him again. She wished she'd studied the blueprints he'd shown her when he first inherited the place.

Leaving the door open, she stepped close, and peered down. The stairs disappeared down into the darkness. Stepping down them would be an adventure, to say the least. It also meant closing the door and becoming part of the darkness. Meg hated the darkness, always had, but tonight seemed the night for an adventure.

It's a good thing I have that tiny flashlight on my keychain somewhere in my purse. She pulled it out and switched it on. The thin beam was strong in the thick darkness, but not strong enough to shine to the bottom of the staircase and reveal what was there.

"It probably leads back down to the cellar," she voiced her thoughts aloud. And since that might be where Quint was, giving yet another tour of that legendary place, she'd venture down and find him.

She left the door open, adventure or not, she couldn't stand being in complete darkness. The staircase went up as well as down, and it appeared old and dusty, but sturdy. Even though Quint said he checked every set of stairs, she tested them, pressing her weight down, standing still on the first step to make sure it would hold her. It did, and without as much as a creak.

She shined her light up, saw only stairs, and decided that her adventure would take her down instead.

It's always better to start at the bottom and work your way up, right?

Her heels tapped softly on each step as she ventured down. This time, she held to the banister with one hand, while shining the light with the other. Only the beam of her small flashlight registered in the tight space. She moved around the center post, and at what had to have been a full story, she stopped and looked around. There wasn't even a door she could use to exit out to what had to be the second floor. She looked up toward the door through which she'd just come, saw the faint light from the windows, and then continued down.

She descended another story, but the steps stopped. The floor beneath her feet was hardwood, dusty, and unused. The entire place smelled of must, and the air was stale and heavy as if it hadn't been opened or aired out in years. Meg shined her flashlight into the gloom and saw a single door, just like the one two flights up.

She sneezed twice then grasped the detailed, although dusty, antique doorknob and pulled open the door. She moved through the opening and stepped into a hallway of sorts. It wasn't the cellar as she thought it would be; there was no cobblestone floor or stonewalls like in the wine cellar. The walls were paneled, not plastered or papered like the rest of the house. Another door stood open before her so she shined her flashlight and peered through it. The room beyond was empty except for a built in bench and a quilt of cobwebs.

She moved down the hall, passing eight rooms just like the first. A large doorway at the end opened into a room containing an empty pool. She stopped.

Everything she'd seen fell into place. The small rooms along the hall were dressing rooms. The pool was white tile, grayed with dust. And yet, her breath caught at the sight of it. Quint wasn't lying when he said it was big. The room was as big as the carriage house, and the pool took up most of it.

Meg shined her light upward and gazed at the white ceiling. Something looked wrong about it, but she couldn't put her finger on what it was. Perhaps it just looked strange in the darkness, the shadows from the small flashlight beam dancing along the furthest reaches.

She smiled ruefully. At least the pool itself had not been filled in or covered during the past century. She hoped it was intact and wouldn't require much work for them to fill it with water again.

The ladders on each side were dug into the pool walls, like holes cut out to create steps. The shallow end closest to Meg needed no ladder, the bottom of the pool sloped up toward her and, at what must have been three feet, there were steps that ran the complete width of the pool.

She closed her eyes and, for a long moment, she tried to envision the room as Joshua and Ellen Montgomery must have seen it; with refreshing, clear water, and tile as white as snow. In her thoughts there was a diving board or slide at the deep end.

She opened her eyes, and gasped at the sight before her.

The pool that moments ago had been dark, lit only by her slight flashlight, was now lit by what must have been a hundred candles. The smell of beeswax hung in the air.

The pool was filled with inviting water, not dust. The grayed tiles now glimmered in the candlelight, the brilliant white rectangles a stark contrast to the cool blue of the pool water.

"Oh…" Her heart hammered in her chest and she stumbled backward, fighting to keep her balance. This wasn't possible. She blinked several times but the room didn't change.

The room, the water, everything was so still she heard her own heart pounding within her chest.

The single word she'd let out in shock no longer echoed off the walls.

"Would you care for a swim, *mon coeur*?"

Meg started and let out a gasp.

That voice…Quint?

She turned to find him slowly approaching. She thought her heart would beat out of her chest. She stared at him, unable to even speak, unable to breathe.

His sparkling blue eyes reflected the light from the many candles.

Her hand flew to her chest as she worked to catch her breath while starring at the man who'd almost given her a heart attack.

"Quint? How—what?" There were so many questions to ask, but she couldn't form a complete sentence.

"I didn't mean to scare you." His voice was soft and seductive. He looked like her husband. He sounded like her husband.

And yet, he wasn't. Was he? She didn't think so.

"Please accept my apology. The last thing I want to do is frighten you, dear wife."

Unable to move, she watched him approach, coherent thoughts refusing to come to her. He sounded so formal. "Quint?"

"Do you like it?"

"Like it?" What was he asking?

"The pool."

She tore her gaze from his and glanced at the pool. The water in the pool was the same color as his eyes. Then she looked up at the ceiling. The wrong plaster ceiling from before was gone. Now a domed glass ceiling invited in the grayness and flashing lightning from the storm. Rain poured against the glass, its sound softer than she expected.

She dragged in a breath. "It's beautiful." She said, her voice ragged and almost not hers. "It's wonderful. It's what I imagined it to be." She was light-headed and still had trouble breathing. "This has to be a dream. I must have sat down somewhere and fallen asleep. There's no other explanation." She still felt her heart racing, still heard her blood rushing in her ears.

"No, Meggie." He reached out and took her hand. "It's no dream. I'm here, you're here. And we are real. I assure you."

She blinked, her attention now at his throat. His tie was different. It was thin and black, and tied differently from the suit-and-tie tie he was wearing in the dining room. Her gaze lifted, from his chin, to his straight nose, to his dark blue eyes. "How did you know I was here?"

"I followed you when I saw you head off into the unopened part of the house. You could have tripped or gotten hurt or gotten lost, and no one would know where you were."

She couldn't look away from him, it was impossible to tear her gaze from his.

"I needed some time away from the party." She felt like she was speaking to him through a fog.

"Yes, there are so many people, so much noise. It has become a bit overwhelming. Did you feel my kiss on your neck when you were resting in the hallway?"

"Yes, I felt...No that's impossible. You weren't there." She had to force a breath through the tightness in her chest. "What the hell is going on?" Her words breathy, but at least she could form complete sentences. "None of this is possible. The swimming pool doesn't just fill up in the blink of an eye. And when did you change your tie?"

He kissed her. His mouth was warm, perfect. It was so easy to melt into his kiss as his lips commanded she do. He let go of her hand. His fingertips on either side of her face brought a surge of heat to her cheeks. She wanted him. Now. The rush of need almost knocked her off her feet. She swayed against him. He held her face tighter keeping her steady. The flashlight she held dropped to the floor with a thud. He reached down again and took her hands in his. He ended the kiss. "Don't worry about my tie. Don't worry about the pool or anything." His whispered words were warm against her face.

She stared up at him. He looked like her husband, the man she'd shared a bed with for the past five years. And yet, he didn't. His stance was different, favoring his right leg. For a moment, she thought he might be a complete stranger. "But—"

He let go of one hand to reach up and place two fingers against her lips. "No buts. No talking. I just want you to feel. It's important that I be here with you, Meggie. Close your eyes."

Meg felt as if he'd somehow reach into her and taken control of her. She could not deny him. She closed her eyes. Her other senses felt instantly enhanced. She felt the familiar touch of his hand in hers, the warmth of his breath, the heat of his closeness.

He turned her to face the pool and pulled her against him. Her back against the hardness of his chest. He held her waist with one hand, his fingers splayed against her lower belly, sending waves of heat into her core. He draped his other arm over her shoulder and pressed his palm against the bare flesh above the scooped neck of her dress. When he spoke, his breath was warm on her ear and neck.

"Open your eyes."

She did. The pool was before her. "But how..."

"Shhh. No talking. Just feel. And imagine how tranquil the water can feel. Would you still care to relax with a swim?"

Right then, she was feeling him pressed against her back, his hand just above the top of her dress and she couldn't think beyond her need for more.

He caressed her skin above her collar bone and the flesh of the top of her breast, and then he reached up and cupped her cheek, his palm warm against her face. She couldn't stop the urge to lean into it.

Meg couldn't think, didn't even want to think. She wanted to lean against him, to feel his body pressed against hers. "This has to be a dream," she murmured aloud. "I fell asleep. I must have. Heaven knows my feet and legs were tired enough. There is no other explanation. There's no way you could change this room in the blink of an eye. There's no way you could..."

"What about if I do this?" He brushed his lips against the hollow of her throat. The pressure of it harder than what she'd felt while standing at the windows minutes before. This time, his kiss sent a shiver through her and into the floor.

She groaned, feeling as if her legs might give out.

"Stop worrying over how this happened, Meggie. Right now, I just want you to feel—feel me, feel us. Feel how much I love you." He reached out and touched her cheek. "You look radiant."

"Thank you," she whispered.

"We could swim, the water's warm. The clouds cover the moonlight and the stars, but we have candlelight."

"Moonlight?" The single word was muffled by the fog in her brain. She glanced up at the ceiling again.

"I can't stop thinking about my making love to you this afternoon. I've thought of little else, Meggie." He nipped her ear. "I want to make love to you again, here, now, in the water." He reached down the front of her dress. She gasped. Her nipple was hard and erect, and he teased it with his finger and thumb.

Meg moaned, closing her eyes and pushing back into him, the delicious sensations he wrought ringing through her. She no longer cared how the room changed. She no longer cared about the party upstairs or who might miss them.

He leaned around her, kissed her mouth passionately, drawing another groan from deep within her. When his soul-reaching kiss ended, Meg again opened her eyes...

...and found herself in the water. *How did he get my dress off?* She couldn't remember, nor did she remember stepping into the pool. The warmth of the water enhanced the magic Quint had done to her nipples.

"How is this possible?" *Breathe in. Breathe out.*

"No more questions, Meggie, just enjoy. Just feel. Do you like this?"

"Yes." She couldn't help *but* question it. "Who *are* you?

"I'm your husband." His mouth covered her lips as the warm water covered her body, his heat radiated into her. The slight covering of hair on his chest tickled her nipples, she shivered as if an electric spark sizzled through her.

Her legs had no more substance than the water surrounding them, and beneath his hands, she was no more than putty molding to whatever shape he desired.

In one explosive moment, he held her, he kissed her, he seduced her.

He slipped inside of her.

She gasped at the intrusion, at the sudden shudder of ecstasy. Fiery passion as she'd never known before, flared through her. Quint filled her completely. Perfectly.

Meg worked to catch her breath, closing her eyes against the delicious sensations of her insides convulsing around him. In one deep thrust, he'd sent her to the stars.

She opened her eyes to find herself once again standing beside the empty pool. The candles were gone. The room was dark except for the small light from the flashlight that lay on the tile near her feet.

Her dress was once again in place, although her breathing was labored, and her heart raced with lingering pleasure. Her lower belly clenched and unclenched as if he were still there, inside her. Her body still quaked in the aftermath of the most passionate lovemaking she'd ever experienced

"Oh, my..." she let out. She took a step sideways to keep her balance on weak legs.

This can't be happening. This didn't happen...

But what didn't happen? Just what the hell *had* happened? Terror immobilized her.

Her gaze flicked around the large room, seeing footprints in the dust and neglect on the tile. She recognized her own footprints. She shivered at the larger footprints alongside hers.

"Meg?"

CHAPTER EIGHT

Meg pivoted in unison with her scream.

Quint stood behind her.

"Meggie, are you all right?"

He looked more like the husband she knew than the man who'd made love to her in the water a few moments before. The blue striped tie she remembered him wearing was once again in place around his neck.

She stared at it for several long moments before turning her gaze up to meet his with wide eyes. She stumbled back. He grasped her arms to keep her from tripping down the slope of the now empty pool.

"Quint?"

Terror surged through her just as strongly as passion had three minutes before. Her panting, gaspy breaths echoed off the walls.

"What's the matter with you, Meggie?" He stared down at her. His voice and expression showing genuine concern. "What are you doing down here?"

"Quint?" She reached out and placed her hand against the front of his shirt, as if to make certain he was real.

He grasped her hands and studied her. "Yes, it's me. Quint. Who else did you expect? Are you all right?"

"Didn't you see—the water—the candles?" She was back to being unable to complete a coherent sentence, much less think a coherent thought.

"Meggie, it's all right." He tried to pull her close. "Just tell me what happened."

She pushed at him, staring at him as if horns grew out the top of his head. Her weak legs almost gave out beneath her. He reached out to steady her, and she had no choice but to let him.

"You didn't see the water?" She managed a complete thought. She looked down, half expecting to find her dress in nothing but a heap on the dusty floor.

"There's no water in the pool, honey." He stared back at her. "At least, not yet. Remember, I told you it would be a while before we could get the pool up and running. I just have too many other priorities."

"You didn't see anyone else?" She panted between her words, still working to gain some sort of control. She stared up at him, trying to reconcile the man who had held her in the water with the man who held her now. She wasn't so certain the two men were one in the same. What explanation had he had for all the things she'd seen? She couldn't remember. Not to mention, she hoped *this* Quint hadn't seen anyone else. The man in the pool had seduced her and slipped inside her so easily. If he wasn't Quint...

I should shut up before Quint gets the wrong idea.

"You were alone in here when I found you, just standing here staring at the pool. Hell, Meggie, I'm sorry. I never meant to scare you like that."

"You were here. You—you—" How could she tell him he made love to her in the pool? She wasn't wet or naked. He'd think she lost her mind. She still wasn't certain now that man had been Quint.

"Yes, I'm here. I what?"

I really should shut up. But she couldn't seem to. "You were here with me, but you were different." She looked at the pool, hoping to find answers to all the questions flowing through her mind. "Maybe it was a dream."

"What were you doing, sleeping standing up?"

She ignored the tease in his voice. "No. I don't think it was a dream. You were here with me." She was sure she'd been awake. It was too real. And it *had* been Quint, and now, as she looked up into his gaze, she recognized his deep, intense look.

"I'm here with you now, and I'm glad I followed you." Before she could comment on the changes in him, he pulled her close again. This time she didn't fight him. She was too weak. He leaned down and nuzzled her neck. "Damn you smell good."

He smelled of the Quint she knew. His embrace felt so familiar. She relaxed in his arms.

"Tell me what you saw." His voice sounded curious, yet still filled with concern. He held her close.

"I don't know what I saw." Her muffled words filtered through his shirt. She suddenly didn't want to tell him anything. She let out a frustrated huff at her own uncertainty. Her lower stomach still quivered from what she felt.

"Maybe it was a ghost."

His light, teasing banter touched a raw nerve inside Meg. She'd just experienced an explosive orgasm before being scared out of her wits, and he wanted to tease her about it?

"Don't even say that." She didn't want to think about it. Thinking about it filled her with feelings she couldn't identify. There was fear, and yet, she welcomed it. She wanted it. She wanted the touch and the passion that came along with the fear. She wanted to be in the wonderful water making love with him again. But it was time to shut her mouth before she said something she couldn't explain to Quint, and most of it she couldn't explain.

"There's a glass ceiling on the other side of the plaster above us." She tightened her grip on him, still to unsteady to let go.

"I know."

She pressed her face against his chest, finding comfort in the calming, familiar sound of his heartbeat.

"Will you be able to uncover the glass ceiling so we can swim by the moon and starlight some day?" She wanted to swim in the pool as she thought she had a moment before.

He kissed her. "Of course, *mon coeur.*" And in those four words she heard the man who had taken her in the pool.

She shifted to look up at him. He looked like her husband still, but it was too dark to see his eyes.

"Are you all right now?" He asked, his voice deep and husky against her ear.

"Yes." It was the biggest lie she'd ever told him. Her insides protested until she thought she might lose her supper. What frightened her now was not knowing what bothered her so much. Was it fear? Was it the undeniable need to feel a stranger's touch, to taste his kiss? "We should get back. You're missing your party."

"No, I'm not." He held her closer, wrapping his arms around her. She felt so small in his embrace.

"Yes, you are, and it's because of me. Let's head back upstairs. On Sunday, when my shop is closed, I'll come back, and we can spend all day exploring this place and learning about the different rooms in the light of day."

Do I even want *to leave?* The room beckoned her. She wanted to stay and swim in the pool, look up at the dark night sky, explore the passion still humming within her.

At the same time, she wanted to run.

Quint turned her to face him. His face was no more than a shadow in the darkness, but now she saw the way his eyes sparkled.

Was it her imagination or did his gaze deepen, grow harder and more intense?

"I could take you upstairs to our room, let you rest for a while, wake you later, and we could do all sorts of exploring tonight."

Meg knew very well what he meant, and she couldn't help but lick her lips. That dream or apparition or whatever it was had left her horny as hell. There was nothing she wanted more than for Quint to take her up to their room and make love to her. Hell, he could make love to her *here*, right beside the pool, in the dust or standing up with her back pressed against the wall. It didn't matter. She barely saw past her burning need.

"What if I want you to take me upstairs and make love to me now?"

He cupped her face with his palm. "There will be time for that later, my love. You've been an excellent hostess all night even after working all day." His kiss was warm but light. "I'll take you up, and you can lie down. Then I'll be back in half an hour or so." He took her hand and the flashlight, and led her toward the door.

"I don't need a nap." She walked closer to him so that her side brushed against his. "I feel wonderful."

Indeed, she did feel wonderful, as if she had an invigorating moonlight swim and tryst.

"Are you sure?" Again, his voice was that of the man who'd seduced her in the pool.

"I'm sure."

He reached out and brushed his fingertips along her cheek. "Have I told you that you look radiant tonight?"

The dream or vision or whatever it was burned through her like the rush of a tidal wave. "As a matter of fact, you have."

The other Quint's words, mentioning making love to her that afternoon, flitted through her memories. She fought down a shiver, knowing answers would not be easy to find.

His smile was slow and sexy. "Then let's go dance. I haven't danced with you all night." He turned away to lead them back to the party.

He led her to stairs much wider than the spiral one she'd ventured down. At the top was a door that brought them out into the other side of the new kitchen.

Between the kitchen and the ballroom, they murmured various greetings to all they passed, and offered many "thank yous" for compliments about the wonderful party.

Once in the ballroom, Quint took her into his arms, his hand at her lower back, his gaze upon her face. "This room is so perfect. What a lovely ending to such an amazing night." She breathed. "I never knew you knew how to waltz."

Despite the late hour, the massive ballroom was still packed with partiers. People danced, stood chatting holding various drinks, or sat on the round velvet sofas. Meg thought it looked like something out of a photograph or even a lot like the painting hanging at the far end of the room.

"You're right. This ballroom is perfect. We won't have any trouble booking it for parties and things. It's even big enough for a wedding."

She waved her fingers at Evan from over Quint's shoulder as they danced past. Her assistant was in a corner talking to a redhead Meg didn't know. She'd seen him from a distance before, he'd been at the bar talking to Melanie Wirthington, and she'd wondered if they were discussing Melanie's new purchase—the Shakespeare books. Evan looked like he was enjoying himself, and Meg was sorry she'd been too busy to talk to him.

"We already have three bookings for it. And this night is far from over." Quint's whispered words were warm on her neck, and she shivered in answer. He used his hand on the small of her back to pull her closer and press her pelvis against his.

She was so happy for him. She closed her eyes and leaned against him, letting him lead her in the perfect dance.

When she looked around again, the room was different, but the same.

Dancers still waltzed. Plush velvet round sofas still circled every post. But now, three large chandeliers above her head lit the room with help from glowing sconces on the walls. Evan and the redhead were gone. The ladies who now danced and stood about the room wore long dresses. Meg looked down at her own dress. She wasn't wearing the short black velvet dress Quint liked so well. She wore a deep blue silk formal. Her low cut neck line revealed the cleft of her breasts. The silk fit tight across her ribs, inhibiting her breathing—or was it from the sudden magical shift in reality?

She looked up at Quint and saw the man she'd taken a dip in the pool with earlier, the man who wore a black tie. She missed a step. *What the hell?* This could not be happening again. Was she losing her mind?

"Relax, Meggie." He tightened his grip on her before she could trip, the steps of the dance just as smooth and perfect.

"What...How...Who the hell are you?" Terror and uncertainty gripped her. It was hard to speak. Her words were little more than whispers.

"I'm your husband." He stared down at her with a knowing gaze, his words just as even as their movements. "You've been tense all evening. Just relax and follow my lead, *mon coeur*."

Like that was going to be possible when her world just took an impossible twist.

A couple—the woman in a bright red dress, the man dressed in black complete with tails, waltzed past them. The woman was smiling and laughing. All around them, people of another era danced.

"You look lovely tonight. I love that dress on you. It makes your eyes look more blue than gray.

"Thank you." She forced the words from her tight chest. Hadn't Quint said something like that when she'd first arrived? She tried to remember.

"You still feel so tense in my arms, my love. Just relax. This party is moving along wonderfully, just as I told you it would. Let the servants do their jobs, and you enjoy yourself for once."

Either she'd lost her mind, or she fell into another dream. *No, this isn't a dream.* There's no way she fell asleep while dancing with Quint. The love making in the pool wasn't a dream either, but none of this could be real. It wasn't possible.

But it was. She could smell the beeswax candles about the room. Her blue gloves matched the dress, caressing her fingers with their softness. Through her right glove, she felt the warmth of his hand in hers. The music filled the large room, drowning out conversations.

"Have I lost my mind?" She stared up at the man who called himself her husband, not believing how calm she sounded.

"No." He was just as calm. His gaze held hers like a vice.

Her heart raced, her lungs were tight. Perhaps if she got some answers, she could relax in his arms as he instructed. "How is this real? How did I get here?" She asked.

He offered her his now-familiar crooked smile. "On the contrary, my dear, it is you who allowed me to bring this all *to you.*" His eyes sparkled just as they had when she'd stood near the pool a short time before.

"I don't understand." Then again, who really understood insanity?

He leaned close, close enough for her to feel the warmth of him, close enough for her to smell the clean, familiar scent of him. The air in the room felt as if it grew heavy. And cold. Meg looked to see if someone had opened one of the many French doors that led to the balcony. None were open. Yet, the chill remained. She shivered his in his arms. He appeared unaffected by the drop in temperature. The hair on the back of Meg's neck stood. She forced in a breath and let it out, expecting to see it. She needed to break free of his grasp, but she could not command her body to do more than follow his lead.

"You are my Ellen, Meg, my soul mate. I have searched for you for over a century. It is your love that allows me to live again. Thank you, *mon coeur.*"

She stared up at him. His words sent her heart racing. She didn't have time to even consider the million questions soaring through her thoughts before the waltz ended and everyone applauded. She applauded with them, her mind incapable of thinking outside the now, her clapping muffled by the gloves snaking up her arms past her elbows.

He kissed her then, his tongue touching hers.

He tasted of wine and spice. Of passion and desire. He tasted of her husband, the man she knew, and the man who had seduced her in the pool, *and* the man who kissed her in their bed earlier that afternoon. He was also the man who had kissed her in the bookstore.

When he ended the kiss and Meg opened her eyes, she was back in the black velvet dress. The room was lit by modern electricity. The ladies in long dresses that swished about the floor were gone.

"Are you okay?" Quint gripped her arms. "You look a bit flushed. You're trembling."

"I don't know." She stared up at him. "I keep seeing things." She tightened her grip on him, her legs, once again, refusing to hold her steady.

"What things?"

She wanted to tell him, but instead she stared up at him, searching for the man she just waltzed with. The sparkle of his eyes and the crooked grin he flashed her were the only resemblances. *How do I tell him that I think* he's *a ghost?*

"Just…things." She had the strange feeling that if she shared it with him, someone might overhear. The last thing she wanted was potential customers thinking Quint's wife was crazy. The room was warm again.

He smiled down at her, and her heart skipped again.

She swallowed hard. "We'll talk about this later."

"Let's get you something to drink." He held her hand and led her from the dance floor.

Meg was proud of herself. She maintained her composure until they reached the nearby bar. Her heart still raced. Her legs felt like they were filled with water. Her skin was hot and clammy, shivers wracking her body. Perhaps it was the excitement of the night. Perhaps it was not enough food or the fact that she'd been on her feet for the past fifteen or sixteen hours.

Perhaps it was because her husband was a ghost.

She wanted to laugh off the idea, but that idea was easier to handle than the idea that she might be losing her mind.

I need more sleep. She wasn't used to staying up this late any more.

Quint brought her a drink. It was warm and chocolaty, and whatever liqueur was in it sent warmth through every vein of her body. It did make her feel better. She sipped it while she listened to him talk with another patron, someone whose name she couldn't have remembered had her life depended on it. All the while, she tried not to stare at Quint.

Then he nodded, offered a good night to the man Meg couldn't name, and took her hand. Bidding everyone they passed a simple good evening, he led her from the room.

CHAPTER NINE

"Where are we going? We shouldn't be leaving the party again." Her heart skipped several beats when the pool came to mind. Would he take her there?

"As far as I'm concerned, for us, the party's over, and it was a huge success, I might add. The bar is closing so the lingerers will filter out to their cars or up to their rooms. Brad has strict instructions not to let anyone who appears to be intoxicated drive, Melanie is taking care of the kitchen, Susan and her helpers are in charge of putting away all the food on the buffet table, and the night crew knows their job when it comes to cleaning up. So my job is done." There was no mistaking his job-well-done tone of voice.

"What a wonderful party you throw, too." Meg was still warm, and maybe just a little tipsy, from the drink he'd given her. Even more, she felt rather giddy from the visions she'd seen, or whatever they were. "Now, where are we going?" She had no idea where he'd even led her. The halls were dark, filled with shadows from curtain-less windows.

"You'll see." Quint led her through the house.

With her hand in his, he led her down another dark corridor, into a large, no *huge*, empty room with a high ceiling. The entire west wall was all glass, and light filtered in from the street lamps that edged the parking lot. It wasn't quite as huge as the ballroom, but it was grand. The windows along the wall gave it an openness that made it look bigger.

"I can hear the ocean beating against the rocks." she whispered, daring to speak no louder for fear of breaking the silence in the cavernous room around her. Still, her whisper echoed off the empty walls. "Was this once a library?"

"It was an art room, a gallery." Like her, Quint spoke in soft voice, but his words were harsh and ragged. "It was once filled with tapestries and paintings and sculptures from all over the world."

Meg looked around. "How sad. Like the pool, it's so empty now."

She inched her way toward the windows, and pressed her hand against the cold glass.

"How sad, indeed. But like the pool, I hope to fill it." Quint's spoke from just over her shoulder.

She hadn't even heard him move. Yet, she'd known he was there, behind her. She felt his warmth. "With what?"

He pulled her against him and turned her to face him. "With books. I want you to have this room. I want you to fill it, Meggie."

She stared up at him in awe. "Fill it with the books from my shop? I don't know if I have enough books to fill it." She grinned. "I doubt there's enough furniture in our entire little house that could fill this room. I still find it so hard to believe that this is all ours." Her voice rose, echoing off every wall.

"Oh, I think you can fill it."

She held his gaze through the soft light from a streetlight that filtered in through the rain-covered windows. "You're certain?"

"Listen to this idea—your books, your shop full of books on this side over here." He motioned to the side of the room on his left with a wave of his hand. "And over here, near the windows," he motioned with his other hand, "you could have chairs and comfortable furniture where your customers could sit and read, maybe even have tea, or coffee and cookies, or something. Through that door over there is a hall leading to the outside, so customers wouldn't have to pass through the house to get here."

Meg didn't even realize she'd shaken her head until Quint responded. "Don't say no until you've at least thought about it. You said yourself, Jackson planned to increase the rent. Well, here, you wouldn't have to even worry about rent."

"I know." Meg listened to the ocean, close enough to hear, but not seen through the darkness. "But I'm not sure it's a good idea to combine the businesses."

"Why not? Your shop is doing great, and combining them would bring in more customers, increasing business for both of us. People who came for your books would smell the coffee, so to speak, and may stop in for a bite at the restaurant, or book a room and vice versa. Besides, it wouldn't be combining them, just housing them under the same roof. Your shop would still be yours. I won't intrude. I won't tell you how to shelve your books. You could have your own lock on the door and set your hours any way you want."

"I don't know..." She spoke each word thoughtfully.

He tilted his head and cocked a brow at her. "I'll charge you rent if it would help you feel better. A hundred dollars less a month than Jackson is charging."

She saw that twinkle in his eyes and laughed.

Then his grin disappeared as he brought her hand to his lips and gave it a soft kiss. "Just promise me you'll think about it for a while."

Meg looked around the room, seeing it filled with tapestries instead of dust. Then she tried to envision it with her books. It wasn't too hard to see. "All right, I'll think about it. I love the sounds of the waves on the rocks."

"I knew you'd like it."

A short time later, they were back to their room, and he opened the door for her.

"Is there anything else you want to show me tonight?" Meg couldn't help but ask before she kicked off her shoes and flexed her toes against the carpet.

"Yes, plenty I'd love to show you now, but there's champagne and a whirlpool waiting for us, and I've waited long enough to show you those."

"I thought you hated champagne. At our wedding, you didn't even sip champagne at our toast. Don't you remember? Tommy Raymond, your best man, filled your groom glass with beer so everyone would think it was champagne." Meg lay back on the bed and took a relaxing breath as she watched Quint.

He slid off his tie and tossed it over a nearby chair. Meg stared at it for a long moment, remembering how different the thinner tie of the man in her vision was.

Then he unbuttoned the top buttons of his shirt. "I never liked peas, either, but I do force them down now and then."

Reaching the champagne and the whirlpool tub seemed to take an eternity. He poured them each a glass of champagne, picked up a perfect, ripe strawberry, and placed it in her mouth.

Him feeding her was as intoxicating as the champagne. His fingertips brushed against her lips. His warm and electrifying touch drew her in.

Then he handed her a glass.

They clinked glasses in a salute. "To a successful party."

She smiled, and still touching her glass to his, added to the good wish. "I'm sure that has already come to pass. So, I want to toast to a successful beginning and a successful future."

"I'll drink to that, too," he said.

With champagne and a bowl of berries in hand, he led her into the huge bath where he lit waiting candles. The candles combined with the water gave her pause as the memory of her vision flooded through her. Her heart quickened its pace.

"What are you waiting for?" Quint still held her hand.

She stared down at the water. "This just made me think of the pool. I saw—"

"Don't think about what you saw right now. I want to just live this moment with you, Meg." He kissed her, bringing her back to the present in an instant. Meg's black velvet dress became a pool at her feet, but she didn't remember it sliding down her body.

The whirlpool was warm and the bubbles pulsated as Meg climbed in after Quint was in and waiting. Quint pulled her closer, seating her on his laps. She didn't know what felt better, the warmth of the water or Quint's hard heat.

Meg let out relaxed sigh. "This is a wonderful massage."

"How's this?" Quint moved her forward and rubbed his palms down her back.

"Even more wonderful." Then she laughed. "The champagne tickles."

The champagne was light, and the bubbles gave her a heady feeling. But it was Quint's kisses on the back of her neck, the hot touch of his hands, his body pressed against hers that made her lose whatever control she had left.

He reached around her and cupped her breasts, tenderly kneading them. "I've been hard for you all night, Meggie."

Meg was lost in the heat that surrounded her, lost in the champagne, lost in the darkness of Quint's gaze when he gently maneuvered her around to face him and straddle his lap. "I thought you'd be too tired for this."

"I'll never be too tired for this. Now, whether I have any energy left afterward..." He finished the sentence with a kiss.

She was as entranced in the water making love with him as she had been in the pool earlier. The beautiful, glorious things he did to her left her weak and wanting. And, somehow, Quint knew, because once he brought her to completion in the tub, he carried her to the bed.

"Do we have to do this now?"

Meg's whispered words were loud in the absolute stillness. "After everything we did earlier, then making love, I'm exhausted."

The room was dark, filled with little more than shadows. Quint held her hand. "It's important that you see this now. It won't take long, I promise, and you'll love it. It goes along with the new beginning for us."

She couldn't even hear their footsteps. The new carpet was plush and warm against her bare feet. She wore Quint's shirt, and the soft cotton of it brushed against her naked legs. He wore a pair of lounging pants, his great chest bare. She paused, allowing her vision to adjust to the dim light.

"Are we leaving the room? We should find something else to wear in case any guests are out and about."

"Shhhhhh."

She didn't feel like being quiet. The darkness sent tingles up her back. "We could turn on a light."

"That would ruin the effect, I think. Did you know we're staying in what was Joshua Montgomery's room, the master suite?" He led her across the room.

"Yes, you told me that. I think it's why it feels so warm and welcoming."

True, the downstairs was all dining and dancing and bar areas, and a good part of the second floor was bedrooms and baths for the Bed and Breakfast, but it was redone to fit a business. This room, however, held a sense of home, the same sense she knew Montgomery felt when he lived here.

Quint let go of her hand.

She yawned and waited. "If you don't have something else to show me, I'm climbing back in bed."

"I have something wonderful to show you. Do you want to see a secret room?"

A shiver rippled through her, but whether it was from his voice, the dark, or the fact she wore only his shirt, she couldn't be sure. "I'd love to."

The idea sent her heart pounding in her chest, and she wondered if Quint could hear it. Climbing back into bed was now the farthest thing from her mind. "I'll bet, after working throughout the house, you know about all the secret rooms."

"Yes, I do."

"Why didn't you tell me about this before?"

"Shhh." This time she felt him hold his fingertips to her lips to silence her. "No questions now, Meggie. Just see what I have to show you, then later there will be time for talk, all right?"

She lost herself in his words, in the deep, richness of his voice. He sounded more like the man who'd been in the pool with her, and the man who'd danced with her. She tried to see him, to see if his grin was crooked or if he favored one leg over the other, but it was impossible. He was nothing more than a shadow in the darkness.

"It feels like home here, doesn't it?" He reached out and touched a panel on the wall.

"Yes." Meg tried to watch him, but couldn't see his exact movements.

"I'd like it to be our home, Meg, ours together."

"I like that idea. I was just thinking that very thing."

She heard him slide his hand along the wall. Then she heard the movement of wood against wood. Through the shadows, she could make out a panel opening, revealing the musty darkness of another room. Like the rooms surrounding the empty pool and the unused hallway earlier, the stale air told her how this room had been closed for some time. A slight touch of cool air brought gooseflesh to her bare legs.

"Wow." Meg tried to see. "What is it?"

"Take a look for yourself." Quint pulled her closer to the opening. There was a taper in a sconce on the wall. He lit it, and the flickering flame cast a soft yellow light in the small room.

Meg looked around, astonished. "It's a dressing room and bathroom combination."

"Undiscovered and untouched. After all these years."

It was complete with an old cast iron tub on one end, something that looked to be a shower enclosure not too far away, and a mirrored vanity on the opposite wall. Dust covered bottles of cosmetics and perfume sat on the vanity. She stepped closer, awed by the century old personal articles. There were hair combs and a large powder puff, a hairbrush with a tarnished silver handle.

She couldn't catch her breath.

"These things belonged to Joshua Montgomery's wife, didn't they?"

"Yes, I have no doubt they were Ellen's."

His certainty intrigued her. But the room intrigued her more. "I feel like such an intruder here. When did you find this?" For another long moment, she gazed about the room. The flowered wallpaper was old and covered with cobwebs of time. The tub was gray, although, she was sure, it had once been white. This was how she'd expected the kitchen to look.

"I always knew this was here." Quint's gaze was hard, colliding with hers through the candlelight like a sudden gust of wind from an oncoming storm.

She looked into the mirror. "You did?"

In the mirror, she saw herself and Quint. They were nothing more than dreamy, shadowed figures, familiar, yet unfamiliar at the same time. Had Joshua and Ellen Montgomery stood the very same way, looking into the very same mirror all those years ago?

"I knew that with your love of history, you'd like this."

He didn't answer her question.

With a soft touch of his hand on the small of her back, he guided her toward the mirror and eased her down on the cushioned seat before it. "What are you thinking, Meggie?

Tell me." His quiet voice was captivating in the small room. The warmth of this breath touched her ear, and shivers raced up her spine.

"I was thinking about Joshua Montgomery in this room. I can just imagine him, maybe, getting ready for one of his many dinner parties, or getting ready for bed afterwards." She stared into the mirror. "Do you know of any other hidden rooms?"

"What if I told you I know everything there is to know about Joshua Montgomery and his house?" He leaned down and touched his lips to the side of her throat. Again, Quint's voice sounded different. Deeper, distinctive, each word more announced.

Meg peered at him in the mirror, one corner of his mouth was slightly higher than the other, not quite the crooked grin of before, but close. "How? That's not possible."

"What if I told you I know about more hidden rooms than this one, and more secrets, perhaps even about the treasure?" His deep, beseeching gaze held her spellbound.

She stared at his reflection in the darkness. "How?"

He slid his hands over her shoulders. "Will you do something for me before I answer your questions?"

"What?" Just as his voice was different, her own voice didn't sound anything like her usual tone. The feelings storming through her were nothing less than a tornado of desire, anxiety, curiosity, excitement, and wonder. Her emotions were all laced together with an unexplainable fear, but of what, she didn't know. She felt safe in this room. She felt safe with Quint. Goosebumps broke out on her arms, and her flesh down the front of the shirt she wore called out for his touch. Yet, she couldn't deny the fear.

The warmth of his hands on her shoulders sent what felt like tiny sparks of electricity over her skin.

"Look into the mirror."

She did.

She saw herself and Quint. His hands were still on her shoulders. She felt him as much as she saw him. His breath on her neck was almost hot. They peered into the mirror as if it held secrets.

It probably does.

Quint drew closer and leaned toward her; his chest against her back. She felt his heart beat and turned to look up at him. "No, don't look at me. Look at us," he said. "There." He indicated the mirror.

Meg turned and looked again, blinking against the lightheadedness that washed over her.

He squeezed her shoulders. "Close your eyes." His whispers sounded as if they were inside her head.

She did as he asked. She couldn't help but obey him.

"Now look into the mirror again."

In the mirror, Quint, as he stood before, was gone. She saw other things—visions. They came to her as they did in the pool room and ballroom. She saw Joshua Montgomery. She more than saw him—she felt his presence. She smelled his clean scent of man and leather. In the mirror he met her gaze. He was preparing for a dinner party.

How is this possible? Quint's hands are still on my shoulders.

"What do you see, Meggie?"

She took a deep breath before she spoke. "Me. You. Perhaps it's Joshua Montgomery." Her own voice sounded as if it came to her through a tunnel. She watched him in the mirror.

Next to her, Quint leaned even closer, still touching her. He moved one hand down her arm, and with his other hand, he reached up and pushed her hair to the side so he could whisper into her ear. "What else do you see? Tell me everything."

"He's wearing black, looking sharp, crisp, perfect. He's adjusting a cuff link."

"What else?"

"He's watching...."

"Watching what? Watching who?"

Me, she almost replied. She stared into the old mirror, transfixed, feeling as if she was floating and watching everything from the ceiling above or on the screen in a movie theater. Yet, at the same time, she was *in* the movie. She was *inside* the mirror. She was the woman Joshua Montgomery watched with evident hunger in his expression. She recognized the same hunger she'd seen in Quint's eyes in the past few days, the same look of desire she'd seen at the pool and on the dance floor. She worried that she'd drunk too much champagne, but the worry was fleeting. "His wife. He's watching his wife. Sitting there—here—in front of the mirror, brushing her hair."

"She knows he's there, doesn't she?" Quint's words touched her with more heat, just like his fingers.

"Yes, she sees his reflection in the mirror." *But more than that, she feels him. Just as I feel him.*

"What else? What is she wearing?"

"A beautiful blue dress. The dress I could've sworn I was wearing when we danced earlier," she whispered.

"What's he doing now?"

"He's stepping closer." Meg saw the man in the mirror glide toward the woman, *her*, his step silent. Yet, whether it was Quint or Joshua Montgomery, she couldn't be sure. "He kissed her on the back of her neck."

Meg gasped as she felt her hair moved aside more. Then there was the touch, just a soft feather touch on the back of her neck. She tried to jump away, out of Quint's grasp, but he refused to let her go.

Instead, he pulled her to her feet, pressing her into him, close enough she felt every contour of his body—his lean, muscular thighs against hers, his ribs and the hardness of his chest against the softness of her breasts, his evident want of her pressed against her lower belly. She also felt the softness of the silk dress against her skin.

She stared up at Quint, meeting his gaze, her heart racing. "How is this happening?" It was hard to breathe, much less speak. Quint kissed her neck. *This* is *Quint, right?*

This was exactly like her experience by the pool. She felt it. She lived it. Yet, it was as if she were someone else.

Quint met her gaze again. "Relax. Look back into the mirror, Meg."

Her heart raced in her chest, pounding so hard, she felt it. "I don't think I should." Yet, she found it impossible not to do so.

He leaned down and touched his lips to hers in an earth-stopping kiss. His touch sent a tingle all the way through her. "Why not?" he asked after he ended the kiss and pulled away.

"I feel like I'm intruding."

"You're not. Don't you want to see?"

"Yes." She wanted to see Quint or Joshua, whoever he was. He was stunningly handsome in his dark jacket, his dark hair neat, his eyes filled with evident longing and desire.

She turned back to face the mirror again, taking in their reflection. He stood behind her and held her against him. The room changed it was now lit by lamplight, not just the single taper. The cobwebs and dust were gone, the room no longer drafty or smelling stale.

"Can you feel how much he loves her?" Quint's whisper was soft against her throat. He took her hands within his own.

"Yes." She felt weak, almost too weak to form words.

"Can you feel how much I love you?"

"Yes." Emotions pierced her like the hot tip of a knife. Yes, there was love, clear and strong. And desire. And need. And wonder. There was even a strong sense of jealousy, but she didn't understand why that emotion was woven in with the evident love spilling from the couple through the mirror.

In the mirror, Joshua slowly unbuttoned the small buttons up the back of Ellen's dress. *Perhaps they weren't getting ready for the party. Perhaps the guests were gone and they were preparing for a little party of their own.*

Meg felt cool air against her skin and realized the buttons on her shirt were undone, exposing her nakedness to the shadowed lamplight.

"How did you do that?" Quint hadn't moved. His hands still held hers. The buttons on the blue dress had been up the back, but the buttons on Meg's large shirt were in the front.

Still, they were undone.

Quint replied with a touch of his lips to hers. He let go of her hands and allowed the soft cotton shirt to slide down her body. It landed on the floor at her feet.

This room hadn't been heated in a number of winters, so Meg should have been cold, but she wasn't. She wasn't the least bit chilled, but still, shivers wracked her body and her nipples hardened. The sensation of floating hadn't dispelled, and she was aware of every sensation and every action, yet she couldn't control her own reactions.

In the mirror, Joshua reached up and cupped her breasts. Ellen's breasts?

Meg felt his hands, her flesh filled with fire beneath his touch. She gasped in an effort to draw in a breath, her eyes closing against the ecstasy. Still she saw everything, felt everything with the greatest intensity, felt every touch, and every emotion with senses that had reached impossible heights.

Joshua kissed Ellen.

Meg felt his kiss, and she felt passion flow into her like a strong, uncontrollable bolt of lightning, instant, blinding, heart stopping.

Joshua touched Ellen.

Meg felt the caress wash over her like a sun-filled ocean wave. It was a caress that centered all its strength in her soul. It caused her core to flutter.

Joshua drew Ellen to the floor, his kiss unending.

Meg didn't remember moving. She felt the softness of the plush carpet against her back. His heat and hardness pressed against her. Was it Joshua or Quint? She didn't open her eyes to see.

His kisses set her on fire.

His touch sang over her.

He filled her completely.

Their love making was explosive, leaving her weak and exhausted and needing more—as desperately as she needed her next breath. The pleasure here, now, was even more powerful than what she'd felt in the pool.

She'd never known such passion, had never felt so loved in her life.

It was the passion she felt in the pool mixed with the love and desire she experienced during the waltz. If she didn't know better, she'd think he'd lit a thousand candles in her soul.

"Thank you, Meg." He whispered at her ear, his breathing fast and ragged.

"For what?" Her voice, much like the rest of her body, quivered in the aftermath of the earth-shattering climax he'd just shared with her.

"Through you, Meg, the transition is complete. You have allowed the spirit of Joshua Montgomery to be where he belongs, which is by your side. You have allowed him to live again."

Meg wasn't certain she heard him correctly. It was hard to hear anything over the blood rushing in her ears, and besides that, it made no sense. "What? I don't understand."

"You have Ellen's soul," he said, his voice haunted and rough. "I recognized you the moment you came to eat lunch all those months ago." He chuckled and leaned down to suck her breast into his mouth. Meg gasped at the touch. "It seems like I've searched for Ellen for an eternity. Then out of the blue, you simply stepped into the house."

Confusion and fear touched her like an ice cube dropped down the back of her pants. "What are you saying? Are you saying you're Joshua Montgomery?"

This can't be real. This must be a dream. You feel like Quint. You taste like Quint. You smell like Quint. Besides, Joshua Montgomery has been dead for more than a century.

"This can be a dream if you want it to be. And I can be Joshua or Quint. It does not matter what you choose to call me. Just as long as you know that I love you."

She must have spoken out loud.

"You became Joshua? What about Quint? Where's Quint?" Her words shook as shudders passed through her.

This had to be a dream. It still didn't make any sense. It couldn't be real. It couldn't be possible. There was no other explanation.

He held her tighter but it didn't stop her from trembling. "Relax. Quint's still here. I just mixed with him. Think of it, Meggie, I have my—Joshua's—business ability. I can take this house and make even more millions with it. And I have Quint's ability to build it into anything I want."

He hungrily pressed his lips to hers, heat poured through her.

"And you, Meg." He paused to kiss her again. "I have you, too. You made it all possible. Your love opened the door and allowed me in. Thank you."

His kisses went on and on, leaving her weak.

Then he entered her again, seeking, finding, and giving pleasure until the world tumbled away, leaving her filled as never before.

Meg opened her eyes and looked back into the mirror. She saw the candlelit silhouettes of herself and Quint in the reflection. She was wearing Quint's shirt, her blue silk dress gone. She sucked in a breath and gripped the edge of the dressing table. "How long have we been here?"

"Not long."

It seemed like hours. His touch left tiny sparks on her flesh. Her insides still vibrated from her orgasm. Her heart raced in her chest. "Did you see that? Did you feel that?"

He tightened his embrace. "Yes, I saw it. I felt it, with you. Just like now I see you, Meg. I feel you, and you feel so good." He sounded and felt so familiar.

She wondered if he tingled with the aftermath of the lovemaking as she did. *Did we even make love at all?* "Was it real?" *Am I crazy?*

He gazed into her eyes, appearing calm. "Yes, Meg, it was real." He kissed her again, and she wondered if her legs would hold her up.

He squeezed her hand. "Come on."

"Wait I want to know—" There were a million things she wanted to know. Like, how did it happen? Could it really be possible that the spirit of Joshua Montgomery now possessed him?

"Not now. Let's go back to our room and get into bed where it's warmer. I want to hold you forever."

He refused to let go of her hand even as he blew out the lone candle and thrust them into darkness. Meg shivered, but whether it was from his touch or the coldness of the dark caressing her passion-heated skin, she had no idea. Her legs trembled, unwilling to hold her erect. Without further comment, he pulled her out into the bedroom and slid the panel door closed behind them. She had no more than a second to glance back into the mirror. She saw the shadows of the two of them through the darkness.

Meg woke with a start and sat straight up in bed.

The room was dark, filled with shadows and the muffled sounds of the night outside. It took her a long moment to recognize their room at Montgomery Manor.

Her heart still pounded in her chest. Her skin was still slick with perspiration from the passion she'd just felt. She remembered leaving the hidden room, but she didn't remember climbing into bed. Had she dreamt everything about that hidden room? No, it had been so real.

"Meg?" Quint sat up beside her. "What's the matter? Was it a dream?" His voice was gruff with sleep, but he sounded like the regular Quint she knew.

"I don't know. I don't know what it was. It seemed too real to be nothing more than a dream." Confusion rolled through her. It *was* real. Her insides still shook with the aftermath.

"You're shaking." He put his arms around her, holding her against the warmth of his chest. "Are you cold?"

She wasn't sure *what* she was. She clenched her jaws to keep her teeth from chattering. She felt and heard the familiar strength of his heart beating. "Just hold me."

"I've got you. Mmmm, you feel wonderful, too. I want to hold you forever."

She pulled away from him. Her dream lover had said the same thing. "There was a room, a dressing room."

"There's a bunch of rooms here, Meggie. Remember, on Sunday, we're going to explore them all. But I think right now, I'd like to just explore you." He moved to unbutton the shirt she wore. His hand on her breast made her shiver.

She couldn't remember ever being filled with so much want before. It was as if Quint's touch now set her on fire, an endless fire.

"But the room," she tried.

"Forget the room." He slid his hand down her belly, and tangled his fingers in the soft fur between her legs. His touch only added to the tremors already inside her.

He kissed her, and his kiss was just as he'd kissed her in that hidden room standing before that mirror. Just as before, she found it impossible to fight the passion, the pleasure rolling through her. She had no choice but to open herself to him.

Much later, she slept against him.

But Quint didn't sleep.

He lay awake in the darkness and listened to her soft, steady breathing. He didn't need to sleep. With the newness of feeling whole, and living again, his energy soared.

And even if his energy hadn't been renewed, he still would not have slept, for he was far too happy.

The transition was complete, and in such a short time, too. It amazed him how easy it was to push Quint Falkner where *he* needed to be, then to allow himself, and the bits and pieces of Quint Falkner's life, to weave themselves together, much like he and Meg had been a short while before.

He smiled in the darkness as he remembered the way he'd allowed Meg to feel his spirit; in the pool, on the dance floor, in the hallway, and in the dressing room. It hadn't been a necessary part of the transition, but it was something he'd wanted to share with her. He wanted her to feel him even before the transition was complete.

Now Joshua Montgomery's spirit was in its place, and the woman who held Joshua Montgomery's heart in her hands slept beside him, his seed planted in her womb. He reached out and stroked Meg's thigh, careful not to wake her.

He had always been proud of the Montgomery name, but he had to give it up now. He had to accept Quint Falkner's name just as he accepted his body and took his place in this life, mixing their souls together. He now knew all that Quint knew, he had all of Quint's memories, as well as he had his own.

Of all the men Joshua Montgomery could have joined, Quint would not have been his first choice. When Joshua's spirit found Meg, Quint was using his joblessness as an excuse to be lazy. But all in all, Quint wasn't a bad sort. Quint had an inner pride and strength, and his spirit, Joshua's spirit, helped him bring those traits out.

And what of Meg? How much would she remember in the morning? Would she question him? Would she demand answers? Would she even believe him if he told her the truth? He had no idea. Besides there was little she could do to change things now.

Did he harbor any guilt for becoming her husband?

No.

He would have done whatever necessary to live beside her again.

His mind raced with ideas. There was so much he wanted to do. He knew the identity of Ellen's murderer, and he would have liked to clear his name, but he wasn't certain that was important any longer. Why waste his time looking for evidence that wasn't there? More important, he planned to restore the house completely. And, above all else, he planned to spend the rest of this life—this chance—with Meg. He planned to share all that he had and fill this house with their children.

He would create a future for Montgomery Manor.

Most important, he planned to create a future for himself and his wife. True, he loved the house. After all, it was *his* creation, but he built it to share with the woman he loved.

He never got that chance.

Now that he had that woman in his arms, sleeping beside him, he didn't care if the house burnt to the ground as long as history did not repeat itself. This time he wanted to grow old beside the woman who held his heart.

Thunder still rumbled outside, although the storm was blowing itself out.

Quint Falkner snuggled up against his wife.

CHAPTER TEN

Meg sat up and yawned.

"Good morning." Quint leaned down and kissed her.

She stretched. "Boy, do I ever feel stiff. What time is it?"

"Ten to nine." Quint buttoned his shirt, but watched her.

"Oh, no!" She tossed back the sheets. "I need to open by nine-thirty."

"What time does Evan get there?"

"About the same time."

Quint stopped buttoning his shirt and leaned close again. His kiss was warm and inviting. "Let Evan open. We could take another dunk in the whirlpool."

"I'd love to, but I better not." She stretched again, her body wakening to the new day. "Although it sure would be nice to sleep another hour or two." She climbed out of bed, deliberately checking if her legs would hold her.

"Tired, are you?"

"Between making love and staying up late dancing and the strange dream I had—yes." For a moment, she tried to put the visions she'd experienced in some sort of perspective. It was impossible. So, she pushed the idea aside, determined to move on with her day. "Besides, I don't want to leave. I guess I'm as caught up in the history of this place as you are, and I'd love to stay and explore. And you've intrigued me with your offer of the art room."

He gave her a flash of his crooked grin before he moved to finish the buttons on his shirt. "Well, as soon as you close later, you can come back, and we can look around together."

"Can I give you some of my ideas?"

"I wouldn't have it any other way."

Meg had to pull away from his next kiss. "I have to go. My shop waits, so do my books."

"If your shop was here, you wouldn't have so far to go."

"I'm still thinking about it."

In the carriage house, Quint settled for a lingering kiss. "When would you like to move in permanently?"

She looked around, a surge of excitement washing through her. "I can start packing things up this week."

"We can use the furniture in our house to fill some of the empty rooms. And our table and chairs would work well in the game room." He held her against him.

"That sounds like a plan. What do you plan to do today? Rest? You deserve to." Meg wished *she* could.

"I doubt it. I plan to look for glitches from last night, see how many rooms got booked, make sure things are in order for this morning's breakfast buffet. We're a go now, Meggie. There's no stopping us."

He gave her another kiss before tucking her into her car. "When you come back and have some time, remind me to show you the secret passage to get from here to the house."

"Are there spiders? You know how much I hate spiders."

Quint laughed. "I always try to get rid of all the spiders, just for you."

"I can hardly wait." She grinned back at him, noticing his grin looked so much like the smile of the man in her strange dream.

He closed her door and gave her one last quick kiss through the open window.

Meg reached the store and unlocked the doors. The shop greeted her with its welcoming antique smell. She took a deep breath, feeling right at home, but wishing she could have stayed at the Manor. In bed. Her romantic night with her husband might be over, but she wasn't quite ready to let it go.

Oddly, the shop all but added to the sense of home she'd felt at the Manor. She stopped and looked around, taking in her shop, seeing everything she worked long and hard to build. True, she had built this into a successful business, but maybe it was time to move it in another direction. She wondered if moving her books to the Manor wouldn't be the best idea. After all, her shop was the *Treasure Hunters* bookstore, and wasn't the Manor filled with historical treasures, as well as having a legend of hidden treasure? Would Quint like the idea of opening part of the house as a historical museum? It would be an interesting concept. And besides mystery dinners, they could host scavenger hunts or treasure hunts. She planned to suggest it to him as soon as she talked to him.

Her gaze caught the vase of roses still on the counter from the day before. The blossoms were still as beautiful as they were when they were delivered. She wondered if their sender had been at the party. Had he watched her without her knowing? The thought sent a chill through her. Would she ever know who sent them?

"Good morning."

Meg jumped. She'd been so caught up in the roses and the night before she hadn't heard Evan come in.

"Sorry, I didn't mean to scare you. It was a great party. Quint did a wonderful job. And the food was the best."

"Thanks, I'll tell him you said so. Who was that redhead you were with?"

He shrugged as if it didn't matter. "Just someone I met there. I doubt I'll see her again. You look happy this morning."

"I am." She didn't say anymore on the subject, unwilling to share her night with Quint with anyone.

"Did you stay the night in the house?"

"Yes."

"I thought about doing that, too, but then I booked a room for Saturday instead when I don't have to come into the shop the next morning. I want to spend more time looking around."

It was another busy day. Business couldn't be better. It just wasn't easy to concentrate. Meg's thoughts were on Montgomery Manor and her night with Quint. Memories of the empty pool weren't too far away, either.

The buzz about her shop was Montgomery Manor's wonderful grand opening. Two customers even admitted to seeing a ghost.

"I saw a pretty woman in a flowing blue dress," said Amelia Middorf.

"Why didn't you point her out to me?" asked Sally Landford. "I was with you almost the whole time."

"You were busy flirting with that white-haired man. What was his name?"

"Stuart Jenkins. And I wasn't flirting for that long. You could have told me she was there," Sally huffed.

"She was no more than a flash. Didn't I read somewhere Ellen Montgomery was wearing a blue dress when she was murdered?" Amelia asked.

"I think so," Sally confirmed.

Amelia looked at Meg. "Do you have any books about the Montgomery Manor here?"

Meg smiled. "As a matter of fact, I have a few right over here." She was glad she'd thought to set up a special display. She led the ladies to it. A short time later, she rang up two more sales as both ladies bought different books, planning to switch with each other after they'd read them.

As she closed the ladies' sales, Nicki Paulson stepped up to the counter. She noticed the books the two had chosen. "Last night's dinner was fabulous and I saw a white, misty figure float across the dining room while I was eating."

Amelia and Sally jumped right into the conversation relaying what Amelia had seen. Meg noticed the way Evan fought to keep his grin at bay as they chattered. She bit her lip to keep from laughing when he added, "I thought I saw something like that, too."

The three ladies were still chatting about ghosts as they went out the door and sent the chimes over their heads ringing.

"What do you mean you saw something like a white, misty figure?" Meg asked as soon as they were gone. "Lies like that might get you into trouble."

Now he *did* grin. "Lies like that will get more customers into your husband's restaurant. The curious always flock in for the unexplained. I couldn't help but notice, though, the glimmer of fear on your face when they talked about seeing ghosts. Did you see something, Meg?"

She turned away so he couldn't see her expression. "I'm not sure what I saw, and I don't want to talk about it."

"If you change your mind, I'm here," he said. He was kind enough to let the subject drop.

Meg went back to work, refusing to say any more about the strange apparitions she experienced in the pool and on the dance floor. The strange dream she'd had seemed so far away, but on the surface of her thoughts at the same time. She kept herself too busy to think about ghost stories.

Besides, it seemed all her dreams—as well as Quint's—were coming true. Why would she want to put a dark cloud over them when it might have been just a series of dreams? Realistic, erotic dreams.

She managed to call Quint late in the afternoon. The party was a success for both of them. He'd been just as busy and hadn't been able to call her.

"Are you about to close?"

"Yes, Evan's already gone, and I plan to lock the doors in the next ten minutes."

"Will you be coming here then?"

"I will in a while. I've got some work to do here. If anything, I need to at least sweep the floor. And if I keep spending all my time there, I'll never get anything done here."

She could almost hear him grin, and she should have known what his next words would be. "You can move your books here and not have to worry about it."

"I'm still thinking about it, don't push me." She'd already made up her mind to move into the art room he'd offered her. It didn't make sense to stay here and keep paying rent when she didn't have to. Besides, the house, the art room or the gallery as she preferred to think of it, seemed to call to her. She *wanted* to be there. It had tugged on her heart to have to leave that morning.

"Okay, I'm sorry. I've got to get back to work. I should be able to get away from here soon. How about I come by there and get you. I have a present for you."

"I'd like that. I'll wait here for you."

"Okay. I'll bring you back here and we'll have a late supper together. In our room—in the whirlpool."

Meg laughed.

"What's so funny?"

"Nothing, I doubt I'll get much work done thinking about you."

He paused for a long moment. "I'll be there soon."

Moments later, she was back to logging in a stack of books. And minutes later, she locked the doors and turned the open sign to closed. The roses on the counter caught her gaze. They were so pretty, so mysterious.

Little did she know, she wasn't the only one gazing at them.

CHAPTER ELEVEN

Meg went back to her office where books piled in stacks waiting for her to log them into the computer. Or she could take a look at the poetry Evan logged in.

Or she could make plans to move her books to Montgomery Manor.

The thought sent a shiver of anticipation through her.

She loved the shop she'd created, but at the same time, she thought it time to move to something bigger and better.

She moved toward her desk, planning to sit down and write out a list of pros and cons of moving the shop to the Manor. And then make a list of what she'd need to do to get the move made.

The lights went out.

"What?" She asked into the sudden darkness.

Before she could take another step, much less reach her desk, grab her phone to call for help, a rough, big hand clamped across her face. The intruder shoved her sideways onto the old sofa she kept in her office.

She fought to maintain her balance. And lost.

She struggled against the strong arms holding her. She lost that battle, too.

She couldn't breathe past his fingers, but with her heart now lodged in her throat she was choking anyway.

Terror raced through her blood freezing her in her place. Her body rippled with fear. For a long moment the world came to a sudden, grinding halt.

The primal need for air took over, she'd fight for oxygen if for nothing else.

She pushed against the hand pinning her to the couch. At the same time, she tried to turn her head.

The intruder grasped a handful of her hair with his other hand, holding her head in place.

She was going to die. Right there. Right then. Meg expected her life to pass before her eyes, or to see a great light or something spectacular.

But there was nothing. Just the petrifying darkness. And paralyzing terror mixed with cold panic she couldn't seem to think beyond. Her lungs screamed for air.

He gripped her hair tighter but released her face. She took the opportunity to gulp in much needed air.

After several long drags of oxygen, she squeaked out, "What do you want?"

Her throat ached with each word.

Who was he? Why was he there? She couldn't imagine someone breaking into her shop for the books. And Evan had taken the cash from the store to make a bank deposit when he left earlier, so there wasn't much money locked in her desk. That left....

"You, Megan."

The intruder's hot whisper hit her like a closed fist.

Did she know that voice? No, she didn't recognize the whisper. Or did she? Was it the same voice that whispered to her on the phone? And who called her *Megan* besides her mother? Like a computer sorting data, she searched for answers but found none.

There was nothing about him she recognized. He wasn't Evan, he wasn't Quint. He was just darkness, just terror, a faceless, nameless specter.

She felt the roughness of his hand on her chin, then on her throat, and into the top of her blouse. A shrieking alarm of invasion and violation lit through her.

I can't let this happen. His identity no longer mattered. Just stopping him, getting away from him was all that mattered.

"No!" The single word was painful in her throat, but she ignored the pain. She clawed through the dark, seeking his face. Her nails raked flesh. Where did she get him?

He let out a hiss of pain and pulled away. Meg took the opportunity to jump up and away from him, but he still held her hair, so she didn't get far.

He stopped her with a sudden snap of pain to her scalp.

"Don't think you're going to get away so easily, Megan. I've watched you for too long. I've waited to have you for too long." He growled into her face.

Meg's stomach somersaulted at the smell of his hot, acidic breath. How the courage scratched through the blanket of blinding terror, she didn't know. "Don't think you're going to get me so easy."

Her words brought a bolster of courage but less pain in her throat.

He ripped open her blouse, the sounds of its buttons hitting the floor in the dark cracked through the stillness like gunshots. Meg jumped, her sudden movement pulled on her already sore scalp, her hair still held in the attackers' hand.

The cool air of the office touched her bare flesh raising a layer of goose bumps along her naked skin.

I can't let this happen. She just couldn't.

She swung her closed fist. The darkness was as much a disadvantage to him as it was to her. Her knuckles made contact with—his neck? Meg ignored the pain spreading through her hand and up her arm, and for the first time he let go of her hair.

She jumped off the couch, away from him.

The office was small, containing her desk, computer, the couch, and stacks of books. She tripped over one stack. Books scattered, and she fell to her hands and knees.

The intruder took that moment to grab her again. He groped for a good hold on her but only managed to get a fistful of her silky skirt.

If she could just get out of the office, into the sales room where it wasn't so confined or filled with obstacles, and where moonlight streamed through the windows, she might have a chance to escape or at least have more places to hide.

She kicked out at him and missed. He'd grown wise, moving out of her path.

Hot tears streamed down her cheeks. *I have to get away.*

She thought she could escape him, too.

No, I can't give up. One last try.

She scrambled for the door through the darkness, so close, but unreachable as he griped her arm and hauled her to her feet. When she kicked out at him again she made contact with what had to have been his shin. He shoved her away.

She fell into the corner of her desk.

The corner felt as sharp and pointed as a double edged sword. It cut into her backbone just above her tail bone with enough force steal her breath and senses.

She fell to her knees again, helpless, letting out a cry of pain, pain that all but vibrated from that spot on her back. The jolt moved all the way to her fingertips.

The intruder shoved her to her back and tore at her clothes. He was heavy on top of her. She couldn't escape.

I can't...I can't stop this. He was going to do what he wanted, and she had nothing else with which to fight him. She tried to scratch at him again, he grabbed her wrists with one strong hand, and pinned them to the floor above her head.

"No!" She screamed the word over and over. She didn't recognize the sobs from her own lips.

His words cut through her sob like a knife. "Did you like the roses?"

His words stopped her fight altogether. "No, no…" Bile rose in her throat.

"You will be mine." His words were harsh, and spoken with determination, as if it was already final.

"Never, no…" She tried to sound just as determined, but it was hard to get enough air. She still tried to escape, but he pinned her wrists above her head.

"Even if it is just for this moment."

"No…" Her throat was rough, scratchy, her voice hoarse as she screamed the single word over and over.

In the next moment, his weight was wrenched from her, and through the haze of terror combined with the sick realization of what he meant to do to her, Meg was aware of another struggle in the room.

Someone else was there.

Someone had come to her rescue. Someone else now fought the intruder. She sobbed with relief and the remnants of terror. The sounds of the struggle came to her as if from a great distance. She was aware of the struggle moving to the sales room. There was a loud crash of breaking glass.

Then nothing. Silence broken by the sound of her own heart racing in her ears.

Meg understood that the intruder was gone, his hands no longer on her body, no longer making her feel vulnerable and dirty. She trembled uncontrollably. Her breaths coming in ragged pants.

Hands touched her again, and she fought weakly. Her sobs, however, grew in strength. Had the intruder returned?

It was a long moment before a voice reached her. A soothing, welcoming voice. Quint's voice.

"Meg? Meggie? It's me. It's me. It's Quint. I won't hurt you." He gripped her face.

She recognized his touch and the sound of his voice and stopped fighting him. "He….He…." She tried to tell him, tried to speak and tell what had happened, but the words refused to come. It seemed to take all of her energy to breathe.

"It's all right. He's gone. I'm going find the breaker box so we can get some light in here, then I'll call the police."

Meg pressed herself into his embrace and clutched his shirt in her fists. "No, don't leave me!"

"Are you hurt? Can you walk?" His voice sounded tight.

"Yes, I think I can walk." She wasn't certain whether she was hurt or not. She felt numb and weak, her legs like rubber.

Quint held her close and helped her to her feet. He held her close, took her with him to the breaker box which was not too far away from her office. He flipped a switch and the lights came back on.

He turned to her, and let out a ragged, heavy breath. "Fuck." He hesitated, then reached up and gently touched her cheek.

"Don't." She tried hiding her face from him, as if convincing him not to look, not to see her, could make all of the horror of what happened go away. "Maybe you should turn the lights off again."

He moved her back into her office toward her desk, pulled out his cell phone, and ignored her request to turn off the light. After his 9-1-1 call, he set her down on the couch.

Only then, did he take time to absorb every detail of her face. "When I get my hands on whoever did this—" He spoke through gritted teeth. His words were so filled with rage, Meg thought he might suddenly burst apart.

She stopped him with a touch of her trembling fingers to his lips. "Don't. It doesn't help me right now."

"It helps me." Undeniable anger laced his voice. His big hands gentle, he closed her blouse, pinching it together when he noticed the buttons missing. "What did he do to you? Did he hurt you? Where did he touch you? Who the hell was he? How did he get in here?"

"I'm all right." She hoped her voice sounded as calm as she was pretending to be. She struggled to keep her teeth from chattering and to make sense of Quint's rapid-fire questions.

"And pigs can fly." Quint saw right through her lie. "I should call an ambulance, too."

"No." She held on to him, refusing to let him reach for his phone again. "I'll be fine, really. Nothing's broken. I'm just shaken up, that's all, and there's nothing any doctor can do to help with that. He managed to rip my blouse, but you stopped him before he got the chance to do anything more than scare me half to death. Did you see who he was?"

"No." Quint's voice was rife with hostility. "And he's damn lucky, too, or I'd already be hunting him down to kill him." He held her to his chest.

Meg heard sirens in the distance.

"How long was he here with you?" Quint's words vibrated through his chest and into her.

"I don't know. It felt like a lifetime, but it probably just a few moments. I had just turned my sign to closed and came in here when the lights went out." Meg clutched his shirt in her fists. She couldn't get close enough to him. He was warm and smelled so wonderfully familiar. She couldn't deny the how safe and secure she felt in his arms.

He pulled her closer.

"So whoever attacked you killed the lights. I thought you'd left when I saw the place dark, but then I saw your car still parked outside. I came to the door to look inside, thinking maybe your office light was on, and I just couldn't see it. I was about to knock when I heard you screaming."

Meg felt him tense as he spoke. He swore and tightened his arms around her. "If I hadn't come in. If I hadn't seen your car and I'd just gone home...."

She shuddered at his words at the thought of what could have happened—what would have happened if he hadn't come in when he did. "I locked the door. How'd you get in?"

"I have a key, remember? You gave it to me a long time ago. It was on my ring with my truck keys, and I was lucky enough to have it right in my hand."

She nodded, thankful she'd given it to him.

When the police arrived a moment later, two uniformed cops found Quint Falkner holding his wife.

By the time the police finished, Meg felt beaten and violated a second time.

Now sitting in the chair behind the counter in the sales room, she snuggled deeper into Quint's coat, which he'd wrapped around her some time before.

"Let me make sure I have everything," Humphreys, the first police officer stated for what Meg thought must be the tenth time. "Neither of you got a good look at the intruder?"

"It was dark." She closed her eyes against the memory.

"No, I was too concerned about getting to my wife," Quint said at the same time.

"Are you sure you don't need to be examined by a doctor?" Humphreys looked at Meg, studying her with his too-observant gaze.

"I'm sure." She wanted to scream that she needed some peace. That she needed a bath to wash off the dirty feeling of some unknown man's hands on her. That she needed a drink of something—anything—wet and warm that would rinse away the dry, horrible feeling in her throat and warm her frozen insides. Most of all, she wanted to scream.

She'd been so paralyzed with fear that all she'd been able to say through the attack was 'no.' And now, she thought if she could just scream, it might relieve some of the pent up terror and frustration trapped within her.

"Do you know of any reason why someone would want to do this?" Humphreys wrote something in the small notebook he held.

"No, but he sent me roses. Or at least he knew about the roses I received yesterday. And he called me on the phone," she remembered.

Quint sucked in an angry, huffed breath as she explained about the roses and the phone call.

"There were roses delivered to Montgomery Manor for her last night, too, just like those." He looked at the roses on the counter.

With the excitement of the night, she'd forgotten all about the roses delivered to the Manor.

"You didn't think there was anything strange about that?" Humphreys looked at them with a scrutinizing glee in his eyes.

"There were several bunches of flowers and plants, even a basket of wine and cheese, sent to the Manor wishing us well for the grand opening last night." To Meg, Quint's words sounded strangled, reminding her of a guitar string tightened too tight. With his brows knit together and his pursed lips and his clenched fists when he wasn't touching or holding her, he looked like a man ready to do battle. She wondered if Humphreys recognized it.

The police moved to inspect the vase. It didn't take them long to discover there wouldn't be much of a lead. There wasn't even anything in them to indicate which florist had supplied them. The card was simple and white, the envelope the same.

"I'll call the various florist shops in the area and see what I can find out." Officer Humphreys' words didn't assure her in the least.

She'd already known there was nothing on the vase to indicate which florist had supplied them, and she didn't even remember the young man who had delivered them except the color of his hair. What a useless detail. She'd been too taken in by the brilliant deep red buds to pay much attention.

"We've checked thoroughly and there's no sign of anyone breaking in. So we think you must have locked him in here with you."

Meg let out a heavy breath. "There just isn't any other way he could have gotten in here with me. I did my usual look around and locked the door when I closed. Quint had to use his key to get in. I didn't think there was anyone in here, but there wasn't much time in between when I locked up and when he grabbed me."

She looked at Quint, recognizing his need to move as he paced like a caged cat. And she, through her own emotional turmoil, saw his emotional whirlwind, no matter how well he hid it from the police.

"You should be chasing the bastard who did this." Quint glared at Humphreys.

She heard the underlying fury beneath the forced calmness of his words.

Humphreys directed his attention to Quint, and Meg was certain by the challenging look in Humphreys' expression that he did, indeed, recognize the rage Quint worked to keep hidden. "We'd like to do that."

Humphreys' words were calm and even, and he sounded a great deal like a cop on a television show. "But we don't have much to go on. And I was just informed by Officer Rankins, who has been dusting for prints, that there are just too many smeared prints on the door handle. Is there anything more you can tell us about the assailant besides his size and the fact he wore dark clothes?"

"I don't know anything else." Quint looked at Meg.

Humphreys narrowed his eyes. "I'm surprised that if you struggled as much as you say, and pushed him right through the glass of the front door, that you don't have a mark on you."

Quint's defenses went up in an instant. He stared at Humphreys for a long silent moment. Then he looked up at the ceiling for a brief moment as if to gather his patience and let out a huff. Again, he grit his teeth as if he was afraid to open his mouth and say something he might regret. "I already told you, I had a hold of him from behind. I tried to keep a hold of him, but he kept slipping away. He wore one of those nylon sweat suits, and I couldn't get a good grip. He also wore a knitted cap. And I never said I pushed him through the glass, I said he ran through it. I was a few feet behind him when he did, so I wasn't near any sharp glass."

"And it didn't stop him?"

"Not much. But seeing the jagged edges of all that broken glass stopped *me*."

"Oh?" Humphreys seemed like a seasoned cop. Skeptical was probably his middle name.

"I wouldn't be much good to my wife if I managed to get myself all cut up and bloody, now would I? Besides, I could still hear her crying. I thought she was more important."

Humphreys didn't answer the question. "And you didn't see what direction he ran?"

"I told you, across the street, past the bakery, that was as far as I could see him."

"What color was the sweat suit he wore?"

"Dark, navy blue, maybe black. And since I heard my wife crying, I was too worried about getting back to her. Since I didn't know if he had hurt her, the last thing I thought of doing was leaving her alone to go chasing after him. To tell the truth, I was just glad to see him gone." Quint looked at Meg again, and for the first time that evening, his expression softened.

Her head hurt, her hand hurt, and her back throbbed. She felt like a million tiny bugs crawled on her skin where the man had grabbed her.

"How was it you could see this man through the dark, attacking your wife, yet she couldn't see him well enough when he was closer to her?"

Quint crammed his clenched fists into his pockets. "I don't think I *could* see him. I heard her struggling and crying, and I just reacted. I just reached out in the direction of her voice."

Humphreys nodded, seeming satisfied.

"Can we go home?" Meg interrupted.

Humphreys closed the small notebook he'd been writing in. "Of course. If we come up with any leads or have any further questions, would it be all right to give you a call?"

She reached across the counter and retrieved one of her business cards. She scratched her numbers on it. "Certainly. If I'm not at home, I'll be here or at Montgomery Manor with my husband."

Quint took the card from her and added his cell phone number and the number at the Manor.

Humphreys nodded and glanced at the card before tucking it in his pocket.

"Come on, Meg, I'll take you home." The anger was gone from Quint's voice.

She looked up at her husband. He looked as tired as she felt. Yet, there was a smoldering fire in the darkness of his eyes, and she knew, without a doubt, that his anger and frustration still raged despite the coolness of his voice. He reached out and took her hand, holding her with unmistakable gentleness, as if she were a treasure he wanted to protect.

She let out a heavy breath. "That sounds wonderful."

He held her close. "You're shivering." He wrapped his coat tighter around her.

"My teeth would still chatter if I let them."

They headed toward the door where two uniformed cops were placing a board where the glass of the glass door used to be. The rest of the town must have been quiet if the officers had the time to help out. The room was cool from the night air seeping in through the broken door. "We'll make sure the place is locked up," one of the officers promised.

"Thank you." Meg shivered against the chill.

Quint pulled her close. "I'll turn on the heater in the car." They headed for the door.

Meg didn't know which was worse, the stiffness that threatened her back and legs, or the overwhelming sense of being stared at.

She told herself they were almost out of there, away from the sympathetic eyes, away from the place where she'd been attacked and violated—a place where she might never feel safe again.

Once the two of them stepped outside, fear gripped her again. It didn't matter that she was tucked beside Quint, warm in his coat, his strong arm around her, and police just inside the shop behind her. She was terrified to be out in the foggy darkness, where an unknown assailant waited. She knew the unknown man was watching her.

CHAPTER TWELVE

Quint peered into the darkness.

Someone waited out there, someone who wanted to hurt Meg. That someone was soulless. Quint recognized the sensation of being in the presence of an evil entity—dirty, heavy, ugly.

Knowing Meg was in danger because of him tore at his heart. If only he'd asked more questions about the roses she'd received at the grand opening.

He breathed, trying to calm himself. Rage still ripped through him—someone touched his wife. Evil was too close. He swore under his breath. He might as well admit it. The cycle of evil and danger was repeating, and there was nothing he could do to stop it.

If he allowed himself to become what he'd been before, a free spirit, he could recognize the evil one. He could soar through the darkness and find the dark color of the evil being, or at least the dark shadow of it.

Yet, in that incorporeal form, he would powerless to fight against it. Also, he didn't know if he could leave Quint's body now that the transition was complete. What he did know, from timeless past experience as his soul joined with other men, was that in his previous form when he did not possess a body, he wouldn't be able to protect Meg.

Quint took Meg home to their little house. He'd been torn between taking her home and taking her to the Manor, but in the end, he knew she needed the familiarity of home.

Meg climbed into the tub in the bathroom behind him, the water sloshing. He wanted to go to her, hold her, shelter her, protect her, promise her she'd be safe with him forever.

But he couldn't make that promise.

History proved that promise couldn't be kept. In his mind, he swore again. How could he stop this cycle, this curse? Why had fate given him another chance if happiness was impossible?

He listened to Meg as he stared out through the darkness, recognizing the sounds of every move she made in the hot bath he'd run for her. He heard her sigh, and knew she'd leaned back in the old claw-foot tub. In his mind, he saw her, knew she closed her eyes. He saw her deep, fiery hair piled onto her head, held in place with one of those springy clips. He saw her lithe body perfectly shaped; and he longed to climb into the tub with her, hold her, and rub and kiss her hurts.

He felt a fresh wave of rage wash over him. Rage he didn't need. Rage his wife didn't need to experience. No, she needed his compassion and his understanding. His rage would help neither of them.

He hadn't always been compassionate in the past. But he was a different man, a new man. He was a man with new attitudes, attitudes mixed with those of the old Quint Falkner.

He turned away from the darkness and faced the fact there was little he could do about the bastard who had put his hands on Meg. At least for now.

But there were things he could do for Meg.

"I brought you a cup of tea." He found her in the tub as he'd envisioned. Except for one thing. She looked smaller, vulnerable, as if swallowed by the large cast iron tub and the water filling it. The room was warm and steamy. The strong scent of the tea he'd brought her was underlined by the floral smell of the soap she used.

"Thank you." She looked up at him.

He ignored the dark circles under her eyes and set her tea on the small table beside the edge of the tub where she could reach it. He leaned against the wall, crossing his arms. He watched his wife and contemplated his next move.

"Why didn't you tell me about the roses or the phone call?" He spoke quietly, hating to confront her, but he had to know.

She avoided his gaze as if she'd known the question was coming and didn't want to face it. "I don't know." She sighed. Then she corrected herself, "Yes, I do know. You were so caught up in the grand opening, and I just didn't want to mess that up for you. Besides I didn't think it was a big deal at the time. I definitely didn't think it was something dangerous. People have sent me flowers and things to the shop before, to thank me for finding a rare book or something."

"It's my fault, too, Meggie."

She forced out a chuckle. "Why? You didn't send me the roses."

He gave her a small smile. "No, but for the past two months, I haven't been here, not long enough to spend time with you—speak with you, see what's going on with you. And I'm sorry for that. It's another reason why I'd like you to move your shop to the Manor. We'd be closer to each other, and we could communicate with one another without having to dial a phone first."

She closed her eyes for a long moment. "Let's not talk about that right now. I want to think about it when I have a clear head and don't have tonight clouding my judgment."

He wanted to push the issue, wanted to make her say she'd pack books into boxes as soon as the sun came up. But he couldn't push her, couldn't take advantage of her vulnerability right now. "I have something else for you, too."

She reached for her cup of tea and paused to look at him.

Quint held up the book.

"A book?"

Her surprise was genuine, if not unexpected.

"Yes, I found it today in a hidden wall compartment, and I knew you'd enjoy it, given your love of books." The lie rolled so easy from his lips. The idea of lying to her left a sour taste in his mouth. Of course, it wasn't exactly a lie. He did take it from a hidden wall compartment. He might have Joshua Montgomery's soul, thoughts, knowledge, but he still had the name, thoughts, knowledge, and upbringing of Quint Falkner. He didn't want to start his new life, this second chance with the woman who'd held his heart through generations, on a lie. But he wasn't ready to tell her the truth, because, despite what she may or may not remember about last night, he knew she wouldn't be ready to accept it.

"A hidden wall compartment?"

"I told you I knew about all of them. I just hadn't *looked* in all of them."

"How many wall compartments do you think are in that house?" She took a sip of tea.

He knew what she thought. She thought about a hidden dressing room and wondered if that room had been real or a mere dream. "I'll show some of them to you tomorrow after work." He set the book on the table beside her tea. "It's Joshua Montgomery's journal."

"What a find." She was astonished. "Thank you." Her voice was no more than a whisper. "Do you think your Mitchell Greensburg ever went through the house looking for all the treasures hidden there?"

"I think he wanted space to run a restaurant and that was enough to satisfy him." He didn't want to explain how he knew that much. He paused. "And Meggie—"

"What?"

"I don't want anything—any secrets kept between us. Ever. If you get roses or phone calls or anything, no matter how unimportant it may seem, share it with me, okay?"

She looked up at him, her eyes soft and teary. "I don't want any secrets, either." She glanced at the book but didn't touch it. Her wet fingers opened and closed, as if they itched to reach out but resisted so she wouldn't wet the old book. He was touched with the care she showed toward the words of Joshua Montgomery's life, *his* life. Thanks to Meg sharing her body with him, sharing her heart, his soul was now free to be with her again.

It was, however, inside Quint Falkner's body.

He had no idea how it happened. He just knew it had happened many times in the past. He didn't mind Quint Falkner's body. He was handsome, strong, smart. It was a good mixture.

He smiled slowly.

Meg, not knowing his reason for the smile, returned it.

"I'm going to make you a sandwich." He pushed away from the wall.

"I don't think I can eat anything."

"You can try. You might feel better. Besides, I'm hungry, too. I'll make us a one big one and we can share it."

"All right."

He was glad she agreed. He didn't want to argue with her after everything she'd already experienced that night. Before leaving the room, he paused and knelt down beside the tub to give her a light kiss. He fought the urge to groan at the readiness with which she accepted it.

She was his wife. *His.*

This time, he would do whatever necessary to keep her. Perhaps history wouldn't repeat itself, he hoped. Perhaps this time, the outcome would be different.

No one—*no one*—was going to take her away from him.

For the next hour, he remained close, though he left her alone to absorb some of the information in the journal he'd given her. His journal. His words. He'd never in his wildest dreams ever thought he'd allow another soul to read his words. But not only did he see them as a bridge to Meg, he wanted to share them with her.

He came out of the shower and found her tucked in their bed, both pillows propped up behind her back, her nose buried in the words he'd written over a hundred years ago.

He knew he hadn't made a mistake in giving her his book, the story of his life, the sharing of his dreams.

"So how is it so far?" He pulled on a pair of flannel pants.

"Extraordinary..." She didn't take her gaze from the page. "It really is Joshua Montgomery's own journal, and I still can't believe you found it. But I'm glad you did."

"What has it told you so far?" He already knew what the book said; he was more interested in what she thought of him and what he'd written.

"Well, he loved his house, his cigars, his books on world history, and his wife." She looked up at him for the first time. "Did you read of any this?"

"As a matter of fact, I did." He chose not to lie to her any more.

She raised her brows in surprise. "Really?"

"Yes, really." He fluffed his hair with the towel he'd wrapped about his waist. Soon, he was in bed beside her. "Why don't you quit reading for now and get some rest."

"I hate to stop. Thank you so much for this. It has helped to take my mind off what happened tonight."

He hated to see her stop, too. Truth be told, the book had calmed her more than anything he could've done. "But I want to hold you."

"I'd like that, too." With evident reluctance, she put the book down on the bedside table and turned to fit her back against his chest.

Quint reached up and turned off the lamp on the nightstand, sending them into darkness.

"No." She stiffened beside him and grasped his arm as she sucked in a breath. "Turn the light on, I don't want to be in the dark."

"Hell, sorry, Meggie." How could he be so stupid? For the first time in a very long time, he felt in tune to her. She'd just been attacked in the dark. He should have known. He switched the light back on.

She let out a long breath she'd obviously been holding. "Can we leave it on for now?"

"Of course."

Desire poured through him, her body against him burned him to his core—but he had to fight it. She didn't need sex, she needed compassion.

"Joshua Montgomery could never have murdered his wife."

Quint wrapped his arm around her, moving her hair away as he leaned close. He drew in a slow, deep breath before replying. He wanted to touch her. He didn't want to talk about Joshua's—*his*—past. But if it helped her, then he would. "How do you know?"

"He loved life, he loved everything around him. He would never have done anything to destroy it. Do you think we'll ever know who killed her?"

Everything she said was true, and the pain of it cut at his heart like a razor. "Maybe we'll see her ghost some time, and we can ask her." He knew very well who had killed her. He also knew there was no way to prove it, no way to clear his name. That hurt, too.

"I'm not joking, Quint."

"I know, sorry." He also knew this was the best therapy for her after the terror of her night, to think of and talk about something innocuous. He tightened his hold on her. She fit so well in his arms. She wore a pink short silky nightgown. The fabric was soft beneath his palms. He held her tighter, wishing he could hold her and keep her safe forever.

"I know this sounds stupid, but I'm exhausted and still I don't think I can sleep."

"Try." Just as he tried to ignore her warmth.

"Every time I close my eyes, I see him, even though I couldn't see him in the dark. I feel his hands on me—"

"Feel my hands now." He caressed her, his lips grazing her throat.

She turned into his embrace. "Your hands feel wonderful."

"You feel wonderful."

For a long moment, they were quiet. Quint gently kneaded her breasts, giving her pleasure while denying himself the passion pulsing through him.

"Make love to me, Quint." Her whisper seemed to touch his heart through the silence.

He wanted nothing else, and she had to know that with the way his arousal pressed against her back. But he wasn't sure it was what she *needed*.

"Let me just hold you for a while." He found he needed to feel her safe and whole in his arms almost as much as he needed to make love to her. With her in his arms, he could reassure himself she was fine and all was right in the world.

What a lie…

Besides that, the rage of earlier was not gone. He moved his hands over and let her softness wash away the anger than lingered. Then he leaned over her, cupping her chin, forcing her to look back at him. "Are you sure this is what you want?"

"Yes. I want to feel your love. I want to feel your magic. I want it to wipe away the dirtiness where he touched me. Does that make any sense?"

No, it didn't. He wasn't sure how his touch could erase that of another. But he was willing to give her whatever she said she wanted.

She reached up and cupped his face, looking into his eyes. Her hand was soft. "Trust me, it's what I need."

He needed no further invitation. In the blink of an eye, he slid the flannel pants down, off and out from under the covers to drop on the floor. He rolled her toward him and brought his lips to hers as he maneuvered her nightgown up her thighs. Then, with all the gentle tenderness he could muster, he rolled her onto him so that she straddled him. His objective was put control back in her hands. Her assailant had held her down. The last thing Quint wanted was to have her feel caught beneath him.

Grasping her hips in his hands, he moved her, guiding her so she could slide onto him. A heartbeat later, he was buried deep within her. He tried to give her the magic she yearned for. She gave it to him.

Surprisingly, the rage he thought still lingered was gone in an instant, replaced by something he couldn't quite name. Magic? Pure and simple love? He thought he was helping her, when in fact, she was helping him. When he kissed her, he damned well thought he melted right into her.

She pulled her lips away. "Know what?"

"What?" His single word was raw and husky. She was so warm, so moist and tight. He didn't want to talk.

"He could never touch me where you touch me."

Quint looked into her eyes. She leaned down to kiss him again. Her words caught in his heart, in his soul.

The new Quint Falkner understood love. He understood that he loved this woman in his arms, this woman who so eagerly and lovingly shared her body as she shared her hopes and dreams.

But he hadn't, until now, understood the power her love held over him. It was, indeed, magic.

He wanted to laugh out loud. The poor pitiful son of a bitch who had mauled her would never know that magic.

Much later, deep in the night, after making love to Meg twice, Quint held her close to him and watched her sleep. "So beautiful." He was careful not to wake her.

There was something about the innocence of sleep that added to her allure.

She turned over to her side. She put her hand under her cheek, which gave her an adorable, younger appearance. He shifted to give her room. It was then he saw the large purple mark on her back.

She must have hit the desk or the corner of the couch. Or perhaps that pig had kicked her. The sight of dark marks in the shapes of fingers on her wrists and dark circles under her eyes made his blood boil. He raked his gaze over the dark bruise on her back, let out a huffed sigh, and grit his teeth before tucking the sheet around her.

In the soft light of the small lamp on the bedside table, he gazed down at her. Then his attention was drawn to the darkness out the bedroom window. He left the bed, being careful not to wake Meg, and made his way it. The moon was high in the sky, and the choking fog was gone.

He loved this new life, this chance with Meg. But he couldn't help but miss the freedom of his spirit flying through the night when he hadn't had a body to possess. Especially now, when he longed to find out who was stupid enough to hurt his wife. The evil spirit could have joined with anyone, just as Joshua had.

Quint gazed out at the trees, their few, long-dead leaves blowing in the night breeze. A small, furry creature scampered along one of the branches, and he recognized the raccoon. He hadn't explained to Officer Humphreys, but his night vision was excellent, as were all his senses. Everything about him was in perfect shape. It was the newness. Quint thought his sharp senses might dull with age as this body he now occupied would, but he wasn't sure. All he knew was his spirit also allowed for strong senses, powerful awareness of everything around him, as well as a deep desire to condition every muscle.

That was how he'd seen through the dark. That was how he'd seen the tall man who pinned Meg beneath him. Yet, because of the cap the attacker wore, and the fact he'd kept his back to the door, Quint hadn't been able to see the man's face.

I should have killed him then. Snapped his neck in two or beat him to death. Either would have been justified in his rescue of Meg.

Yet, when he'd seen that man on top of Meg, all he'd thought was getting him off of her. He'd needed to make sure she was whole and safe. He'd needed to erase the look of terror he saw on her face. He hadn't considered killing the man until seconds later. Then the man had managed to slip away, and it was too late. He couldn't leave Meg to chase him.

In her sleep, lost in the pitfall of a dream, Meg moaned. Quint let go of the darkness out the window and turned to his wife. He would do whatever necessary to keep his wife safe this time.

In past lives, he had ignored the danger, had thought no harm could come to her, and still she had paid the price.

It would not happen again.

Now, he switched off the lamp and slid into bed beside her, taking her in his arms to ward off whatever tried to invade her sleep.

CHAPTER THIRTEEN

"I think you should stay home today, or at least come to the Manor with me, but don't go to work. Let Evan open. He can handle it." Quint watched her dress and knew that, though she'd slept, she didn't look like it. The dark half-moons beneath her eyes were evidence of her restless night.

"I have no idea what needs to be cleaned up or fixed. I don't even know how I feel about stepping into the shop, but I can't let this scare me into a closet where I never want to come out again."

She adjusted the blue sweater she'd just pulled over her head. "I can't wear this." And she took it back off again. She reached for a gray one.

Quint worried about her. Fashion was never a problem for her. "I think you need a break. You need to get over the trauma you experienced in a place where you should feel safe; that's not hiding in a closet."

"I know, but I think I need to do this. It's like getting thrown off a horse. I need to get right back on."

He didn't agree. He'd been thrown off a horse. This was a hell of a lot more frightening. "Fine. I'm driving you."

"You *have* to drive me. My car's still there."

"Oh, right." He gave her a half grin. "And I'm staying with you. If I feel you need to leave, I'm taking you out of there. Understand?"

"Sure."

She was quiet all the way to the shop. He parked next to her car and climbed out.

"Maybe I was wrong," she said as she stood in the parking lot staring at the busted door of her shop.

"What?"

Meg jumped at the sound of his voice as he came up behind her, and Quint touched her arms to calm her. "It's all right, Meg. It's just me. Don't do this to yourself. I think you need some time away from here. Let me take you to the Manor."

"No. If I put off coming in here, I may not ever want to come in here."

"I don't agree. I don't think this is a good idea." But he had no choice but to follow her as she stepped into the shop. He said nothing, just watched her as she looked around before moving to her office.

"What a mess." She stared at the disarray on her desk and the books scattered all over the floor. She looked lost, like she didn't know where to begin.

He fought the urge to pull her into his arms or pull her back out to his truck.

She stood at the office threshold. She turned to face him and he saw fear in her eyes. "Do you think he'll come back?"

"I'm going to call someone about getting a better security system put in, at least until I can talk you into moving your books to the Manor. I don't want you to be afraid here."

She looked into her office again. "I don't know if that'll help me. I've already got an alarm system."

"I'm talking something with cameras."

"I don't know if that's what I need, either. Besides, how did he get in here in the first place? Did I lock him in with me? If I did, a security system isn't going to help, cameras might not, either. The door was locked. I remember locking it. And what if he comes in as a customer? Will I even recognize him?"

"Officer Humphreys gave me a phone number for a victims' group. Maybe it would be a good idea for us to check it out."

"Us?"

"I want to help you, Meggie, as well as—"

"As what?" she asked when he stopped in mid-sentence.

"As well as get over my own anger. Every time I think about some unknown man putting his hands on you, attempting to hurt you, I want to break something, preferably his neck."

Meg forced out a chuckle.

"What's so funny?" He didn't feel like laughing. Nothing about this was funny.

"My emotions fluctuate between fear and fury, terror and anger. I look in my office, and I see so many weapons on my desk—the letter opener, a nail file, my keys. I could have even gouged him with a pencil. But I didn't even think to try and reach any of it. I'm terrified that he'll come back, and at the same time, I hope he will. Because next time, I'll think differently."

Quint drew in a harsh breath and pursed his lips to keep from arguing with her. The thought of Meg being attacked a second time stopped his heart. She might be angry and determined to mete out revenge, but if his memory served him right, the intruder outweighed her by eighty pounds. Quint didn't want to tell her she had no chance against this man, with or without a letter opener. He was grateful, instead, to see her spirit, even if it was fear and fury bolstering it. He was grateful she wasn't cowering in the corner, her spirit broken by a man who would've hurt her or killed her, given the chance.

"Do you want me to call the victims' group? I could do it before I call somebody about a security system and call someone to replacing the glass in the door."

She stared into her office and didn't answer for a long moment. "Yes, I guess. It wouldn't hurt for us just to talk to someone."

"That's what I thought." Another lie. Meg needed no one but her husband, but he wanted to play this her way and let her have what she believed she needed.

He started to walk away, but she grabbed his attention. "And you know what?"

"What?"

"Before we spend money on a security system, let's talk more about moving into the Manor."

He liked that idea, but he hated that it was brought on by her terror.

"Are you sure?" He needed to make sure it was what she wanted. If she was pushed into moving, it wouldn't work. The last thing either of them needed was for her to blame him or regret the move.

Meg didn't get the chance to reply.

"What happened to the door, Meg? What's going on? The cops came by my place at last night and woke me up, said there'd been a break in, asked where I'd been since you told them I had a key."

They turned at the sound of Evan's voice. Meg tried to pull away from Quint, but he held her with arms that refused to let her go. Evan stared at them, his expression filled with concern and curiosity.

Quint glanced at Meg before he spoke. "Someone broke in."

"Yeah, so I see. So I heard. But broke in for what? What was taken? I had already taken the daily deposit."

For a moment, neither Quint nor Meg answered. "Nothing that we know of yet." Quint gave her arms a slight, reassuring squeeze.

Meg turned and looked up at him as if to say, *We know what the intruder wanted. We know what was almost taken.*

Evan swore under his breath and fired of a litany of questions. "When? Why? How? Were you here, Meg?"

Meg gave a few answers, only what was necessary, telling of how there had been an intruder, how Quint chased him, and that the man ran through the glass door.

Quint interrupted. "Do you think you could let it go for a while? Meg's really upset about the entire ordeal."

"Sure. Sure." He looked at Meg. "What do you want me to do?"

"The same thing you usually do this time of the morning."

Quint wondered if Meg meant to sound so snappy. Evan either ignored it or didn't notice.

"Open," Evan put in.

"Right."

"You're sure you want to open?" Quint looked from one to the other.

Meg sighed. "Yes. I think we need to show whoever did this that he can't put a damper on my business."

Quint couldn't help but smile at her spirit, even though he didn't agree with the idea.

"Okay." Evan sent another long look at Meg then set about opening the shop.

Meg still hadn't moved from the office door. "What are you going to do?" She asked Quint.

He looked down at her, sweeping her into his dark gaze. "I thought I'd stick around here for a while. I already called Brad and told him what happened. He can handle things while I'm gone."

The smile she gave him seemed false, forced.

"I'd like that," she said.

"What would you like me to do? What do you need?"

Meg drew in a deep breath. "Could you move these boxes of books out of my office? If I get the chance, I want to go through them, and I don't want to do it in here. Most of them have been logged into the office computer, the rest I can log at the computer on the counter." She laughed hesitantly.

"What?"

"I'm not sure about what to do."

"I said I thought you shouldn't open." It wasn't quite the same as I told you so.

"Not about that." She paused and looked around the office. "About the books. If I *do* move into the Manor, the last thing I want to do is put these on the shelves here where we just have to move them again. At the same time, they should be out where customers can see them."

"Meggie, I can move them as many times as it takes. Stop worrying about it."

"I know."

"I'll take them out to the counter right now. When you want them moved again or put on a shelf or even thrown into the trash, just let me know."

She chuckled again at his joking tone. But he thought she looked like she fought the urge to cry.

After a long moment, he let her go. He almost moved back to her when he saw her shiver at the sudden absence of his warmth.

Quint carried the two boxes out to the sales floor and put them in the corner near the counter where they were out of the way of customers trying to reach other books. Then he reached for the phone book and pulled out his cell to make the calls. He needed to get some estimates on security systems with cameras. He wanted to be ready to install something if Meg changed her mind about moving to the Manor.

Evan walked by with a few books tucked under his arm.

"By the way, Evan." Quint stopped him. "Where were you about seven last night?" Quint wasn't even certain why he needed to ask. Evan was a loyal employee to Meg. If he wanted to hurt her, heaven knew he had plenty of opportunity every day. It was just the fact he had a key to the shop that had him asking. That, and Quint wondered what Humphreys might have asked him.

"At home. I had just got there after stopping and grabbing some supper after taking the night's deposit to the bank. I fell asleep on my couch watching TV and didn't know anything about the break in until the cops woke me up, why?"

"Alone?"

"Yes, as if it's any of your business, why?" There was no denying the sudden defensiveness in his voice.

"Because you're the only other person with a key to this place, that's why. And since there was no break in, we don't know how the guy got in, *unless* he had a key. Or he was already in here hiding, and Meg locked him in with her. You didn't happen to notice anyone in here when you left, did you?"

"Yeah, well the cops already asked me the same thing. Do I look like I ran through the door? Do you see any cuts on me? And no, I didn't notice anyone here when I left."

"No, I don't see any cuts on you." Quint stared at him, watching his reaction. He saw nothing but questions in his eyes. Either Evan was a very good actor or he knew nothing about the break in.

Quint saw worry and concern in Evan's clear gaze. "Besides, I'm here all day, sometimes alone. If I wanted anything, why would I wait until after closing to take it?"

"Good question. I apologize for accusing you." Quint looked down at the phone book until Evan drew his attention again.

"Is Meg going to be all right?"

"I think so." He hoped so. If the need to sleep with the light on was all she suffered from this, he could live with it.

"He frightened her pretty bad, didn't he?" Evan spoke softly, so Meg couldn't hear.

"Yes, he did."

"I'll be frank with you."

Quint waited and said nothing, letting Evan go on being totally frank.

"I respect Meg, and I respect you. I wouldn't want to do something to change that. But if I did—if I wanted Meg in some way or I wanted something here in her shop, I wouldn't go about it in some low, dirty way like breaking in and terrorizing her. I'd come right out and tell her my feelings and let her make the next move."

Quint respected Evan for being straight forward. But it still didn't explain why the intruder hadn't had to break in. Or why Evan assumed the intruder wanted Meg. Neither Meg nor Quint had gone into detail about what happened. "Why would you think the intruder was here for Meg?"

Evan shrugged. "It was just an assumption. There was no money; I'd taken the night deposit. And there are valuable books out here on the sales floor, but none of them were touched. So what else was this guy after? Since a secret admirer sent her roses."

Quint said nothing, neither confirming nor denying Evan's thoughts. He supposed anyone with a brain could make the same deduction, but it didn't answer the questions of why and how. Thinking like Evan, Quint couldn't help but wonder why this man would choose to stalk Meg. Why not just approach her, talk to her, flirt with her?

"Are you going to stick around?" Evan broke into Quint's thoughts.

Quint stopped flipping through the phone book, his defenses raised like the force field around a space ship in a science fiction movie. How was that Evan's business, if he were staying or not? Hell, the whole terrifying experience had made him as jumpy as it had Meg. There was no logical reason to take any of it out on Evan, but it didn't stop the frustration that wanted to lash out at everyone. He met Evan's gaze and forced calm into his voice, revealing none of his inner turmoil. "I thought I would, why?"

"Meg would be happy with that."

That Evan would know what would make Meg happy perked Quint's interest in a heartbeat. "She would, huh?"

Evan gave him a half shrug. "She's been trying for years to get you in here, hasn't she?"

Had she? Quint searched his memories and was left uncertain. But he licked his lips, put on his best poker face, and put a cap on his instant frustration. This was a part of unchartered territory when it came to knowing the real Quint Falkner. The idea he rarely came into the book shop left him burning with anger. His deep breath curbed it, but didn't drown it completely.

Later, Quint watched Meg organize books on the nearby shelves. Her movements were random, little real purpose in her task. She seemed to just need to move and feel busy, she didn't seem to have anything specific to do. He looked back at Evan and couldn't stop the returning suspicion. Meg might be happy, but would Evan be happy if he stayed?

CHAPTER FOURTEEN

Quint was reluctant to leave Meg's shop.

"You've got your own business to take care of. You can't stay here and babysit me."

He stared at her. "Are you sure you'll be all right if I leave?" He wasn't certain *he'd* be all right if he left. He wanted her safe, in his sight. He still wanted to wrap his fingers around something and squeeze. His heart would sing if it could be the throat of the man who attacked her.

"I've been all right all day."

Her words didn't help convince him. She still avoided her office like the plague, still hadn't eaten anything, she jumped every time the chimes above the door sounded, and she watched every male customer as if he were her attacker.

She rolled her eyes at him as if his leaving was no big deal. "Go to work."

"Are you trying to get rid of me?"

He tried to keep his voice light, joking. He didn't want to leave her. He laced his fingers through hers.

"No, but I have to admit, I don't know how to act with you in the shop. I'm not used to you being here so much."

"I've missed out on a lot in your life, wife." He squeezed her hand. "And I'm sorry."

He saw his apology stunned her. She stared at him as if she had no idea how to reply.

"By the way, I have something else for you."

"Another present?" Meg's small smile was the first genuine one he'd seen since her attack.

"It's not much. It was with the book." He pulled out the coin he'd taken when he retrieved his journal, and handed it to her.

She stared down at the coin in her palm and her eyes widened with surprise. "Wow, it's a half dollar, dated 1895. Are you sure you want me to put this in my shop? You could keep it at the Manor, put it on display, which reminds me... I was thinking you should open a small museum at the Manor."

He liked the way she was thinking, beyond the attack, to something more positive. "I could. I'll put you in charge of planning it."

She looked up at him before looking down at the coin again. "Or you could sell this and use the money to make more renovations."

"You keep it here. I want you to have it."

Perhaps I should tell her. He wasn't sure it was necessary to tell her who he was, who his soul had possessed previously, or how he knew everything there was to know about Montgomery Manor, including where more coins were hidden. An entire treasure, as a matter of fact. "I'm sure we'll find enough other stuff to use in the museum. But for now, I guess if you're sure you don't need me, I'll go. Are you sure you're all right with my leaving?"

"I'll be fine." She continued staring at the coin.

"I'll call you later or I could even come back in a little while, bring you and Evan something to eat since you haven't had lunch."

He moved close and kissed her.

The kiss ended, and she leaned back and studied him.

"What?" he asked.

"I don't know. You taste like you, but you kiss different. It's like there's an electrical current in your kiss that wasn't there last week."

"You don't like it?" He knew what the difference was. He'd even told her the night they made love in the hidden dressing room, when her connection to him completed his transition. But she thought it was all a dream. She still hadn't said a word about it. Perhaps she didn't remember.

"I do," she replied after some hesitation.

"Then I'll kiss you like that more. Later."

She scratched her head and color came to her cheeks. "That sounds nice."

"I'll see you later."

"I'll either be here or home." She flipped the coin over and looked at the back side.

"Don't go home alone. If you leave here, come to the Manor, and make sure to call me first to let me know you're on the road." He tried to keep the worry out of his voice, but until he was with her and knew she was safe, he would worry.

"I'll stay until closing tonight, too, and keep an eye on her for you."

Quint hadn't noticed Evan was close enough to hear them. He didn't reply until Evan moved out of hearing. The truth was he didn't believe Evan or his supposed openness about his feelings for Meg. Evan was secretive. Meg had said so before, when Evan brought her remarkably valuable books, refusing to tell her where he'd gotten them.

At the same time, Evan had always respected Meg. And it was true, he did spend hours alone with her, so if he wanted to hurt her, he had ample opportunity.

Quint waited a moment before reaching out and cupped Meg's chin. "Call me if you need anything—and I mean anything, Meggie. I love you." His kiss was feather-light. Still, the touch of her lips left him hot.

He turned and left.

He hoped to hell his words, his touch, left her feeling loved. From what he'd seen so far, women of this era were too independent. This was a fast paced age, where people didn't take the time for something as simple or meaningful as a heart-felt hug. For Meg, he intended to change that.

Once Quint was gone, Meg regretted letting him leave. Even with Evan cleaning up fragments of glass, and the sunlight pouring through the huge front windows, it was easy for her imagination to run wild.

Evan was the only other person with a key, and he knew his way around the shop in the dark. She looked at him. He wore a long-sleeved shirt under a V-neck sweater. Was he hiding cuts he received from running through the glass door?

She shook her head to get rid of the idea. Evan wouldn't hurt her. She tried to convince herself that any of her frequent customers would know their way around her shop in the dark. It didn't help.

She was almost positive Evan wouldn't hurt her and neither would any of her regular customers.

Before she could dwell on it further, the bells over the door chimed in another customer. It occurred to Meg then—how did the intruder get passed those bells even if he'd had a key? The bells would have been enough to warn her. There was no other explanation than he hid in her shop and she locked him in with her.

CHAPTER FIFTEEN

He watched Megan from a distance.

He licked his lips with anticipation. He had the vague impression she knew—*felt*—him watch her. It added to the eagerness rushing through him like lava. When he was first drawn to Megan, he never guessed there'd be such a rush. Was this anxiety the same for a panther hunting its prey? He shivered at the memory of Megan's softness against him.

He tore his gaze from her and glanced down at the newspaper in his hands. BREAK IN AT LOCAL BOOKSTORE. SUSPECTS QUESTIONED, the headline read.

He fought the urge to laugh.

Some poor patsies had taken the heat for him, unless it was media propaganda and the police had no suspects at all.

Not that he worried, he would never be a suspect.

He sat in the coffee shop across the street and watched Megan through the window. Windows made up the entire front of her shop, so it was easy to see her every move. Things couldn't be better, he thought, as he looked back to Megan. She was edgy. She watched the movement of everyone in the shop, and fear darkened her gaze when someone inadvertently bumped into her. He smiled at her fear, liking it, tasting it, smelling it. Like rich perfume, it brought fire to his blood. He licked his lips again. He wanted her to be afraid of him, almost as much as he wanted *her*. It gave him more control over her. For the first time in forever, he had the advantage, and he loved the sense of power it brought him.

He thought it strange how his desires and goals changed after turning his thoughts to Megan. At first, he just wanted the treasure he suspected was hidden somewhere in Montgomery Manor. Then he considered Megan. His want for treasure hadn't gone away, he just added his desire for Megan to the list of wants. He could have it all. No one could stop him.

And soon he would have her. Then he would have the treasure, too. He tossed the newspaper into the trash and finished off his coffee. Then he slipped out of the coffee shop. He crossed the street and peered through the bookstore windows. Damn, she was so close, he felt her.

She stood behind the counter, checking out a customer's purchases. She didn't notice him.

CHAPTER SIXTEEN

Quint arrived at the Manor and found Brad Mills rubbing the bridge of his nose with his finger and thumb. "Are you okay?"

"I would have never thought murder could interest so many people, but this murder mystery dinner idea has done wonders for the Manor. I'm sorry *I* never come up with the idea. If I had known what this type of entertainment could do Montgomery Manor, I would have talked Greensburg into staging one. I've had so many calls, I made the executive decision to book two dates. And that's on top of the lunch crowd, which is, well, crowded." Brad explained as he followed Quint into his office.

Quint chuckled. "If you like the murder mystery, wait until you hear some of the other ideas I have for this place. Most of the murder mysteries I'm checking out are comical. I plan to stage a murder where contestants have to solve the murder, tell where and how it happened."

Brad's eyes widened. "Wow, I like that idea, too."

"Yeah, and if you come up with any more games, just bring it to me. Meg mentioned something like a scavenger hunt. But I'm open for more ideas," Quint commented as he reached for the stack of messages on his desk. *Wait until Brad saw the things that would show up in the museum.*

"Can I ask you a question?"

Quint ignored the message in his hand to meet Brad's gaze. "Of course. Is it another idea for the Manor?"

"Not really. I just wanted to know how *you* know so much about this place. I mean *I* worked here for years with Greensburg, and he never mentioned knowing you or even having a distant cousin. He never spoke about half the things you know about this house. You seem to know about secret passages I never knew existed."

Quint shrugged. "It just took a little investigating. Mitchell Greensburg probably kept you too busy to do much of that."

"Well, that's true." Brad agreed. "I'd also like to thank you for keeping me on here like this. It's given me the chance to learn about this house, and, if you don't mind my saying so, it's as if you belong here. Ever since you stepped in here, I've had the feeling we met before, but I can't, for the life of me, figure out where."

"Well, you're welcome, and you're doing a great job." He tipped his head thoughtfully. "I don't remember meeting you before. But if *you* remember, you can refresh my memory." Quint didn't need to reminisce about where he might have met Brad in the past. His thoughts were consumed with Meg and her stalker. Being here, away from her, tore him in two. He wanted to send movers to her store to start packing her books to get her moved to the Manor.

As Quint looked at Brad, he realized it felt as if Brad belonged at the Manor, too. In a turtleneck and jacket, Brad was sleek and perfect for his role as manager or host, not a dark hair out of place.

Quint wondered if talking about business would move his worry for Meg to the back burner for a while. "Fill me in on this morning. How did things go?"

"I've had so many calls this morning, more people letting us know what a great grand opening it was. And as I already told you, I made two dates for murder mystery dinners since so many people made reservations."

"That's great." No, it didn't move his worry for Meg at all.

"People want to know if the dinners have a theme."

Quint grinned and although his thoughts were still with Meg and he wished she were here with him, he felt the tension leave his face. "Yes, there's a murder." He leaned back against the large, oak desk and crossed his arms. The dwindling scent of fresh paint still lingered in the air.

"They know there's supposed to be a murder."

"Let me see what I can come up with and I'll get back to you on it. Actually, I'll talk to Steve. He sounded like he had a few ideas. I think he's been to a few dinners. I'll let you know."

"As long as Steve doesn't want all the characters to be construction workers with hammers and saws." He laughed. "What's on the agenda for today, besides serving the best food in the area?" Brad leaned against the door jam.

"I'm calling in a crew to clean and inspect the gallery, the old art room. I'm trying to talk my wife into moving her book shop there." Quint couldn't help but notice Brad's surprise with him raising his brows and stepping away from the door jam. Quint also noticed Brad's effort to hide it.

"You're giving her the gallery?"

Quint raised a brow in question. "You have a problem with that? Did you have other ideas for it?"

"Not at all. I read the story in the newspaper about the break in at her shop. It sounded like more than what you told me since all you told me was there was a problem at Meg's shop and that you'd be late."

"It was nothing major, didn't keep her from opening this morning." Nothing major? That was the biggest lie he'd told so far, even as he hid how much Meg's attack affected him from the rest of the world. He wondered if he would watch every patron who ventured through the door, suspecting they were Meg's attacker.

"Did they take anything? The paper didn't give many specifics."

Quint shrugged as if the break in was no big deal. "They broke in the front door. As far as we can tell nothing's missing." It was another lie. A single man broke *out* the front door, and Meg's sense of safety was cut to pieces. He couldn't hold up the pretense that everything was fine for much longer. He needed to do something with his hands before he choked someone with them; maybe put on some work clothes and find a hammer to swing. "Is there anything else I need to know?"

"No, I just wanted to touch base with you."

"All right. I'm going to check out a few things then." Quint left his desk and walked past Brad without offering an explanation.

Let Brad get answers to his questions from the newspaper. He headed toward the registration desk where the second vase of roses still sat. This was the second set of flowers Meg's secret admirer had sent. There was nothing to indicate who'd sent them. He wanted to toss them into the trash as Meg had done with the other vase, but he thought better of it. If, by chance, Meg's attacker came here, he wanted him to see they weren't afraid. They would never cower in the corner. They were going on, doing business as usual, just as Meg was in her shop.

Quint, however, did more than go on with business. He studied everyone, looking for any sign indicating cuts left from going through the shop's glass door.

A short time later, he called Detective Humphreys to see if anyone matching the intruder's description had been treated for cuts at the local hospitals. No one had. Since Brad left for a late lunch, Quint handled the remaining lunch crowd before calling a crew to inspect the gallery.

By the time Meg reached the Manor later that evening, Mother Nature was beating down the coastline. Wind whipped against her car like an animal trying to get in as she drove. The rain pounding against the roof sounded like a Rock n' Roll drummer. The downpour covered the windshield just as the fast as the wipers smeared it away.

Meg rolled her shoulders, working to ease away the ache left from a mixture of tension and fatigue. She pulled into the carriage house and parked, then leaned her head against the steering wheel for a long moment.

I should have gone home, where I could rest and take a long hot bath, read some more of Joshua Montgomery's journal, and just unwind. At least she had the journal with her in her purse, so wherever she wound up for the evening, she could fulfill *that* part of her wish. Besides, a stay in the whirlpool tub would be better than a hot soak in the regular tub at home.

Quint insisted she come here and not go home alone, but because she didn't want to wait around at the shop until Quint could come and get her, she came to the Manor. Deep down, she was glad she'd not argued with him about coming to the Manor. For as the darkness once again settled around her shop, she knew she had to walk through it to her car. So, she made the decision to take up Quint's offer to move her book store to his gallery.

She saw Brad when she rushed through the front door to escape getting any wetter from the rain. No doubt he thought she looked like a rat that had just climbed out of the swimming pool, but he greeted her by taking her hand.

"Meg. You're soaked to the skin. Why don't you head up to your suite and get warm and dry. I'll let Quint know you're here, and I could have some dinner sent up."

She stared at him for a long moment, everything he'd said sounded absolutely wonderful. Yet, his hand in hers was colder than the rain. "Thank you, Brad." She slipped her hand from his.

His smile didn't quite reach his eyes.

"But I'm not really hungry." She stared at him. "I would, however, like to get my hands on a copy of one of the books about the Manor, maybe one you sell here in the gift shop. Do you think you could find me a copy?"

"Sure." He glanced toward the dining room. "I'll have one sent up to you."

She smiled at him. Her comment about not being hungry was a lie. She did want something hot and filling to eat, but she wanted to order it herself.

She headed for the stairs, planning to call room service or come back for something as soon as she'd gotten settled.

"You've only been here once since Quint redid your suite. Can you find your room on your own? Because I'll be glad to show you."

She glanced back at Brad. Leading her to her and Quint's suite was even more personal that ordering her dinner for her, and the last thing Meg needed was to feel Brad's coldness all the way to her room. "I think I remember how to find it, thank you so much for all your help. If you greet all the customers like this, the place will do great. Keep up the good work." As she moved past the bar on her way to the stairs, she paused to greet to Melanie Wirthington.

"Here, take this cup of coffee up with you." Melanie poured a steaming cup of java and placed it on the bar. "It will warm you up. It's hazelnut, and it's delicious."

"Thanks." Meg reached for the cup. "I love those earrings you're wearing." It was hard not to notice the shiny old-fashioned diamond earrings dangling from Melanie's earlobes. "They reflect off the lights above you."

"Thank you. My sister gave them to me when I started working here. She said she thought they fit the era and décor. She's into vintage and has that kind of fashion sense."

Meg covered her mouth and sneezed.

Melanie chuckled. "Bless you. Go up and get dry before you catch a cold."

Meg took a sip of her coffee before moving. "This is really good."

"Glad you like it."

Meg moved away as Melanie left to wait on another patron.

Quint found Meg in their bedroom a short time later.

The television was on, but he noticed she wasn't watching it. He watched her from the doorway for a long moment, smiling. Her hair was wet, and she was wearing one of his shirts. There was nothing sexier than a woman wearing her man's shirt. She was reading the journal he'd given her and on the bed beside her was a copy of one of the books about the Manor.

"Meg?"

She jumped at the sound of her name. He wanted to kick himself for startling her. She had enough fear to contend with.

"I'm sorry." He sat beside her on the bed.

"It's all right. I was just so engrossed and with the TV on, I didn't hear you come in."

Her voice was deep, and it brought a wave of desire to mingle with his lust at seeing her in his shirt.

She accepted his quick, but warm and hungry touch of his lips. She licked her mouth and looked at him. "You taste like cigars."

"I received a box of them as a gift at the grand opening and thought I'd try one. It wasn't too bad." It wasn't a lie. He had received a box of cigars as a gift. In his life as Joshua Montgomery, he'd thoroughly enjoyed his cigars. It was good to taste them once again.

"How are you, *mon coeur*?" he whispered against her. Her skin was warm and soft. Her hair smelled of flowers. He fought his desire to press closer to her.

He tried to kiss her again, but she avoided him. He let her.

"Okay, admit it," she pressed, "you did more than just flip through this journal."

"All right, I admit it, yes, I read it. I didn't want you to know because I didn't want you to feel bad that I don't read any of the books in your shop." Like the comment about the cigars, that wasn't a lie either. He had also read through the books about Joshua Montgomery's house and life they sold in the Manor gift shop. He wanted to make sure everything written about Joshua Montgomery was the truth.

"It's all right. Besides, this is all so interesting. And I guess you know then that Joshua Montgomery called his wife, Ellen, the same nick name you've recently started calling me. Is that where you came up with the idea?"

Yes, he'd called Ellen that pet name, and now he called Meg the same because she held his heart in the same way. "Need I give away all my secrets?"

She shared his smile. "No, I guess not." Her gaze moved to the book and read, "'Something is bothering my lovely wife, Ellen, *mon coeur*.'" She emphasized the last two words. "'I have tried to discuss it with her, but she evades me at every opportunity. I know, however, that with time, I will get to the heart of the matter.' I wonder if he ever discovered what was troubling her."

"He did." As well as his renewed strength and heightened senses, his memory was as sharp as ever. Quint remembered the incident well, as if it happened yesterday. Much to his dismay, it did happen yesterday—to Meg.

"Don't tell me, I want to read it." She obviously didn't hear the sharpness in his words.

He let go of the horrible memory and smiled down at his wife. But she didn't see, her gaze was back on the words written in the book. He'd been given a second chance at life, and he would not dwell on the horrors of things he could no longer change. He would dwell on the here and now, and do whatever he had to do to hold on to this chance with Meg.

"People come here hoping to see his ghost." She looked up at him again. "That reminds me, I looked through this other book. It says that there's a legend that Joshua Montgomery *did* hide treasure somewhere in this house. It hasn't been found."

Oh, yes, he did. Just like he hid the paintings between the floor joists and the jewelry he'd given Ellen behind stones in the wine cellar. And he hoped to hell to share it with Meg soon. He hoped to spend a lifetime sharing it all with Meg. "How exciting."

Just as she didn't hear the sharpness of his tone before, she also paid no attention to the flatness of his reply.

"It also says that he recited poetry to Ellen in French." Meg was more absorbed in the books and the history than she was in his shifting emotions.

"Do you know what else I heard about the Montgomerys?" He leaned down to kiss her. This time she let him.

"What?" Her single reply was no louder than a whisper. *Finally*, he'd distracted her...with his lips.

"He and his wife used to spend a lot of time out near the cliffs, the two of them together, watching the sea crash against the rocks in its wild glory. I bet he even made love to her out there. But I read where he'd hold her hand and recite French poems. Would you like me recite French poetry to you?" His words were broken up by soft kisses on her neck and face.

Meg sighed with his feather touches and let out a small giggle. "The only French you know is '*mon coeur*.'"

He paused. He moved his hand to cup her breast, and her nipple hardened in the warmth of his touch. He smiled at her through the soft light. Then he spoke, words she couldn't understand, that held the rhythmic ring of an accomplished poet.

She stared at him, amazement on her face. "That was beautiful. Where did you learn that?"

"I always wanted to learn, so I did."

"Really? Because that sounds pretty lame."

He shrugged. "Really. The first time I learned Joshua Montgomery entertained a French ambassador here, I thought maybe I might get the chance to do the same. So I thought I'd better learn."

"Right..." Her voice was filled with disbelief and suspicion. She narrowed her eyes at him.

"I learned as I was working on the renovations." At least that wasn't a lie since it was during the renovations that he'd become a part of Quint Falkner's being and their knowledge had blended.

She stared at him, filled with questions. The Quint she knew had plenty of time to learn a new language while he was a couch potato between construction jobs before taking on the Montgomery Manor, and he didn't even learn how to put in a load of laundry. "I don't believe you."

"There's probably a great deal you've yet to learn about me." He kissed her cheek.

"Like what?"

He deepened his gaze, looking down at her as if he could drink her in. Then he leaned close and kissed her, his mouth urgent and eager against hers. "I want to make a baby with you."

Like the French poetry, his words caught her off guard. So off guard that she turned her head away when he tried to kiss her again.

"What?" That same Quint Falkner who couldn't do laundry pushed aside the idea of a baby every time she brought it up. He always gave her the excuse his job was too unpredictable for kids and her shop kept her too busy. Now he wanted one?

"I said I want us to have a baby."

"I heard what you said."

He tried to kiss her as she spoke.

"I don't know..."

"What's to know?" His kisses grew in urgency.

She turned her head to force him to talk so couldn't distract her with kisses. "Well, for starters, you just opened this place. From what you've told me, there's still so much to be done before it's the way you want. I'm just now growing comfortable with the business in the bookshop, which, by the way has been going very well, thanks to the opening of this place, I think. Thank you very much. Then if I take you up on your offer and move the store, it's even more work." She took a breath and relished in the feel of his kiss against her neck and the way he kneaded her breast. "You're distracting me."

He refused to be deterred. "No, *you're* trying to distract *me*. People have raised children through worse things."

"I know, but I want to be able to devote time to our kids. I don't want to struggle, juggling work and kids." She sounded like he did last year when she'd suggested starting a family.

"Loving you and dealing with this house will never be a struggle, and neither would loving the children we create together." He slid his hand into her shirt where the heat of his touch felt like it melted into her flesh. He couldn't mistake her response beneath his palm, as well as the sudden quickening of her heart.

He brought his lips to hers. And Meg felt like he reached right in and touched her soul. The book slipped from her hand and fell to the floor. For the next hour, Meg completely forgot about Joshua Montgomery's journal as Quint kept her mind and body occupied.

Later that night, Meg lay awake listening to the storm rage outside, lost in her husband's touch.

He pressed up against her back in his sleep. His now relaxed groin pressed against her tailbone, his chest against her back, his knees against the backs of her legs. His breath played against her hair. His right arm held her. Though he was relaxed in sleep, his hand splayed over her flat belly. He had fallen asleep quickly after making love to her, unbothered by the lamp light.

He didn't snore. He never had in the time that Meg had known him. His breathing, however, was deep and even, and its rhythm brought her comfort.

And now, a storm, equal in strength to the one beating against the windows, raged in Meg's soul. She drew in a heavy breath as she ignored the storm and brought Quint's words to mind.

A baby. Children.

He wanted children.

The Quint she knew six months ago had referred to his own brother's daughter as nothing more than a pain in the ass. She knew *that* Quint had been out of work, sitting on the couch, debating starting his own construction business, so she understood children would not have been an easy subject for him.

Now, he wanted a child of his own. He'd never, in five years, mentioned that he wanted children, and she'd had been too busy trying to get her business off the ground to push the issue. True, she saw children in their future. In fact, she considered the idea a few months before, before they owned this house, before he'd been consumed with the work that came with it, when Quint had been without a job and seemed to be stuck to the television. Now she wasn't so sure they were ready for children.

This business in the Manor was so new, and her business was going very well, and both businesses took a great deal of time.

Face it, Meg, a little voice inside her said, *you're just afraid it might burst the bubble you've been in for the past few days. A baby crying at night would put a damper on your new romance and the passion Quint has ignited in you. Not to mention squash the excitement of this house.*

The admission scared her. The thought of children, of Quint wanting them, frightened her, too.

Other thoughts terrified her just as much. All of them mixed and mingled in the pit of her stomach like a bad meal eaten in haste. The changes in Quint were too many to count. The simple—though not so simple—way he looked at her was enough to tell her he'd changed somehow. Even tonight, when he'd startled her with his presence, the look in his eyes was so different from the construction worker who came home, gave her a peck on the lips, and asked what was for supper. The look in his eyes tonight was sparkling, mysterious, dark, and passionate. It called to her and turned her heart cold at the same time. She didn't remember much about the strange dream she'd had the night of the party, but she did remember the strange eyes of the man in her dream. Quint's eyes.

His smile was crooked, just like the man in her dream, just like Joshua Montgomery in the photographs in the books she read.

It was also impossible to mistake the way Quint now favored his right leg, but twice he'd shrugged it off as nothing when she'd questioned him about it. In one of the books she'd read, she learned Joshua Montgomery loved horses, but had injured his ankle when he was thrown from one.

Then there was his attitude, not just about her but also about everything, a new sudden drive to push forward, following his sudden change in profession. From construction worker to entrepreneur. He was filled with ideas about the Manor and he planned to see each one through as soon as possible.

And there was all the time he'd now chose to spend in her shop, when she hadn't been able to get him in there more than twice in the past six months.

Also, there was the fact that they'd made love every day for the last week, something that hadn't happened during the entire course of their marriage. She wasn't complaining, she just didn't know what to make of his new, heightened libido.

And he'd smoked a cigar.

And spoke French.

Hell, he hadn't ever said so much as one word in a foreign language, or indicated that he'd even had the desire to do so, in all the time she'd known him. Did she dare believe he'd referred to her as 'my heart' or learned poetry simply because he'd seen it in Joshua Montgomery's journal and he hoped for a chance to entertain a French ambassador? Every minute of every day, she learned more about the stranger who held her, the stranger she *wanted* to hold her. Perhaps a spirit really had possessed him. Or perhaps he had been—as Evan pointed out the day of the grand opening—jealous of her until now.

And hadn't he said something about coming alive again during that strange dream she'd had in a hidden dressing room. Now, as she tried to think about it, all thoughts jumbled together in a hazy, unfinished puzzle.

She wouldn't say that Quint, himself, frightened her, but he did make her question things and wonder—but no answers came.

What scared her most was that she didn't really want answers. She wanted to stay lost in his arms...and this house. For the first time in her life, she felt sheltered. She felt cherished in a way she thought only existed in the books in her shop.

Then there was her shop. She sighed. She had to face it, she may never feel safe there again. Earlier, the dark had felt as if it smothered her, and all she'd done was look out the window at her car in the street.

Why did the unanswered questions pile up now that Quint was asleep? They had been so easy to ignore when he made love to her. She needed to make a move. She needed to feel at least that she was moving forward. "Quint? Quint?"

"Hmmm?" He sounded more asleep than awake, yet he answered her quickly as if he was *not* sleeping as deep as she thought.

"I don't know if I'm ready for the children thing, but I'll start packing up my books tomorrow to move into the gallery, if the offer still stands." Her words were loud, even against storm outside.

"It will take a few days, maybe even weeks to get the gallery ready, so take your time. Do you want me to come and help you?" His voice was deep and rough. Maybe he had been asleep.

"No, just let me know when the gallery's ready."

He leaned up and gave her an absent kiss. "Get some rest, Meggie. We'll talk more about it in the morning."

She lay still in his arms and closed her eyes, but it was a long time before sleep took over.

With the light of dawn, Quint found the storm and his wife gone. Just as he'd known she didn't sleep—because he didn't—he knew when she quietly slid out of bed. He also knew when she left their suite. But he remained quiet and let her leave. He didn't want to hound her by always needing to know exactly where she was going and what she was doing. As soon as he was dressed, he discovered her standing in the gallery with a cup of coffee in her hand.

"Did you have any of the breakfast the kitchen set out for the B and B guests?" He gave her a good-morning kiss.

"I'm not hungry yet. I'm too busy studying this room, looking for the best set up. Do you think the bookshelves would work out better running parallel to the windows or not? I can't decide."

"You might get more feasible room if you run them perpendicular to the windows. You'll also get the light from the windows shining between the rows." He pointed with his hands as he talked. Then he took the cup of coffee from her and took a sip before handing it back.

"That's true."

He turned and studied her. "Are you all right this morning?"

"Of course, I'm all right. Why wouldn't I be?"

He didn't like the way she avoided looking at him as she replied. "You experienced a pretty frightening attack, that's why. Sometimes things like that can have a delayed reaction." He didn't think he should have to explain, but he did anyway.

"I'm fine, really."

"Is that why you were awake in the middle of the night telling me you'd take me up on my offer?" He took another drink of coffee and thought the two of them could share a Danish, too. He'd feel better if he could get her to eat something. She still didn't look at him.

"I just thought it over, that's all, and I came to the conclusion that it would be more feasible to have my books here. Why pay rent at all, when it's going up, when I don't have to?" She shrugged as if her decision to move was no big deal.

"That's true," Quint agreed just to appease her, considering he didn't believe her. He knew her well enough to know there was more to this than simple rent. Just as he knew she'd tell him what she was thinking when she was good and ready. Until then, he'd be better off waiting until she was good and ready, too, instead of pushing the issue.

They walked around the room, talking and discussing the shop . He coaxed her into eating a bagel as they discussed the work that needed done until it was time for Meg to leave. He didn't stop her from hurrying home to shower and change before she opened the bookstore. She said planning the move was what she needed to put the nightmare of her attack behind her. She insisted she would be fine.

He should have stayed with her.

CHAPTER SEVENTEEN

It seemed to hit just before noon—Meg began having trouble coping. Later, she'd write it off as some type of delayed reaction, just as Quint had mentioned. The thing was, she didn't recognize it as any reaction. In fact, she didn't recognize it in any way at all. Nor did she see it coming.

She still jumped at every noise. Then she worried that every customer was a potential stalker. Every man who came into the shop watched her with a knowing look that made her to feel as if a million tiny bugs crawled over her. She was afraid to be left alone, and at the same time, she trusted no one. And she continuously felt she was being watched. Her hands shook. And no matter how much coffee she drank, she couldn't get warm. There were moments when she had to clench her teeth to keep her teeth from chattering.

As the day went on, the dread increased. It didn't help that the door had been repaired.

She was inside a fishbowl, with everyone outside watching her.

She picked up the phone, dialed the police department, and asked the girl who answered for Officer Humphreys.

Humphreys came to the phone right away, but it did nothing to ease Meg's growing fear.

"Have you found anything yet?"

"I'm sorry Mrs. Falkner." He sounded as patient as always. "We're doing everything we can, but we don't have much to work with."

"I know." She couldn't keep defeat out of her voice.

"We're making hourly sweeps of the neighborhood. Would you like one of our officers to come inside your shop?"

"That would be nice." Maybe seeing a uniformed officer with a gun would make her feel safer. The truth was she didn't know what would make her feel better.

"And Mrs. Falkner?

"Yes?"

"It might be a good idea if you call the victims' help line number I gave you. They can help a lot."

"I will." She planned to, she really did. But at the moment, she thought staying busy with the best solution.

A uniformed officer arrived about twenty minutes later. He greeted her and told her he was Officer Garrett. He refused the cup of coffee she offered. Though she tried to stay positive, she felt no safer as he looked around her shelves of books.

She called the victims' group number.

"This is Jill." The woman who answered sounded pleasant.

Meg explained her situation, doing her best to keep from sounding like the helpless victim. She learned the group met every Tuesday night at six. This disappointed her; Tuesday was still a few days away. She declined the offer to talk to someone now.

She should have.

Her thoughts again and again returned to Montgomery Manor and moving her books there. She didn't regret her decision to move in the least. She wanted to start packing today. She felt safe in the Manor. It was where she most wanted to be. Her shop was no longer home. Indeed, it felt alien, dirty, and invaded. Its smell no longer welcomed her.

And everything she touched, she couldn't help but wonder if the intruder also touched it.

"What are you doing?" Evan's voice came from behind her, and she jumped for what must have been the fiftieth time that morning. "I just took those books out of boxes last week."

"I'm packing them back up." She didn't look up or hesitate in her task. "We're moving the shop into Montgomery Manor. Quint offered me the gallery, which will be great for the shop."

"Do you think that's a good idea?" Evan's asked in an uncertain tone.

She just wanted to be at Montgomery Manor, with Quint, but she didn't voice that. Instead, she paused and looked up at him. "Yes, I do. Besides the increase in rent may hurt us, and I don't need to worry about it."

Worry consumed her, but about what she couldn't say. No matter how hard she tried, she couldn't shake the fear that gripped her. The lunch she'd tried eating earlier was now a twisted, hot knot in her stomach.

It was Evan. She looked up at him. Evan attacked her. Forget the fact that the police had already questioned him, forget that he hadn't seemed to know anything about the break in.

Meg was certain he was her attacker. He had a key to the shop. Anyone who saw him would know he was an employee, and wouldn't even question his coming into the shop. He would know his way around in the dark. He knew Meg stayed late that night, and he would have recognized her car parked outside. And he, most of all, would not want her to move the shop into Montgomery Manor where there would always be people around. "I don't have to justify anything to you." Her words were sharp.

His brows knit in confusion and question. "I didn't ask you to."

She couldn't hold it in any longer. The fear inside her felt like a cold hungry monster eating away at her stomach. "I see the way you're looking at me."

He raised his brows at her comment. "What way am I looking at you?"

"Oh, don't play games with me. Why don't you just tell the truth?" Her voice rose several octaves, and people in the shop turned to look at her. The last thing she needed was everyone staring at her.

"Meg?" His voice softened in an attempt to calm her.

She glanced around. She felt hot and cold at the same time. Her throat burned and her heart pounded in her chest. She looked back at Evan, who watched her. Everyone watched her.

"What's the matter, Meg?"

She wasn't safe there, wasn't safe with Evan. She didn't know how she knew that, she just did. She had to leave. She had to get away before he tried to hurt her again.

"I have to go!" She grabbed her purse and headed for the door without reaching for her sweater. The sun fought against the clouds and won about thirty percent of the time, but there was no rain or fog, for which she was grateful.

She ignored Evan's call, pushed her way through the newly repaired door, and raced to her car. She thought of going to the Manor, but by the time she jumped into her car and slammed the door, she shook all over.

The last thing she wanted was for Quint or his employees to see her like this. She would go home, have a cup of tea, calm down, perhaps take a nap and come back to work as soon as she felt better. It tore her heart to think Evan had hurt her. One part of her still argued that Evan would never hurt her, but she pushed the part away. She planned to call Officer Humphreys as soon as she got home and tell him he should question Evan again.

On her drive home, she thought someone was following her. She wanted to drive around, make sudden turns to make sure the blue car in her rearview mirror followed her as she thought it was, but she was too eager to get home. She parked in front of her own house, but she couldn't get out of the car and make the dash to the door. Terror held her in place. If she got out of the car and raced to her door, whoever followed her would know where she lived. She couldn't worry about that now. She just needed to get inside. She forced her legs to move, just as she gulped air into her lungs.

The air was cold, and the sun now offered no warmth. She shivered, but her cheeks burned hot. Bile welled in her throat. She grit her teeth to keep them from chattering, and her chest tightened. She still felt sick and couldn't stop her hands from shaking.

What was wrong with her?

Meg ran inside, slammed the door behind her, and locked it. Then, she leaned back against it and tried to catch her breath. She couldn't let whoever was following her get in. The small house was silent except for the rushed sounds of her breaths and the loud thudding of her heartbeat in her ears. She felt as if it had been years since she'd stayed in this little house, a house that had always felt like home to her.

She swallowed hard, but her throat was dry and rough. She looked around her house. She should feel safe here. This was home. Why did she feel so threatened? She didn't know. Perhaps she *should* have gone to the Manor after all.

There was no one here. She was alone, but there was no threat. Right? So why didn't she feel safe? Something was wrong, and it took her a moment to realize what it was.

When she arrived home, the front door was unlocked. Had she left it unlocked after coming home to shower and dress earlier? She didn't think she had, but she couldn't remember. Had Quint come home for something and forgotten to lock it? Or had someone else been in the house? Was there someone waiting for her in another room even now?

Meg couldn't move. The man who stalked her, who attacked her, was in her house.

The phone on the small table rang. She jumped and let out a scream that echoed through the house.

The phone rang a second and third time before she moved. She picked it up in the middle of the fourth ring, expecting it to be Evan looking for her until she saw the caller ID read "Restricted." "Hello?" Even after she found her voice, it was no more than a whisper.

"Megan." The long, stretched out whisper of her name sent chills up her spine.

She couldn't breathe, couldn't force her lungs to work past the terror, much less reply. It was the man who attacked her. Did that mean he wasn't in her house? No, he could call her home phone from a cell and be anywhere, even in her own kitchen. How could he know she was home? Only Evan knew she'd left. Unless he was watching her, following her as she thought he was.

"I'm watching you, Megan."

"You're lying." She managed to work her voice into a harsh whisper. She knew he wasn't lying, but she wanted to put on a brave front. It wasn't working.

"I like the blue scarf you're wearing." He really was watching her.

The scarf around her neck suddenly felt like a noose.

"I'm coming for you, Megan." His whispered threat was enough to send her teeth chattering. "Soon you will be mine forever."

CHAPTER EIGHTEEN

Horrible thoughts rushed through Meg's mind.

She would have screamed, but when she opened her mouth, nothing came out.

She wanted to tell him that he was nothing more than a coward, a slithering worm that hides in the dark and whispers threats over the phone.

She wanted to tell him to kiss off and that he couldn't scare her.

She wanted to tell him she would call the police as soon as she hung up.

But the hair on the back of her neck couldn't have stood up more if she'd been struck by lightning. And the truth was he did, indeed, scare her. Right then, she was terrified to the point that she couldn't seem to form any words no matter what she chose to say to him. Nothing else ever frightened her that much. She shivered uncontrollably.

Since he terrified her to the point words were impossible, she hung up on him.

Moments later, she was still clutching the receiver tight enough to turn her knuckles white. She fought to catch her breath.

One breath.

Two breaths.

Three breaths.

Several more breaths later, she felt somewhat normal. At least she didn't have to concentrate on breathing.

The phone rang again.

This time, Meg didn't jump. In fact, she wasn't even startled. Maybe she'd expected him to call again. This time she was determined to say something, even if she had to put on a false bravado. She pressed the TALK button. She offered no greeting. She said nothing at all as she put the phone to her ear.

For a long moment, there was no sound at all. She waited. Her heart beat so hard in her chest, she was certain the stalker on the other end of the line could hear it. She waited for the long, drawn out sound of her name. Much to her surprise, it never came.

"Hello? Meg?"

Meg let out her breath, not knowing until then that she held it. "Quint—"

"What's the matter? What's wrong?" Quint's voice was urgent, filled with concern. "Evan called here and left me the message that you'd left. Why are you home, are you sick? Why didn't you come here?"

She did feel as if she might throw up, but she didn't tell him that. She didn't even know what to tell him or how to describe the panic she'd felt when she left the shop. "He called." She stuttered. "He called here."

"When? What did he say?" Quint didn't need to ask her who.

She quickly explained the phone call in breathy short sentences as her legs gave out and she sank down the wall to sit on the floor beside the door. "I think he's been in here, too, the front door was unlocked."

"Listen to me." Quint fought to keep his voice in control. "Brad just got here. I'm going to tell him what needs to be done today, and then I'll be there. In the meantime, I'm calling the police and they should get there before I do, all right?"

"All right." Just hearing Quint's voice had calmed her nerves to the point she no longer shook.

"Will you be all right until I can get there?"

"Yes." At least she thought she would be—as long as the whisperer didn't call again, as long as she didn't have to face anything else that sent her heart into overdrive.

"I'll be there as soon as I can."

"Thank you." Just then, she loved him so much, her heart ached with it.

There was a pause. Then, "Meg?"

"Yes?"

"I love you."

Her heart raced as if she'd never heard him say those words before. "I love you, too." She'd spoken softly, but her words were no longer breathy whispers.

Just hearing Quint's voice gave her strength and courage. She refused to let this sick person, whomever it may be, frighten her into cowering in the corner. After Quint hung up, she could breathe normally again.

The phone was dead in her hand. Yet, her heart still raced in her chest.

Why was all this horror happening now?

Her business was doing great. Her husband loved her. Her life had become the picture of perfection she'd always dreamed about.

She couldn't let someone scare her. Not now, not *ever*. She replaced the receiver, expecting it to ring again at any moment. She stayed where she was on the floor, daring not to move a muscle, until she heard the sirens draw near.

Forcing her body to move, she opened the door to Officer Humphreys. By the time Quint arrived a few moments later, she was calmer.

Officer Humphreys talked about phone taps since there was no way to identify the RESTRICTED number, but there was the problem of keeping the caller on the phone long enough for the trace to work.

The officer reminded her of a television doctor about to tell his patient there was no cure for her horrible disease. Meg had trouble focusing on Humphreys' words. There were too many technical terms that made no sense.

Quint couldn't touch Meg enough. He held her close to him, laced his fingers through hers and held her hand. Knowing someone stalked her turned his heart cold.

"We'll increase the patrol to every half hour. And it might be a good idea to change your phone number."

Officer Humphreys' suggestion made sense, at least on the home phone. "What about our cells?" Quint asked.

"If he hasn't called on them, he may not know your number."

"I'll need to keep my number at the shop," Meg said.

Quint tightened his grip on her as she snuggled closer to him. She felt cold to the touch. He willed his body heat to warm her.

He gently cupped her chin and forced her to look up at him. "Why did you leave your shop, Meggie?"

"It's so hard to explain. I felt like the walls were closing in on me, and every customer was the man who attacked me. And Evan—I was so certain it was Evan. I had to get out of there, I was shaking and felt so sick—"

"It was a panic attack." They both looked at Officer Humphreys when he interrupted. "I've seen it happen before."

Quint tightened his embrace.

"But I shouldn't have left." Meg sighed. "I shouldn't have left Evan alone. We were so busy, the place was full of customers, and I just left him."

"When he called, I wasn't near the desk. But in the message I got, he said he could handle it. He's just worried about you." Quint didn't add that he was worried about her, too. "I want you to pack more clothes. You can stay at the Manor with me until we decide what to do."

"I'd like that. I want to be there. It just makes me frustrated that he's scared me into doing this."

"Do you still have the number for the victims' group I gave you?" Officer Humphreys stood as if to leave.

"I already called and found out their meeting times, but maybe it would be a good idea to talk to someone now. I have the card in my purse. I'll call again," Meg said.

Humphreys nodded, pulled out a card, and handed it to her. "This is a number of an actual counselor, not just for the support group."

"Thank you." She glanced at the card before slipping it into her shirt pocket.

Quint fought the urge to ask for his own card. He wanted to make sure Meg went, but he didn't want to force her. Enough had been forced on her. "Do you need me to help you pack?"

She gave him a hesitant smile, but her lips trembled.

"No, I can do it. But, thanks."

It was hard for him to let her go, even though it was just to the bedroom they shared.

"This is a typical reaction," Humphreys said.

He didn't reply. There was nothing typical about any of this. This was his *wife*.

Meg's gasp from the other room echoed through his soul. Quint raced to the bedroom and found Meg just inside the bedroom door.

There, drawn on her mirror, were two eyes.

CHAPTER NINETEEN

Humphreys called the crime scene techs. As far as Quint was concerned, Meg was victimized, yet again, as they were stuck in that house for several more hours while the techs dusted every single inch of the house searching for fingerprints. Her stalker was someone smart enough not to leave any.

"It's so quiet, now that the crime crew is gone." She remarked, her expression and voice tired. "Why do you think this is happening, Quint?"

The flatness of her voice was as frightening as their situation. He helped her climb into his truck so they could finally leave for the Manor.

He threw her bag into the back of the truck before climbing in and answering. "I don't know." Maybe it was because he owned the Manor. He couldn't tell her that. He also couldn't tell her that history repeated itself. The truth of it was a knife slicing through his heart.

"But why has he targeted me like this? Do you think I might have a disgruntled customer or something?"

He started the truck before reaching over and taking her hand. He was pretty certain this was not a disgruntled customer. No, an unsatisfied customer would just demand his money back. "Don't blame yourself, Meggie, not for any of this. I think this is just some sick person who probably doesn't even *have* a logical reason." At least that was what he hoped. In his past, this had always happened because of greed.

Meg gaped at him. "Really? Do you think he's doing this for no reason?"

He shrugged. "I only know I'm going to keep you as close to me as possible until this guy is caught. We'll get through this together, and we'll be just fine, you'll see." He offered a reassuring smile. "Did Humphreys say he'd tap the lines or check the phone records for the shop?"

Meg spent the rest of the trip to the mansion telling him about her choices—or lack thereof. They discussed the idea of the phone tap, and Quint had already called the phone company for a number change. He worried that it might be a waste of time and not help them at all.

What had helped most was the hour Meg spent talking to the two women from the victim's group. They came directly to their house while the police dusted for fingerprints. They seemed to know what to say to calm Meg. They promised to be available any time between then and Tuesday when the entire group met. Quint didn't regret calling them in the least.

On the way to the Manor, he and Meg talked more about the victims' group. To Quint, their conversation reiterated what the two women had said. But Meg had connected with the two other women, so like when leaving the light on, if that helped her, he was all for it.

He drove with his left hand on the wheel and he never let go of her hand with his right. "I'll talk to Brad about putting in a few more hours so I can be with you Tuesday night, and just be more available overall. I'd feel better if you hired someone else at your shop, too, so you can have more time away."

"Thank you. I'll put an ad in paper this week and a sign on the counter. I feel so stupid that this is affecting me so much." She watched him as he drove. "I'm sorry about all of this. You just opened and you've been so excited and way too busy. You don't deserve this."

"Neither do you."

He parked in the carriage house of the Manor. Already the house all but called out to him. This was his home. He hoped he could convince Meg to feel the same. He recognized so much of Ellen in Meg, but would she recognize the house as he did? At least she didn't argue about staying there or moving her shop there.

Right now, she needed *him* more than the house. He squeezed her hand. "Would you feel better if I put everything else at the Manor on hold and stayed with you at the shop while we get everything moved into the gallery? If Brad can't work overtime, I'll hire someone else to help, too."

He'd put his plans to open more of the house on hold. For Meg, he was willing to sacrifice the time. Besides, hadn't he been too proud in the past? Hadn't it cost him his wife, Ellen?

In the end, that same pride had cost him his own life.

He couldn't think of the past right then, and he refused to let anything else dark happen within the walls of his house. No, he would do whatever was necessary to keep Meg safe, to keep her by his side.

"No, don't do that." There was no hesitation in her reply. He knew her pride answered for her. "I'll be fine. I just need to take things slower, one step at a time, like Carol from the victims' group said." She looked up at the Manor. "At least I hope I will be." Her words slowed and softened to a whisper, then she looked up at Quint. "I feel better just being here at the Manor with you. I think I'll be all right if I can avoid that closed in, everyone's-out-to-get-me feeling."

He led her toward the door. Today was not a good day to take her through the tunnel from the carriage house into the main house. "If you get any of those feelings, promise you'll call me."

"I will. I'll be careful and cautious, and not let myself get caught anywhere alone. Besides, just knowing you're close is all I need." She looked at him.

He was instantly caught in the sparking fire in her eyes. Damn, how he loved this woman. "I know it sounds selfish, but I want you with me as much as possible."

She leaned her head against his shoulder. "I want to be with you as much as possible, too."

Soft rain began to fall.

"We'd better get inside in case this is the beginning of another downpour." He tightened his grip on her as, hand in hand, they dodged the raindrops and made their way to the massive front doors. Quint pulled the door open and ushered her inside—into the welcoming, enticing aroma of spices and bread.

Brad stood near the hostess stand with a girl Quint introduced as Stacey, the lunch hostess. Brad greeted them both. "Are you feeling better?" He looked at Meg. "When we got the message you'd left your shop, we thought you might be sick."

"I'm better, yes, thank you."

"Are you hungry at all?" Quint squeezed her hand. "You could get something to eat."

"I'd rather wait and eat with you whenever you decide to eat."

Quint took note of her forced smile. And it worried him she didn't want or maybe didn't think she could eat.

"I still feel horrible about leaving the shop."

"I told you, Evan said he could handle it." With her hand still tucked into his, Quint led her toward the stairs. "I know you don't want to combine the businesses, but at least if you had your books here, on days that you were swamped, I could lend you some help."

"I know."

"If you're sure you don't want any lunch, at least let me get you something warm to drink, and you can come with me to the gallery. I think you'll be surprised at the changes

I've made in a very short time. I was going to order some tables and chairs and things, but then I thought it would be better to move the shelves and the furniture you already had in your shop, and then see what you need. I also wanted you to pick out what *you* wanted. But now, I think you should take it easy for the rest of the day. You're still pretty shaken up, aren't you?" He pulled her close and tucked her beside him, his arm around her waist.

"I know it's strange, but it comes in waves. One minute, I feel fine, the next I want to crawl into bed and cover my head. I guess I could spend some time reading more of Joshua Montgomery's journal." She took in the activity all around her. "Wow, things are hopping here."

No one stood around idly.

Quint followed her gaze and admired the activity. A housekeeper dressed in an old-fashioned black dress complete with a white apron strolled by holding an armload of towels. A man wearing a crisp white shirt with black pants and suspenders carried a tray with a tea pot and several cups and saucers. The fountain room was filled with people. He noticed what looked like a group of students on a tour.

"Just another day at the Manor." Quint smiled down at her. "I think it'd be a good idea for you to find a nice spot and read some more of Joshua Montgomery's journal. I'd like to know your thoughts on it."

Two couples passed them, and he greeted them. It amazed Meg how he remembered their names.

"Let me read a little more first."

A half hour later, Meg stood in the gallery warming herself up with a cup of French vanilla cappuccino. It wasn't a hot cup of soup, but Quint thought it was better than nothing.

"The wood floor looks like we could ice skate on it. And I didn't notice how dirty the windows were before until I look out them now and see how much light comes in and how well I can see the beautiful sea in the distance. Were those chairs just extra ones you found somewhere, because they look perfect for this room?"

Quint was glad she liked the few changes he'd made, but he was far from done. "I found them in one of the empty rooms and thought you might like them."

"Oh, it smells so good in here, like orange. And don't tell me, were those paintings hidden between the floor joists?"

Quint looked at the three huge paintings were hung throughout the room.

"These *originally* hung in this room, and yes, I pulled them from their hiding places." Quint studied her reaction to his handiwork. "If you don't like them in here—"

"They're perfect. I never knew you had that kind of decorative touch." She looked around. "Why do you suppose all the paintings were hidden?"

"My best guess?" *Which wasn't a guess at all.* "Joshua Montgomery knew he was in trouble after Ellen was killed. He knew being caught with a bloody knife in his hand and his dead wife at his feet wouldn't bode well, and he was right. His entire estate, his money, his art that he loved so much, everything stood the chance of going to the highest bidder or being left for vandals. I suppose he hid it all to protect it the best he could."

"I'm glad he did."

The first painting was a masterpiece of a woman sitting on a bench in a garden, her long, flowing skirts sweeping the ground. A small boy dressed in knickers and a blue cap and white shirt sat beside her as she read a book to him.

The second painting was of two young people, also in a garden. The young man pushed his blond-haired lover on a wooden swing. It was very distinctive. Her hair blew in the breeze. Her smile was lovely. The love the man felt for her was evident in his expression, in the way he watched her.

The third painting was that of a sailing ship in the distance, its huge sails caught in the beacon from the lighthouse on the nearby rocky shore.

Quint stepped up behind her and placed his hands on her arms as she studied each work of art. "It's easy to decorate this place. All I have to do is work with what's already here. Brad's been a big help. He knows this house." He paused. "As soon as you feel comfortable, we'll start packing your books and get them moved in, too."

She leaned back against him and sighed, and Quint gave her arms a loving rub.

"I think I'll just sit in here and enjoy the view, get used to the room for a while. It's so much bigger in the light."

He leaned down kissed her cheek. "I'll be in and out if you need me. I need to help man the bar."

"Why? Is Melanie sick?" Melanie was about the only person Meg could remember because Melanie had ventured into her shop so often.

"No, it's just busy."

Quint left her alone, but Meg knew he didn't go far. He also left the door open so she heard the noise from the not-too-far-away restaurant. Sitting and watching the sea calmed her. She pulled the journal out of her bag and, once again, let the words of Joshua Montgomery's life, in his precise, even, perfect script, calm her further. The words written within the old book told of hidden rooms she planned to explore and French ambassadors, parties, business deals, the ups and downs of Montgomery Shipping, and family happenings. Most of all, it told of his love for his wife. Each journal entry, each day with Ellen, was an adventure.

Ellen and I swam in the pool this evening. I had planned to surprise her with a midnight swim under the light of the full moon, but she had surprised me by already having the room lit with what must have been a hundred candles. Making love to her in the water with the stars overhead is the most wonderful experience I have ever known...

Meg's heart pounded as she read the words since she hadn't just seen that night, she had lived it. *Ellen and I climbed among the rocks behind the house, and watched the tide come in. The powerful waves crashed upon the rocks. I could have stood there and held Ellen's hand forever...*

Then the words began to take on a familiar ring, one that sent shivers up Meg's spine.

Ellen and I shared lunch in bed today. I cannot begin to describe the experience.

Today, Ellen received roses from an unknown admirer. I believe her when she tells me she doesn't know who sent them. I plan to use some of my contacts to discover this person's identity.

I have purchased another vessel today—one of the grandest ships of all time. I'm sure she will serve my company well. I will talk to Ellen and we will plan a holiday to Europe on her next spring. Ellen would love that...

Then a week before Ellen's murder:

Ellen finally confided in me what troubles her, and it is impossible for me to contain my fury. It seems my partner, and long-time confidant, Mr. Windsbrook, touched her in an inappropriate way the night of the Ferguson's ball. I have never known Windsbrook to show interest in my wife, and I am uncertain as to why he has now. Yet, she informed me that he cornered her, held her against her will, and tore her dress before she escaped him. She bears the bruises still. She also tells me that he confessed to sending the flowers. I was forced to meet with him this morning and dissolve our partnership as well as our relationship. It took everything within my power not to strangle the life from him. Even now, I find it difficult to write, perhaps tomorrow will be easier when my anger has simmered. I will take Ellen on a holiday so she may recover from this violation. Ellen, my love, also gifted me with the most wonderful news–my child lives within her. I feel as if I leap from complete happiness at the prospect of our child, to wishing still to murder Windsbrook. I now wish we had never planned tomorrow night's Halloween ball...

The last entry was dated October 30, 1899. Meg's heart pounded. Ellen Montgomery was stabbed to death in the cellar on October 31, 1899, during the Halloween ball. Within a month, after a quick trial, given the circumstances and Montgomery's worth, Joshua Montgomery was hanged for her murder. He had declared his innocence to the end. But the fact that dinner party guests discovered Joshua Montgomery standing over her body holding a bloody knife in his hand seemed to be all the jury heard and understood. To make matters worse, witnesses for the prosecution testified they thought Ellen Montgomery had a lover, or that she received roses from an admirer. Then in the weeks just before the murder, obviously before Joshua Montgomery was aware he was going to be a father, the servants had witnessed a terrible argument between Joshua and Ellen over the idea of children. He had wanted them; she hadn't been sure she was ready. What also didn't help was the fact that Ellen's family was in South Carolina and Ellen had, on numerous occasions, voiced her dislike for the northern coastal winter climate, as well as her desire to live somewhere closer to her family.

Most everyone today knew those details. Meg had heard most of the tales, had even read about a few in the book they sold in the Manor. But Joshua Montgomery's own words painted a different picture. How could Ellen have a lover when she without a doubt had a very devoted, romantic husband who shared so much with her? How could she even have the time? And if he were as devoted and in love as his words implied, he could never kill her, Meg reasoned. Also, Ellen had been pregnant, which Meg hadn't known until now.

Meg didn't believe Ellen had a lover, but the question of an admirer nagged at her thoughts. An admirer who sent roses could be enough to stir up suspicion. What if Joshua killed his wife in a fit of jealous rage? It was known to happen, and it was known to happen to the least suspected people. Had the journal been a mere ploy to convince a jury of love just in case they found it? But no one had, until now. And what about this man Windsbrook? There was very little written about him anywhere else. He was known as the silent partner.

Meg stopped and looked up to find Quint had returned. His gaze met and held hers, and he smiled at her before he came into the room carrying a box on his shoulder. "I'm just bringing in some outlet boxes. You have electric lights, but few outlets. I don't know when the electricians will be able to work or how much trouble it will be to keep your shop open while outlets are put in."

She stretched and sat up straight to work out the kink that tried to form in her neck with all the reading she'd just done. "Don't worry about it. I can move in when the room's ready, and it will take some time to organize the shelves before we can reopen, anyway. This is a great room, thank you."

"I should thank you. You let me keep this place."

"I'm glad I did. I'm glad *we* did." She stood up and set the journal on the chair she'd vacated. "The first book in my shop here."

A surge of pride washed through him. "Would you sell it?"

"No, it's not for sale. It's way too valuable. If anyone had known it had existed all those years ago, no doubt it would have been used as evidence. It may have even been enough to convince a jury of Joshua Montgomery's innocence." Meg stepped closer to him. "I think it should be kept our secret, at the very least, it should be behind a case in your museum."

"So you're convinced he was innocent?"

She stepped closer to him. It was impossible not to. She felt so much better, and safer close to him. In no way did she regret her decision to move the shop. "Pretty much, yes."

He peered down at her. "But something else is bothering you. I see it in your eyes."

She swallowed hard, coming to terms with what she'd discovered in Joshua Montgomery's journal. "It's happening again. Here. Now." She spoke slowly, despite the certainty and fear that tugged at her heart.

"What?" He set the box of outlets down and pulled her into his arms.

Meg had the uncanny feeling he knew what she was talking about.

"Everything that happened to Ellen Montgomery. She received flowers. She was assaulted. It's all the same, right down to having lunch in bed with her husband." Meg licked her lips to moisten her suddenly dry mouth.

Quint tightened his embrace. "It's not happening again."

Was he trying to convince her or himself? Meg couldn't decide.

"History is not repeating itself, Meggie. Windsbrook was a partner. I don't have a partner. Ellen's assault was a secret until she told Joshua. This is not the same."

"It feels just as scary as I'm sure it was for her." She leaned against his chest wishing she could melt right into him. "You feel so wonderful."

Quint breathed in a deep breath, filling himself with the flowery scent of woman and whatever Meg used to wash her hair. He wished he could just hold her like this forever. He leaned down, turning to rest his cheek on the top of her head.

"I'm not going to let anything happen to you, Meggie." He spoke the promise from his heart. He didn't tell her how Windsbrook had framed him. He didn't tell her how Windsbrook had tried to kill *him*, and that Ellen had stepped in the way. The situation now with Meg's attacker was different. The flowers from an unknown admirer may be similar, but Windsbrook hadn't attacked Ellen. He had tried to seduce her. He had touched her, tried to be her lover. He had embraced her and refused to let her go, but he hadn't grabbed her in the dark, or slammed her against the desk, or terrorized her. Ellen had explained to him all the subtle moves Windsbrook had made, and how he attempted to seduce her once they were alone. It had made Ellen angry and perhaps a bit frightened and leery of him, but at least Ellen and Joshua knew what and where and who the problem was.

No, this was very different from all that happened to Ellen.

Yet, he had to face the fact the danger was there. The danger could not be ignored.

"If I have to stay with you every moment, Meggie, I will. I won't let anything happen to you."

"Here you are." Brad grabbed their attention as he spoke from the doorway.

They both looked up. Brad leaned against the doorframe and held a long box.

"I've been looking for you two. This was just delivered for you, Meg."

Quint stared at the pure white cardboard box but didn't move. In his arms, Meg didn't even breathe. *Fuck.* He looked down at her. The color that drained from her face was replaced by an expression of sheer terror.

The wide ribbon holding the box closed was blood red and tied in a large, beautiful bow.

Brad brought it to them.

"I'll take it. What florist delivered it?" Quint's voice was hard.

"There's no card. I wasn't at the desk when it was delivered." Brad set the box on the chair atop Joshua Montgomery's journal. "And Stacey said she didn't see it delivered, either. She said it was just sitting on the counter when she came out of the office, and it has Meg's name on it."

It tore Quint in two to let her go. He couldn't help but notice she didn't move. He turned the box and saw Meg's name in block letters on the top. It didn't say Meg Falkner, it said Megan Falkner. "Thanks for bringing it to us."

"You're welcome," Brad said.

Quint's heart quickened its pace as he peeled off the bow. He didn't want to open it in front of Meg. She had dealt with enough. Hell, he didn't want to open it at all.

"Perhaps we should just give it to the police," she said.

He didn't like the flat tone of her voice. He glanced at her. She still stood like a statue. "We will." He had no choice but to open it. He didn't want to wait for Humphreys. He looked at Meg for a moment before pulling off the box lid and peering inside. She stepped close to peer into the box, too, and her warmth and closeness touched him like a soft breeze. Her sharp intake of breath was loud in the quiet room.

The roses inside the box were black.

CHAPTER TWENTY

Meg's fear came in one huge wave after another, sometimes in waves strong enough to almost knock her off her feet. Then when one swell passed, she felt all right for a moment before the next one hit her.

Amazingly and unexpectedly, in between those waves of fear, came anger. There were moments when she shook with anger. She took a deep breath and tried curbing the raw emotions before her knees gave out. But it wasn't easy.

Why now?

She had no answer. Was there ever a better time for stalking? She didn't think so.

She wasn't even sure she wanted an answer to her question. She just wanted the fear to be gone. She just wanted to work her business and spend this special time with her husband. That wasn't too much to ask. She wanted to explore the Manor without fear lurking behind every corner.

The emotional roller coaster left her drained. After her second visit with Officer Humphreys, in which he asked more questions for which no one had answers, Quint insisted she go upstairs and rest. All the while, Quint continued asking her if she was all right.

If she had to lie and say, "Yes, I'm fine," one more time, she'd hit him with something. The anger was back in full swing, and if she wasn't careful, she'd take it out on Quint.

He didn't deserve it.

Besides, she wasn't fine at all, and she wondered if she ever would be again. She hated that she wasn't fine. She hated lying to Quint. But she didn't dare tell him anything different. To avoid telling him anything at all, she agreed to go upstairs and rest.

But rest did not come easy. Rest did not come at all.

In fact, within the cozy love nest apartment Quint had so lovingly put together, she thought she just might go crazy.

She lay down and allowed Quint to cover her with the quilt. He kissed her softly.

She looked up at him after he ended the kiss. "I wish that could go on forever."

"What?"

"Your kiss. It's wonderful and safe, and I can get lost in it."

The smile he offered was small but touched her heart just the same. "I've got a few things to do, but I'll stay with you if you need me."

"I'll just take a nap. You don't need to stay for that." She hoped she wasn't wrong.

"I promise I'll be back in a little while, no more than a half hour. I'm carrying my phone, so you can call me any time you need anything." He moved to the door. "If you get hungry, I've stocked the kitchen with a few things, and there are drinks in the fridge, or you can call downstairs if you want something else. The specialty soup for today is tortellini and it's delicious. It might warm you up inside."

"I'll be fine." She lied again, and closed her eyes. "Maybe I'll call down later for a bowl, or maybe I'll come down and sit in the fountain room for a while. I love that room."

Quint slipped out the door. As soon as she heard the door close, she flipped back the quilt and stood, too antsy to lie in bed.

She paced for a few seconds, then turned on the television in the living room, shuffled through the channels, found nothing interesting, and turned it off again all within sixty seconds. She looked through the kitchen cabinets, but the thought of eating any of the snack crackers she found turned her stomach. Maybe she would have a bowl of tortellini soup in a while, that sounded better than anything else.

She searched for the latch that opened the hidden door to Ellen's secret room. She couldn't find it. Perhaps that night really was a dream.

Meg had too much pent-up energy to stand still. She moved about the room but stopped in front of the desk in the corner. It was covered with plans, obviously plans for future renovations.

Quint had already drawn changes for the pool room. There was also a page showing the gallery that would be her shop soon.

Yet, most of it didn't make sense. The plans looked new, the paper crisp. But after studying the plans for a long moment, she realized they looked old fashioned, the writing not Quint's usual print for dimensions and instructions. The g's and p's were loopy, not at all the way Quint wrote them.

Maybe someone else drew these plans.

She reached for Joshua Montgomery's journal without a thought. The g's and the p's were the same as those on the plan. In fact, all the letters were the same.

She forced in a breath. How was this possible? The walls of the suite closed in on her. She dropped the journal on the desk and moved to the window.

The surf splashed against the huge rocks of the Massachusetts coastline in the distance. Finally, without a word, she slipped into Quint's oversized coat and headed outside. Perhaps some fresh, salty air would clear her head and allow her to find perspective.

Once outside, she took a deep breath of moist air and relished the coolness of it. She may never put things into perspective, but at she felt invigorated with the sky for a roof over her head.

How long had it been since she'd gone for a walk, or even been outside without dashing through the fog or dodging raindrops? Weeks? Months? She couldn't remember. With the cold, damp weather and all the work at her shop and the Manor, she'd been too busy for something as simple and mind-freeing as a walk.

She moved about the garden that, in the summer, would be a rich with circular hedges and plots of flowers. Now, it was moist, gray, and barren. There were benches and stone paths, as well as dry, empty fountains. It wasn't hard for Meg to imagine what the garden would look like on a bright, blue-sky summer day.

But, for now, the earth beneath her feet was soft and showed hints of green under a blanket of old leaves and thawing grass. She didn't care that mud coated her shoes as she made her way toward the rocky cliffs.

The ocean was vast and beautiful in its strength as it crashed upon the rocks. She watched the tide come in. Such power, so stunning—and it was right in her own back yard.

Well, if there was one thing she could thank her stalker for, he made her see things differently. She looked at the ocean with a newness and a certain joy that she didn't remember having before. Even in the misty air, the lighthouse in the distance was bright. It lit a warning as well as a welcome, blinking in her direction.

Yes, she now saw things in a different light. Never again would she take anything for granted. Never again would she hesitate to take a moment to be thankful for all that she had, even if it was the simple splendor of nature around her. If anything, her stalker had shown her just how important things were.

Meg stayed within sight of the house where Quint could see her if he looked out so he wouldn't have to worry about where she was.

She stared out at the spray rising up from the rocks and thought about the roses. Black roses? Hell, where did someone even *get* black roses? At the least, the police should be able to discover where the stalker had managed to get his hands on them. Just how many florists kept black roses in stock, anyway? The anger was back. She took a deep breath working to calm herself, but now she didn't attempt to push the anger away. It was, after all, much easier to handle than fear.

"I can be strong like the rocks." Her words were lost to the sea breeze and the loud surf.

Someone dared—someone was stupid enough—to send her black roses. They thought it would scare her and they'd get away with it. Well, when she found out who it was, she would rub his face in those macabre flowers. A new, devilish idea swept through her mind. She'd prop the black roses up on the bar just to show the world she wasn't afraid anymore. She chuckled at that idea, because she *was* afraid. Those black roses came from someone with a black heart and black thoughts.

Still, she wished she wasn't afraid.

So as soon as the police caught the stalker, she thought the fear would die. Then she'd pack her books, move them to the Manor gallery, and her business would be better than ever.

She looked up at the sky. Her plan was positive. It was the direction she needed to move. At the same time, she did her best to ward off the lingering fear.

She put her chilled hands into the pockets of Quint's coat and tried to think of one person who benefited from stalking her.

No one but Quint.

Quint had wanted her to move into the Manor.

Because of the stalker, now she was.

Quint wanted her to move her shop into the Manor.

Because of her attack, now she was.

She stared out at the surf but didn't see it.

Could it be Quint?

She knew it was a wild idea, but the idea refused to leave.

Quint was always absent when the whisperer called. He had a key to her shop, and he would know his way around in the darkness. She had been so traumatized by the attack, she might have missed that there weren't two people there in the dark with her. Quint could have made it seem as if there were. Also, he admitted he knew she'd left the shop in a hurry, that Evan had called him. He would have had enough time to give her a whispered call to scare her, and then pretend to be the hero coming to her aid. He could plant boxes of flowers addressed to her anywhere in the Manor. He was the boss, the owner; no one would even question his phone calls or any boxes he carried around. And there was no doubt, that in the past months, Quint was not the same man she married.

She didn't know why her thoughts had taken such a diabolical turn. In the history of their marriage, Quint had never been more loving, more attentive.

And yet, like the fear and the anger, the thoughts couldn't be ignored.

She was terrified of her own husband because of the thoughts in her own head. He was the man she should trust above all others, would he really scare her like this to get his way? Would he go to such treacherous extremes to get what he wanted? The questions worked like a chisel, chipping away at her heart.

Part of her tried to tell her Quint would never do such things, while another part continued reminding her of what he gained by moving her into the Manor. Besides, look at the business he'd drummed up using the buzz about the break in at her bookstore. All the mystery and publicity brought in the customers.

She turned back toward the house. No, Quint wouldn't do this to her. He'd never been deceitful, never been anything but loving to her. Besides, he was surrounded by so many people here at the Manor. Everyone here could probably vouch for his actions. She was allowing this stalker to get to her, make her think crazy things just as when she mentally accused Evan. *Bastard.* More than ever, she hated that she rode this see saw.

She needed to find Quint, just hear his voice, feel his arms around her.

Going back in, she passed a glass greenhouse conservatory that all but called out for exploration. But she ignored it and entered the Manor.

Stacey stopped chomping her gum long enough to give Meg a surprised smile when she walked in.

"Do you know where Quint is?"

"I haven't seen him in a while. You can call him if you want, he has his phone." She stuck a pencil behind her ear and then reached for the ringing telephone.

"I don't want to call him; I'll just find him." Meg had to wait a moment until Stacey hung up.

"Well, earlier this morning he and Brad talked about going through the wine stock in the cellar so perhaps they're down there."

Meg walked away after a simple, "thank you," and headed toward the cellar. She wasn't certain she wanted to venture down there. There was something ominous down there that left her fill with cold. But Quint's embrace would warm her.

Meg passed patrons and workers on her way down to the cellar. She was so lost in need to find her husband she couldn't remember who she'd passed or who said hello.

She travelled through four more doors until she found the spiral stairway leading down into the cellar. Because she'd almost fallen coming up this stairway on the night of the grand opening, she clung to the rail as she moved down. It would be too ironic for her to fall and break her neck and never get the chance to know who her stalker was. She wondered if her accidental, mysterious death would bring in more curious customers. She chuckled in the silence at the thought.

Her soft-soled shoes didn't make a single sound on the uneven cobblestones, unlike the night of the tour when she'd worn heels. Also, unlike the night of the tour, every other sconce on the wall was lit. The soft light cast dancing shadows around her, giving the cellar an eerie, creepy atmosphere.

Meg pulled in a breath. It wasn't dark, but the shadows were enough to increase her pulse rate. She wondered if her attack would forever make her afraid of the dark. It was just another reason to be angry with her attacker.

She came around the corner and ran right into Quint. At his sudden appearance in the low-ceilinged, tunnel-like room, she let out a startled cry.

"Whoa!" Quint cried. "Hell, Meg, what are you doing here? You should be upstairs resting, not sneaking up on me like that. If you needed me for something, you could have called." He carried a small wooden barrel on one shoulder. He set it on the floor. "Can you believe some of these still have wine in them? I'm almost afraid to open them to see if it's any good."

The last thing Meg wanted to talk about was whatever kind of fermented grape juice might be in the barrel. "I needed to find you, to talk to you."

"No, you need to rest. You look pale. Have you had anything to eat?"

"Don't order me around, and don't patronize me." She forced determination and strength into her voice.

Quint stared down at her, blinking a few times before replying. She saw contemplation and perplexity flash on his face, and she wondered what his next words would be. "I'm not trying to order you around or patronize you. I'm just worried about you. I hate to point it out to you, but right now, you are as anxious as a cornered doe."

How coincidental that he would be able to describe just how she felt. But she didn't let him know he was right. Instead, she got right to the topic at hand.

"I just was watching the surf and I had this crazy idea that you are the only one I know who really benefits from stalking me. And I…" She couldn't go on. Her words did sound crazy. She hated like hell her stalker did this to her.

"Me?" He sat down on the barrel, putting himself at eye level with her. "What are you talking about?"

"The phone calls, breaking into my shop, the roses, they all scared me and got me to move everything into this place. Tell me how crazy that sounds."

He stared at her for several seconds as her words sank in. "You think I would scare you on purpose to get you to move to this house?" His words, when he did speak, were slow and precise, as if he couldn't believe he had to utter them at all.

"No, I don't, not really. I know it sounds crazy—just look at what you gain when I move in here." Meg tried to keep an argumentative tone out of her voice, but it was impossible.

He crossed his arms over his chest as he continued staring at her. "And just what do I gain—except to have my wife close to me? Except to make up for lost time these past months when I've hardly seen you."

"Well…" She had to think. "You could run my business, just as you run your own."

He laughed, and his body relaxed. "Meg, we've been through all this. I don't want to run your business. I never have before, and while I'm here to help you if you need it, I still don't want to run it. I know that, in the past few weeks, my ideas about books have changed. And I've been in your shop more than usual, but that doesn't mean I want to take over your business. You're running your business fine all by yourself, just as you always have. And I'm sorry, but look around, I'm just a little busy here with my own business."

"And why have your ideas changed?" Her tone changed from argumentative to curiosity and just a bit challenging. She faced him with her arms crossed. Maybe if she could put one thing into perspective, other things would be easier to face. "Hell, even your handwriting's changed."

He took a deep breath. "I don't think now is a good time to get into that. All you need to know is that I support your business, and I love seeing you so happy in it. I'll help you when you ask me to, but I don't want to run it—not in any way, understand?" He peered into her eyes as if to gauge her response. "Now, what else would I stand to gain?"

For a long moment, she stared at him, digging for a reason, at least a substantial reason. "Tell me why you've changed so much." She said instead.

"Meg, right now we're sticking to the subject. What more would I stand to gain?" He got off the barrel and drew up in front of her.

He reached out, but she stepped back out of reach. "Don't try to distract me."

Quint let her. "You don't have an answer, because there isn't one." He sighed, and the sound of it echoed off the walls. "The thing I'd stand to gain is having you closer to me, and that's all I want. Having you here would mean we could break away and take a lunch together...in bed like we did the other day. If you want. I know I sure enjoyed what I ate for lunch." He winked at her and allowed a moment for his words to sink in. "I didn't do anything to scare you. I would never scare or hurt you. It's true, I offered you a place here, but only because I want you safe. I missed you those months while I was here working. But once I started, I couldn't quit until I was finished. I thought if you were here, too, we could spend more time together, at least see each other more often, even if all we did was pass each other in the hall and wave. Then when all this stuff with the stalker started, I thought *you'd* feel better here with me, that's all. And I *want* to keep you safe. I know *I* feel better having you here. I like knowing you're upstairs or at least within these walls where I can get to you if you need me."

He raked his fingers through his hair. "Damn, Meg, you have no idea how I felt when Evan called to say you'd left. Then when I called you and heard the fear in your voice, I thought I'd go crazy before I could get to you. That,

Meggie, is the reason I want you here. But if you don't want to move here, fine. I don't care." He corrected himself. "Well, I do care, because I'll still miss you when you're at your shop across town. It's true that I'll keep asking you to move here, and I will keep finding reasons for you to move here. But I'm not the kind of snake who would try and scare you into moving here. Because if you're not happy in this house with your business down the hall from mine, then fuck it all to hell, I don't want you here."

Meg heard the hurt and anger in his voice, and she was sorry for her quick actions. "I'm sorry. I should have never...I hate what this bastard has done to me. I've blamed you. I've blamed Evan."

Quint let out another heavy breath. The glare in his eyes told her he was trying to keep from getting angry at her. "It's what he's done to both of us. Just knowing someone— someone we don't know—put his hands on you and tried to hurt you feels like a disease eating away at my gut. And the last thing I want is for you to feel the anger and frustration that comes with that. But be honest with me, be honest with yourself. Do you want to stay here? Do you want to move into this house with me?" He stepped closer, and this time, she didn't move away. He reached out and took both her hands in his.

She let him. It was too difficult to deny him.

He stared into her eyes. "This house is part of you, don't you feel it, Meggie? Don't you feel it call to you? Just close your eyes and answer, yes or no?"

Somehow they'd stepped back to another place, another time. Meg closed her eyes for a long moment, then when she opened them again, she found herself staring up into his eyes. She was certain, absolutely certain, she no longer stared into the eyes of her husband. He looked like her husband. He sounded so much like her husband. And yet, at the same time, he was once again the man who touched her in the pool, the man who held her on the dance floor, the man who made love to her in the dressing room.

She didn't answer his question—at least not yet. "Tell me why you've changed so much." Her words came out in a whispered breath.

He held her close and answered just as softly into her ear. "You may not be ready to accept it."

"Tell me." She didn't know if she was ready or not. He was so close she felt his heart beat in his chest.

"You already know why. Your heart recognizes mine. Everything you saw, everything you felt the night of the party was real, Meggie. Those weren't dreams you experienced the night of the party. They were real, like doorways allowing Joshua Montgomery to be here, inside me." He let go of one of her hands to place his hand over his heart for a moment before taking her hand again in his.

Joshua was somehow Quint. Quint had somehow become Joshua.

Meg stepped away from him. This time, he didn't release her hands when she tried to put more space between them.

"It's not possible." She tried to inhale, but her chest was tight. Her heart raced. Although why her heart raced, she wasn't certain. She wasn't afraid, not of the man who held her hands. She wasn't even afraid of the idea her husband was not the same, although she was intrigued. "How?"

"It was all through you, Meggie, you and the love we have shared for generations. I coerced the old man who owned this place to leave it to Quint, just as I coerced Quint to keep it. I did it all to be with you." He spoke as if it were as simple as that.

She shook her head. "No. I don't believe it's that simple, even if it is true."

"Are you willing to deny what you saw—what you felt—in the pool when I made love to you with the room filled with candlelight, while we danced in the ballroom, while we made love in our hidden dressing room?" He paused and stared into her eyes. "Can you deny what you felt when I made love to you in our bed at lunch?"

"Except for the lunch in bed, those were just dreams." She still stared up at him. Shivers passed through her, and yet her face burned hot enough to make her feel lightheaded.

"Were they? Is this?"

He kissed her. Passion raced through her in an instant, passion equaling then surpassing the passion of her time in the pool, her kiss at the end of waltz, and the wild, out-of-control love he made with her in that small dressing room—the secret room she couldn't find again. The flame he sent into her felt like liquid fire from her lips down her neck and into her chest, where her nipples hardened, pressed against his chest, and continued down to her abdomen then between her legs.

If she'd had the strength, Meg might have pushed herself away from him. Yet the will, the very want to push herself away from him, was swept away. After a heartbeat, the heat of his kiss touched her tongue. Then she melted against him. He left her with no choice but to want more, need more, just as she needed oxygen to live.

It was Quint who broke the kiss and pulled away enough to gaze down into her face. He looked into her eyes. She tried to see the truth of his fantastic words his eyes, but she was lost in their blue fire.

With one hand on each side of her face, he held her. "Can you deny what you feel with me, Meggie?"

"No." Although she could deny him nothing, her answer was the truth.

"Do you really think I would hurt you?" His words were hardly more than a whisper.

"No."

"Good." He drew her into another kiss.

He kissed her until her knees refused to hold her upright. Then when she thought he'd lower her to the cobblestone floor or press her against the wall and make love to her there in the cellar, he broke the kiss, leaving her weak and shaky.

"I talked to Brad." His voice was rough and raw. "He has no problem with staying late and taking care of the supper shift tonight. I think we need to spend the evening together—get cozy in our suite, start a fire in the fireplace, enjoy some time in the whirl pool tub, cook ourselves some supper, just be together for a while. It's been so long since we've been able to do anything like that. What do you say?"

It sounded lovely. It sounded like it was what she needed. Making love to him right now sounded pretty perfect, too. "I'd like that. Can we start right now?"

He offered her his now-familiar crooked grin before he drew her closer and gave her one last quick kiss. "I'll continue with more when we're upstairs. If you want to christen the cellar sometime, we can do that when all the employees are gone for the day."

He hoisted up the barrel again and balanced it on his shoulder. "And Meggie?"

She met his gaze. "Yes?"

"Are we going to have to have this discussion again?"

She knew what he meant. He needed to know her thoughts about Joshua Montgomery. He needed to know if she still accused him. "I don't know." At least it was an honest answer.

He nodded in understanding, but his expression hardened. "It might not be a good idea if you discuss it with anyone else, though. I'd hate for the new lady of the Manor to be labeled as crazy."

She said nothing, but she agreed with him.

He met her gaze again and licked his lips as he still tasted her. "Will you try and remember one thing for me?"

At the sight of his tongue, she needed it on her body. "Yes. What?"

"Just remember that I love you. I always have." He spoke in a way that said if she remembered that, everything else was easy. "Can you find your way back upstairs?"

She nodded. "I think so." She was certain she could find her way anywhere but back into his arms.

Later, Meg talked to Evan. He reassured her the day at the shop had gone well and he had no problem locking up or making the night deposit. Then Quint kept his promise. They shared a quiet supper together complete with candles. They spent almost the same amount of time in the whirl pool. They made love in front of the fire. In the afterglow, Meg snuggled closer to Quint and knew he was right. Time together was what the two of them needed.

What she didn't know was just how close terror waited.

CHAPTER TWENTY-ONE

Three weeks went by uneventfully.

Uneventfully, that is, in regard to Meg's stalker. There were no phone calls, no roses, no threats, for which she was grateful. Her three visits to the victims' group helped ease her anxiety. Although she and Quint still slept with the bedside lamp on.

As for the move into the Manor, it was *very* eventful.

Three weeks after she decided to move, the gallery was ready. Meg and Evan closed the shop for a few days to pack and move the books. The building felt odd and empty, and somehow *lonely* with every box she and Evan packed. The main room of the store echoed with each spoken word. The hollow sounds filled Meg with sadness about leaving and, but at the same time, anticipation to move into the gallery.

The move was what she needed. It filled her mind, so she didn't get preoccupied with idea of Quint being a changed man. She *called* him a changed man. She couldn't bring herself to say the word 'possessed.' Besides, she still saw so much of the old Quint. There were times when, while watching him swing his hammer or place his pencil behind his ear, she thought he wasn't different at all. He still wrote with his left hand. He laughed with his easy laughter as always. Meg found a great deal of comfort in the familiar way he, once again, wore work jeans and a denim shirt with a tape measure clipped to his pocket.

But there were differences. What she found most different was the way he looked at her. The old Quint looked at her with familiar ease. So now, the evident desire in his eyes wasn't a bad thing.

Before she and Evan had packed the books, she and Quint moved out of their little house. Little by little, they moved their furniture into the Manor, along with their clothes. She hadn't stayed another night in that house, not after the eyes were drawn on the mirror with her own eyebrow marker, so leaving wasn't difficult. The suite felt more like home every moment after the little touches she added, like family pictures and her own dishes. And when she had some time, she explored the Manor.

In fact, her time was so full, it was almost easy for Meg to forget there was someone out there who wanted to hurt her.

She bent down to retrieve yet another box of books. Evan and Quint, and two men Quint brought with him, Jim and Terry, did most of the heavy work. They moved box after box of books to a truck to deliver them to the gallery. Yet, every now and then, Meg managed to get her own hands on a box of her treasures. It was slow and frustrating, because she had to pack up the books before they could move the shelves.

It was when she stood back up with the box in tow that the dizziness hit her. In an instant, heat filled her face, and she thought she might lose the cup of coffee she'd downed a short time before.

"Meg?"

Quint was beside her. He placed a hand on her elbow. With his other hand, he took most of the weight of the box she held.

"I'm all right. I just got a little dizzy." She tried to keep her words light as if the dizziness was nothing. "It's probably because I didn't eat much breakfast."

"You didn't feel good then, either."

She wished he hadn't reminded her. "I'll be fine." She tried to smile. "I think I'm just excited that this move is finally happening."

"Sit down for a while." Not all the chairs in her shop had been loaded with boxes yet, and he led her to a lone, hard folding chair before he took the box from her and set it back on the floor.

"I think I'll be fine."

"You look pale."

"Thanks for letting me know." She did her best to keep the sarcasm out of her voice and keep her words light so he didn't know just how fast the room spun, but it wasn't easy.

He met her gaze. "Even Evan noticed when we got here this morning."

"Quint—"

"Just stay sitting, humor me. Don't make me sound like your boss. I think we'll go ahead and take what we've got loaded on the truck to the gallery. You can sit on the floor and unpack books. But please stay off your feet and stop trying to do a man's job when there are four of us here to do it."

"I really am fine."

"Well then, make me feel better and just sit here for a few minutes while I put these last two boxes in the truck. Then ride with me to the Manor, and let the rest of us finish with the packing."

Meg watched him walk away. He carried the box of books as if it weighed nothing. Perhaps she had been overdoing it these past weeks, but there was just so much to do. She was eager to be done with moving. Like the house she and Quint had shared, this shop no longer felt like home; not after the stalker invaded it.

Yet, she didn't like the idea of Quint and Evan, and two men she didn't know, packing her treasures. Evan understood the value of her books, but she wasn't sure about the others.

At least she didn't have to feel bad about leaving. Mr. Jackson already had two potential renters.

Just as she was eager to get moved in, she was also eager to be at the Manor. It was home now. How she'd ever been frightened of that big, old house, she had no idea. As soon as she got there, she planned to change out of the slacks she wore and put on a pair of comfortable jeans, maybe even some leggings. Her clothes felt too tight.

Quint came back for the second box. "Ready?"

"Sure." She stood up, and was forced to pause as another wave of dizziness washed over her. "Ohhh…"

"Hey!" He grasped her arms and lowered her back into the chair she'd just vacated. "You really aren't feeling well, are you?"

"I don't know." She took a deep breath and tried to get her bearings. "It doesn't make any sense. One moment, I feel fine, the next, I can't stand up."

"Take a few deep breaths."

"I am. Maybe I've just been trying to do too much."

"Yeah, maybe." He continued to hold her arms, watching her with true concern in his eyes. "As soon as I get you to the Manor, I want you to have something to eat. I know it's early, but we can still eat lunch."

They reached the Manor a short time later.

"It's pretty convenient to have this door so close to the gallery, too," Meg said as Quint parked near it. Then she argued with him about her ability to carry in a box of books. "This one's light, and I'm all right now." She carried it through the door and down the short hall to the gallery before he could stop her. The weather was clear and warm for the spring day, and they left all the doors open on their way in.

"Fine, but it's the only one you get to carry. Why don't you go to the counter and find something else to do while we unload the shelves from the truck so we can put them up. Or go to the kitchen and order some food brought in for all of us." She agreed, and Quint watched her until she couldn't see him when she rounded the corner.

Meg moved to the new counter. It was old-fashioned oak that matched the woodwork of the room. She set down the box she carried and took a deep breath. "I love the smell of this room."

It was a combination of lemon and orange and the wood polish on the floor. Her first load of books had arrived.

Absently, she pulled out her calendar. If the move continued to go as planned, she and Evan could have the shop open by...

She counted off the days on her calendar. Yet, before she could calculate an idea for a grand opening another realization hit her.

Her period was late.

Hell, why hadn't she noticed that before?

Well, because she'd been caught up in the move and the grand opening of Montgomery Manor and all the plans Quint had for the swimming pool and everything else, that's why.

Oh, and she couldn't forget that someone had stalked her.

For a moment, she thought she might faint. She held on to the counter and did her best to look normal so as to not attract Quint's attention. The last thing she needed was for him to notice how sick she must look, since she felt it.

Pregnant.

She was almost too afraid to think. Was it even possible? Of course, it was possible. She and Quint made love every night, some times more than once. And the pills she took were not one hundred percent effective. It was, after all, the dose that worked best with her. Besides, she couldn't be certain, but now that she thought back on the week of the grand opening, she probably forgot a pill or two. She might not want to think about it, but she couldn't *not* think about it. Her period had always been like clockwork, every thirty days with or without the pills, not one day more, not one day less, since the first time she'd got it all those years ago in the middle of Mrs. Eller's 8th grade math class.

For the first time since she'd finished reading Joshua Montgomery's journal and had argued with Quint over the idea, she thought again how history repeated itself. She had received roses. She had been assaulted. If indeed she were pregnant, she would be just like Ellen Montgomery. And what had Quint said? Something about her spirit and Ellen's spirit? Was it even possible?

She looked up at Quint and forced a smile. He caught her gaze and smiled as he set down another box of books.

Meg couldn't help but shiver. And she wasn't so sure she could swallow any lunch.

CHAPTER TWENTY-TWO

The next day, Melanie Worthington arrived for work early. With Quint gone on the bookstore move, Melanie was pretty much in charge of the bar. She wanted to put everything in order before any rush. Because there were no more spaces left where she usually parked, she was forced to park in the lower parking lot on the other side of the carriage house. At least it wasn't raining. The bar was as she'd left it the night before, except now there were clean glasses that needed to be hung by their stems on the rack above her. She hung them after she checked the ice machine and found there was plenty of ice, and the fountains were hooked up and ready.

She was out of house wine. It was a good thing she noticed now instead of in the middle of happy hour rush. Quint had shown her where the house wine was kept, and she had time to make a few trips to the cellar to get it herself.

Melanie loved the cellar. It was cool and musty with a hint of grape in the air. The lighting was what she would consider romantic if she were a romantic person, and if she wasn't on a mission to get a few bottles of wine.

She had her hand on a bottle when a sharp creak caught her attention. It was more like a crack, and it reminded her of an axe splitting a log as it echoed through the tunnels around her. She followed the sounds until she came to a larger tunneled room filled with stacked barrels. In the middle of the room, one barrel was in pieces. Dark liquid, obviously what had been the barrel's contents, covered the floor about the scattered splinters of wood. The strong odor of fermented grapes filled the room.

"What the—" Melanie stared at the mess.

That was when she felt him. Not that she was given much time to distinguish the touch. She recognized the feel of hands—very strong hands—that grabbed her and pulled her back against a broad, hard chest. One hand came over her mouth before she could make a sound. The other arm clamped about her throat before she could breathe.

Panic and terror gripped her in the same instant, and grew as she tried to fight and realized she was no match for whoever held her. Her efforts to kick out and lash out were useless. The entire length of whoever held her pressed against her back. Bile rose in her throat. This couldn't happen to her, she thought with disbelief. It just couldn't, not here, not in the wine cellar of Montgomery Manor.

But it was. Hadn't Joshua Montgomery's own wife been murdered right here in this very tunnel?

That thought rushed in before Melanie could stop it. She fought and fought with everything she knew. In the end, all it won her was a fist in her face and a darkness that clutched her with the same strength as the man who held her. Just like the man, it was a darkness she couldn't fight, a darkness that swallowed her whole.

CHAPTER TWENTY-THREE

Meg wasn't quite sure what woke her. The house was quiet. There was no storm. A bloodless moon was setting low in the sky streamed in like a beacon through the cloudless night. Dawn was not far away. Quint slept beside her. Without making a sound, she slipped out of bed and put on her green robe. She didn't want to wake him.

He'd had a hard, busy day. He'd wanted to help her move more books, but Melanie hadn't shown up for work, and the lunch and supper crowds had been crazy busy. So she worked to remain silent as she tiptoed into the bathroom where she'd hidden the pregnancy test that proved her suspicions true. Quint's child grew inside her.

It had been more than thirty-six hours since she'd first suspected, and she still hadn't told him. She needed time to think—away from him.

Her books were moved into the house. All she had to do was unpack them.

What better place to think than in my new shop? She slipped her feet into her fuzzy slippers.

The hall was lit with soft light, and Meg made her way to the gallery without meeting anyone else who might be up at four in the morning. Apparently no one was. She thought this might be the thing she didn't like about living here. What if she and Quint wanted to go for a moonlight swim? What if they wanted a simple quiet walk in the garden?

What would their chances be of running into patrons who stayed all night in one of the Bed and Breakfast rooms?

They would just have to plan those times and make up a few no admittance signs. Now that she thought about it, she remembered the hidden stairs leading to the pool. They would have to be off-limits to patrons so she and Quint could use them to reach the pool in the middle of the night. And they *would* use them because she would insist there be times when she and Quint could sneak away for time alone. She also planned to insist there be times where they took in no patrons, where they would have the house all to themselves, and the staff could have some time off, and they could walk around the halls in their underwear if they wanted. She stifled a giggle at that idea.

In the gallery, she looked at the many boxes and the empty shelves.

Several of her usual customers had already visited the Manor and asked when she planned to open.

She wanted to be close to Quint. She wanted her shop to have the same atmosphere as the rest of the house. Wasn't a shop of centuries past what she'd always tried to achieve? And here, in a house so rich with history and mystery, her dream could come true.

The gallery was lit by moonlight streaming in through the wall of glass, wiping away the dark that threatened. In fact, the large room was inviting. She took a deep breath. Tomorrow, she would unpack her books. And, plan a grand-opening sale.

Maybe she should have a grand opening party like Quint planned. After all, that was a huge success.

She closed her eyes for a long moment and saw the room—with its rows of shelves filled with her books, with tables and comfortable chairs to the far right, tea and coffee and snacks available, perhaps even a few coupons for the restaurant. She could have a few nights when she left the shop open all night for the people who booked rooms in the Bed and Breakfast. Or she could make her shop part of the murder mystery dinner, when Quint finished finalizing it. She'd add a few small wall shelves with candles to create a romantic atmosphere, add a few original antique pieces of furniture, perhaps a fountain on a smaller scale to match the one in the fountain court outside the dining room.

It was wonderful to think of such plans and let go of the fear that had plagued since she'd seen the positive reading on the pregnancy test. Now, she wondered how to tell Quint. She was on an emotional roller coaster, up and down and around in circles and loops. One moment, she was happy and excited, and the next she was terrified.

She opened her eyes and took in the room once more. Then her gaze moved beyond the room, through the glass. Just in the corner, at the edge of the large window, she saw the corner of the glassed greenhouse. Of all her exploration in the past three weeks, she hadn't yet been able to make her way there.

The greenhouse was lit with a single light.

Quint never said anything about the greenhouse or the endless gardens. There was too much work inside the Manor to worry about the grounds. Because of her move to the Manor, she was certain Quint had no plans for the outside until spring was in full swing; and it was time to prime the gardens.

She stepped closer to the window and peered out. She reached out and touched the cool glass. Now that she was closer she saw the greenhouse in its entirety. The light within was little more than a soft glow, perhaps a lantern or a few candles, yet it seemed so bright in the dark of night.

Despite the fact she wore nothing more than her plush green robe and slippers, she ventured out the gallery door leading to the outside.

A shiver moved through her. The dampness of the grass beneath her feet seeped through her slippers and touched her toes. She did her best to ignore the cold, but it added to the iciness that reached in and grabbed her heart. Like the lifeless fingers of a dead hand. She should get Quint.

Yet, she knew if she took the time to rouse her husband, whoever was out here would be long gone. So, she would just take a look and see who it was. She could tell Quint later.

The door of the greenhouse opened soundlessly. Meg stepped into its tropical warmth. There was a strong, earthy smell that hung in the air like thick smoke. Many of the plants were dead, nothing but brittle, brown leaves in pots of dried, cracked dirt. But some of the plants were green, showing signs of life, and most that were living looked newly manicured.

Someone was working to make the greenhouse the "green" space it was meant to be. Meg was just glad to see it intact. Its walls, its roof were made of sheets of glass, none of which were broken or showed signs of age or neglect. Perhaps Quint hired someone to care for it and get it back to working order, just as he'd hired a gatekeeper, once again opening the gatehouse.

But at four in the morning, who would be out here?

Meg stared up in awe at the bright moon low in the sky, and she remembered reading about the greenhouse in Joshua Montgomery's journal. Joshua Montgomery considered working in the greenhouse a form of therapy, his hands dirty with soil as he worked with various plants. A camp lantern hung on the wall, filling the room with light and a soft hissing sound. The lantern, bright moonlight, and filtered light from the nearby parking lit the entire building.

There were dusty tables and old clay pots, many of which were broken. In the center of the room was a huge fountain—a mother and small boy, carved in stone. If the fountain were functioning, water would pour from the boy's hands and flow into the pool surrounding them. But no water flowed, and the small amount of water that was in the pool was dark and stagnant.

She stared at the fountain for a long moment. Like the gallery, she saw so much potential. This greenhouse would soon be something admired, something loved by all who entered. She would just have to find ask Quint who he'd hired to care for it so she could share her plans.

Near the far end of the aisle in front of her, there was an old iron table with matching chairs. They were dust covered and the seat of one had a ripped cushion. They seemed so out of place even amongst the dirt and the dead plants. She'd replace them as soon as she got the chance.

The back door at the far end around the corner of tables and plants closed with a thud. Her heart slammed against the wall of her chest. After a moment to calm herself, she silently hurried to the corner of the room and peered down the aisle that led to that door, but whoever had been in the house with her was already gone.

She ducked low and crouched down to avoid being seen. After a long, quiet moment, she peered over the top of the table, and through the glass wall beyond it; and she saw him.

He was nothing more than a shadow in the night that floated toward the house, and he went in through the very door she'd exited.

Again, she thought she should go get Quint, wake him, bring him out to the greenhouse and tell him someone was in there in the middle of the night. But the idea seemed silly because there really wasn't anything wrong. Perhaps, like her, someone couldn't sleep and found solace in having his hands in the dirt. She could just hear Quint now, "You woke me, Meggie, to bring me out here to show me all these dead plants?"

Whoever it was simply worked to restore the place. And that would be a good and helpful thing to Quint. Perhaps it was even meant to be a surprise for Quint just as the rest of the house had been a surprise for her. So maybe she shouldn't tell him. But she did want to know who had been in here. She stayed low, making her way toward the back door he'd exited.

It was then that she saw the roses. The sight of them stopping her short and catching her breath.

They were in huge pots, and they were beautifully cared for in all their glory. In fact, they were the prettiest roses Meg had ever seen. Simple yet, complex, perfect with buds and opened blossoms, they grew in various colors. There was golden yellow, pink, white, blood red, just as the buds that had been delivered to Meg, and on the very end there were perfect blooms in deep purple, almost black.

She didn't wait around to see if the mystery man returned. She ran out the same door that just swung shut and headed to the gallery as fast as she could. It was, after all, the closest door into the Manor, and Meg didn't know if any other door would even be unlocked at this hour. This time, she didn't notice the chilly air or the wet grass, at least until she entered the Manor, and noticed how warm it felt. She noticed, too, how loud her breathing sounded in the dead quiet of the room around her, and she paused to take a few deep, calming breaths.

She had no choice but to tell Quint about the greenhouse. He had to know about the roses. She should call Officer Humphreys. She headed toward the stairs but stopped short and backed up to get lost in the shadows.

Someone stood between her and the stairs, someone who used the door leading to the cellar stairs.

The rage working through her burned in her soul. This might be the person who stalked her, the person who sent her roses and called her on the phone. If it was, she wanted to kill him, but she wanted to cause him some pain first. And she needed to know for certain. She couldn't waste the time to get Quint. By the time she made her way upstairs, woke Quint and waited while he put on clothes and came back to the cellar, whoever it was could be long gone. Then she might never know. There would only be the roses. And those roses couldn't tell them who grew them. The opportunity to stop the stalker, if the person she now followed was her stalker, would be missed. Meg couldn't let that happen, not when she was this close to discovering his identity. Not when her rage required she get her hands on him.

She didn't think about the danger. She didn't even feel any fear. Boiling anger had her sneaking closer, working to find out who attacked her, who had terrorized her. Absently, she picked up a box cutter from the counter in the gallery. She thought about those roses, and her blood boiled.

Meg watched him go through the door to the cellar stairs and heard his muffled steps on the spiral stairs before the door closed again. She counted slowly to ten and hoped that was enough time for whomever it was to reach the bottom so that by the time she opened the door, he wouldn't know she followed.

Slowly and silently, she opened the door and peered down. He'd left the light at the bottom on, and the door was open, but there was no one in sight. She made her way down. She planned to stay at a distance, not confront him at all, just see who it was so she could tell Quint and Officer Humphreys. There was, however, a problem for her. The tunnels of the cellar seemed endless, and she'd only been down there a few times.

She didn't know them, and she could get lost if she weren't careful, especially in the dark. No, she corrected, if it was dark, she wouldn't stay and follow him, she couldn't. If he turned out the lights, she'd be back upstairs in a heartbeat. She wasn't ready to face those echoes in the darkness just yet, perhaps never.

Still, darkness or not, in order for her to stay close enough to follow him, she would have to stay close enough where at times he might be able to see her as well.

She stepped into the soft light of the wine cellar. The cobblestone floor was cool against her feel through her wet slippers.

He recognized the stone walls and the bottles of wine in the rack against the wall. Quint even saw the dust covering them. He could almost read their labels if he looked hard enough. There was also that musty thick smell in the air that he now knew so well.

The dream was so vivid, so real. Quint was so much a part of it, every detail recognizable and acute. Still, somehow within the dream, Quint knew he slept, knew he dreamed.

He also knew he didn't want to dream this dream. He'd dreamed—no lived—this dream before. Deep in his gut, he knew it was bad. This was more than a bad dream; this was a staggering living memory that had a horrible ending.

He wanted to force himself awake but didn't know where to begin. The last thing he wanted was to look around. Yet, deep within his nightmare, deep within his soul, there was the knowledge that he had no choice but to face the horror.

He didn't want to see the blood on his own hands, either. He tried to close his eyes. Yet, as with all the other aspects of the dream, he knew the blood was there. Sticky and warm on his skin, and he looked down. In the heavy air, he smelled the strong, coppery smell of it.

The burn of bile rose in his throat.

He wanted to scream at the sight of so much blood, but there was no sound. Beyond the red covering his fingers and dripping to the stones on the floor, was the body.

A woman.

His heart hammered against the wall of his chest, bringing pain with each breath he dragged in.

She was a woman with wavy hair, the color of dark flames, and she wore a flowing dress of vivid blue. He knew she had eyes just a shade darker than thunderclouds. And all of it—all of her—was splattered with blood.

She was his wife.

Oh, please no....

He closed his eyes and refused to look, to see the truth.

He didn't want to look any more.

Quint started awake.

He worked with every ounce of energy to control each breath and slow his racing heart. Did he cry out as he woke? He must not have, because he didn't wake his wife. He wanted the dream to fade away and leave him as dreams usually did.

Why would he dream this now?

His breathing reached a normal rhythm, and he listened to the sound of it through the silence.

He wiped the beads of sweat from his brow. His wife was fine. He was fine. There was no blood, at least he didn't feel its sticky wetness, didn't smell its sickening copper scent in the air.

Still the dream had been so real.

Even now it played over in his mind when he closed his eyes.

With remnants of the dream filling his senses, he reached behind him for Meg. He needed to know she was safe with him.

Her side of the bed empty. He turned in heartbeat. His heart raced when he saw she was gone. Without hesitation, he slid out of bed and walked to the bathroom. He squinted against the light, staring at his hands to ensure they weren't coated in blood. Meg wasn't there.

He turned on the faucet and rinsed his hands. The coldness of the water cooled the hot feeling left behind from the blood in the dream. He splashed water on his face. The shock of it took his breath away a second time, but the frigidness was enough to wash away the dream and wake him completely. He held the towel to his face for a long moment. It smelled of Meg.

He thought about the dream, not about *what* he dreamed, but about the reason behind it. Why would he dream it now, after all this time? He glanced down at the counter and stopped short.

It didn't take but a split second for him to recognize what he stared at.

A pregnancy test—a positive pregnancy test.

He and Meg were going to have a baby. His heart took a sudden leap.

A baby…

The nightmare…

He needed to hold her in his arms. He needed to feel the warmth of her. He needed to find her. Know she was safe. Know the baby she carried was safe. Now. He pulled on a pair of sweats, a shirt, and his shoes before he headed for the door.

He didn't question why his instincts told him to look in the cellar first.

Meg thought she might very well be lost in these catacombs. More than once, she lost sight of her mysterious leader and had to stop and listen for the sounds of his footsteps, before she backtracked and found him again.

She followed him into what looked a great deal like the room she'd been in weeks earlier when she'd argued with Quint, but things were out of place. Now there were barrels stacked around, so she wasn't certain it was the same room.

She stopped and looked around.

I must have taken a wrong turn. Dang. He's getting away.

Someone grabbed her from behind.

She'd fallen right into his trap.

He held her fast, her back pressed against him.

"Oh, Megan." The heat of his whispered, harsh words touched her neck and sent a shiver down her back.

His voice, the sound of him speaking her entire name as her stalker did with each phone call, filled with terror, paralyzing her. For a long moment, she couldn't even breathe. There was no doubt he was her stalker.

"Do you know how long I've wanted to hold you like this?"

Meg drew in a ragged breath and tried to squirm away. He held her fast and pressed her back up against the rock hardness of him.

"Don't think you can get away again, my Megan."

With one arm around her neck and the other draped around her body, there was little she could do, and getting away didn't seem like a possibility.

She tried to scream, tried to fight, tried to squirm out of his grip. The shrill cry she let out was meant to wake the dead, but she only managed a short scream before he clamped a large, strong hand over her mouth.

She fought against the way he manhandled her. Held in his grip, she struggled and managed to stomp on his foot. He let out an oath in her ear, but held her tighter. Reaching up, she managed to catch his arm with the box cutter. He was bigger, stronger, and he seemed to anticipate her every move. He let her go enough to grasp her wrist and squeeze, forcing her to drop it. She groaned as it hit the stone floor. He tightened his grip on her again, ignoring the blood dripping from his wound. He was close enough she felt the heat of his breath on her hair and still, she had no idea who he was.

Again, her rage outweighed her fear. How dare this man put his hands on her—again? How dare he threaten her? Stalk her?

She thought of the black roses and stomped on his foot again. She thought of the terror he'd given her with his phone calls and the eyes painted on her mirror, and she drove her elbow into his ribs with all the strength she possessed.

No more. No more would he hurt her or frighten her.

The pain in his foot or his ribs or the combination loosened his grip. Just enough that she was able to turn and see him. She stared at the man who had terrorized her for the past weeks.

Quint heard Meg's voice, and his heart hammered against the wall of his chest. What was she doing down here? Her words echoed through the passageways of the cellar, and Quint ran down the first one. He had no idea which direction to go. Sound was so strange down here. It bounced off the stones of the walls and echoed through the tunnels. It sounded as if she argued. His dream lingered in his thoughts. He thought he smelled blood.

This could not happen again.

He would not allow it.

No, he couldn't clear Joshua Montgomery's name. He had no evidence to back up the idea that his partner had murdered his wife any more than he when Ellen had been killed. He'd come to terms with that, just as he came to terms with the knowledge that loving Meg and spending his life with her would be enough. She carried his child.

Sudden recognition dawned. He was almost to the room where Ellen had died, where he'd tried to save her and stop the flow of her blood...

CHAPTER TWENTY-FOUR

Brad.

Meg was so astonished, she stared at him for a long moment.

Her hesitation gave him the chance to tighten his grasp on her. His hands were hot, but a shiver lanced through her to her soul. He held her tight enough to hurt her arms.

"You!" Her single accusing word came out in an astonished breath.

"Yes, Megan, it's me." With her in his grasp, he hauled her to the other side of the stacked barrels.

She tried to kick him again, tried to break free. She resisted every step, but she was no match for his strength. "My husband trusted you with his business." Just like Joshua Montgomery had trusted his partner, Windsbrook. Why had she never noticed Brad's muscles, his strength, his build, and his agility? Because he kept himself hidden beneath heavy sweaters, she realized. As she'd followed him from the greenhouse, he'd worn a jacket he had shed before he grabbed her. Now, he wore jeans and a tee shirt that showed his muscles and a recently healed wound snaking its way up his left upper arm. Was that nasty looking gash from running through the bookstore's glass doors?

She glanced to the other side of the stacked barrels and her heart stopped. Melanie Wirthington was tied up on a simple wooden chair, her mouth covered with a large piece of silver tape.

"But why?" Meg didn't take her gaze from Melanie. She saw fear in Melanie's expression, and knew that her own expression must mirror that fear. At least Melanie didn't appear hurt.

"Why, my sweet Megan?"

She hated the way he said her name.

"Look around you. Because of this house...at first." He spoke as if he were reminding a child about the school rules.

"This house?" She needed to keep him talking long enough to think of a plan to get her and Melanie out of there unhurt. She'd intentionally left Quint sleeping, and he was two stories above her. He wouldn't hear her no matter how loud she screamed. Would whoever manned the front desk hear her? She had to do something, or history really *was* going to repeat itself. She let out a cry as he twisted her arm behind her back. He used rope to bind her wrists before forcing her to sit down on an old stool he had nearby. She'd noticed the deep bruise on Melanie's cheek, so Meg didn't fight him. She wanted to keep her wits about her, and the last thing she wanted was his fist in her face. Besides, she well remembered her last struggle with him. There was no way she could out fight him.

She might not be able fight him, but she may be able to out fox him if she didn't let her fear get the best of her. She had to keep a clear mind. So, she let him bind her hands together behind her back.

But she did something she'd once read in one of her horror/stalker books. She inhaled enough air to expand her chest and tighten the rope on her arms. If she remembered correctly, when she exhaled again, the ropes would be looser.

Brad leaned over her, his breath hot on her cheek as he spoke. "Yes, this house. I worked for Quint's miserable old *distant* cousin for years, and what did I gain for it?

Nothing. He didn't even leave me a trinket or an old coin. I never knew he had a cousin to will this place to. But it was so nice of your dear husband to allow me to keep my job." He reminded her of a hissing snake.

She turned away from the lingering scent of whiskey on his breath, but she didn't miss the sarcasm that dripped from his words. "If you were unhappy with the arrangement, you could have said something. Quint listens to you."

Brad chuckled and tore a piece of nearby cloth, tying it around his arm where she'd cut him. She was sorry she wasn't able to do more damage. "Unhappy with the arrangement? What do you think Quint would do about my unhappiness? Give me the house? Share the treasure? Doubtful, Megan, very doubtful. At the very least, he would have rented me a room, I suppose, which, by the way is not what I need or want."

She heard hate in Brad's voice. She said nothing, knowing he spoke the truth. Brad must've hated Quint after Quint changed his mind about selling Brad that house. He probably hated Quint as soon as he learned of the inheritance. "So I thought if I couldn't have this house, which should have been mine," he checked the knots at her wrists, "then I thought I should at least have some of the treasure."

Again Meg met Melanie's gaze. Meg fought the urge to struggle against the ropes holding her wrists together. If there was any chance of freeing them at all, she wanted Brad far enough away not to notice.

Melanie stared at her with wide, fear-filled eyes.

"Treasure? You think there really is a treasure?" Meg searched for answers and stalled for time. She steered away from the subject of what Brad thought should have been his.

"Oh, there is a treasure, Megan. I've watched Quint find pieces of it every day—paintings, silverware, coins. I can almost smell it, can't you?"

She watched him. "I only smell grapes."

His cold gaze bore into her. "Then you don't see what I see. I see the real treasure." He stared at her in a way that needed no explanation. "The real treasure walked right through the front door, wearing a cute, little skirt, and a sweater that made me want to slide my hands up under it."

"That's why you had to terrorize me?" She did her best to keep her voice calm, to sound in control even when her insides were knotted together with icy fear. Her throat ached as she fought not to scream at him.

"Oh, Megan. I know how much Quint loves you. Any fool can see it. He'd do whatever you wished. I wanted to scare you into selling the house or at least scare you enough that Quint would have to devote all his time to you. I wanted him away from here, but I know he doesn't frighten easily. And then something else happened."

"What?" She was almost too afraid to ask, even though she could guess.

"I wanted you for myself from that first time Quint brought you in here to meet me."

That frightened her more than anything. The hair on her neck stood up. "You sent me roses."

It was a statement, not a question. She wanted to talk. She didn't want to think about any of this; thinking about it allowed the horror to set in.

He answered her anyway. "Yes, it was a wonderful gesture, don't you agree?"

"They didn't frighten me," she lied. It seemed like forever ago when the roses were delivered to her shop, yet it was a month ago. They didn't frighten her at the time she received them. But now she knew he grew them here in the greenhouse, and she knew he grew them with intent to send them to *her*. That frightened her now.

"I saw the way you displayed them at your shop. They looked perfect." He maneuvered a barrel closer.

Meg stared at him. She remembered that Quint said there may not be an evident reason for the stalker's actions.

And he was right. Brad's confessions didn't make any sense to her. Brad said he wanted her, but he wanted to scare her so Quint would give up the house. Did he like enjoy scaring her? He sounded like it. "What about the phone calls? Why did you call me?"

"I wanted to let you know I was always there, watching you, always thinking about you. Because, Megan, I *was* always thinking about you."

"And you were in my house."

He smiled at her remark. The simplicity of the act added to her already building terror. She had the uncanny feeling he may very well smile just that same way when he killed her and Melanie. "I wasn't sure if I should do that or not. It was so risky, it gave me such a rush to be in your bedroom, to touch your things. Touching your panties was such a thrill. So many of your things smell like you, all soft and pretty, did you know that?" He paused but when she didn't reply, he continued. "Besides, I wasn't sure when you'd see the eyes I drew on your mirror. You two spent so much time here, I didn't know if you ever went back to your little house. When your assistant called to leave a message for Quint about your leaving the shop, I hoped you went home. Then when Quint said *he* had to get home, I knew you were there, and it was all worth the effort. Quint contains himself so well, but I knew he was upset. And I knew when he brought you here that you'd seen my eyes."

"But scaring me backfired, didn't it?" Meg already knew the answer. She moved her hands behind her, testing the tightness of the ropes, careful to stay unobserved.

"Ah, yes in two ways."

"Two ways?"

He moved closer, but she didn't move. She didn't even breathe.

He reached out and touched her throat. His fingers caressed her with something just shy of tenderness, and bile rose to meet it. "First, the more I watched you, the more I wanted you." His voice softened. "You were so close, but so untouchable. Yet, you belonged in this house. You, Megan, are meant to be mistress of this house."

She didn't feel like the mistress just then. She felt as helpless as an infant, but she said nothing.

He was close enough to kiss her, and she let out a huff of relief when he didn't.

"Second, my tactics didn't scare you out of the house, they scared you into the house. And even though I want you here, it was right where I didn't want Quint to be all the time, where he could watch my every move."

Brad moved away again, and Meg breathed to calm her fraying nerves.

The terror gripped her like icy fingers that refused to let go. She was certain Brad was going to hurt her. She thought he planned to kill her and Melanie. How else could he insure his escape? She didn't want to die, and the last thing she wanted was to die down here in the cellar, just like Joshua Montgomery's wife, Ellen.

"But do you know the best part, Megan?"

There was a best part?

She didn't want to know, but she had to stall for time. She had to keep him talking. "What?"

"Touching you." He spoke calmly and lovingly. "That night in your shop when I felt you beneath me, your breasts in my palms, and every time you allowed me to take your hand—I have never felt anything so soft."

He drew close and touched her face.

She recoiled.

He laughed.

"Tell me, how did you break into my shop in the first place? The chimes over the door would have told me someone had come in." She needed to give him something else to think about other than touching her. Besides, it was the most plaguing question on her mind. Although she had ideas, she needed to know for certain.

He stepped close to the barrel he'd moved a moment before. His grin was disingenuous. She thought he might very well reach back and pat his own back at any moment. "I didn't break in."

"You didn't?" She'd been pretty certain of that. But she needed to know the details as much as she needed to keep him talking.

"I came in before you closed. I hid behind those stacks of books in your back room. I watched you through the crack of the door the whole time. You even came in and grabbed a stack of books and took them into your office, and you never knew I was there. I watched you sweep the floor and lock the door. It was so quiet, I don't know how you didn't hear my breathing or my heart beating—because I'll tell you, Megan, it was beating hard while I watched you."

"So you just watched me and waited?" Meg's sudden anger replaced her fear. It just as quickly built into rage. It boiled through her to the point she thought he'd see smoke rising from her.

He looked away, from her to the barrel, and she took that moment to test her bonds. She could twist her wrists. The rope scraped against her, burning her skin. Yet, she rejoiced—she could move her wrists, she could get away.

"Again, you made things easy for me, Megan. You chose not to leave. I studied the layout of your office and I tripped the breaker to turn out the lights. Your skin is so soft. I was amazed at how soft your skin is."

She imagined a billion tiny, dirty bugs crawling all over her skin.

"So what are you doing down here?" Meg worked to keep her voice light and even, and hoped he didn't hear the tornado of fear and rage that twisted through her. At the same time, she hoped the barrel he was studying kept his attention a little longer. More than anything, she hoped her change of subject lasted.

She didn't care what he did down in the cellar. Her only care was escaping him and helping Melanie.

"I'm looking for the treasure." Brad's tone was strange and flat. He sounded menacing, more dangerous than ever. "I knew, when Quint told me he offered you the gallery for your books, that I couldn't scare any of you away. I wasn't sure how to get rid of Quint and yet keep you here, Megan. Am I wrong to say you'd follow Quint wherever he would go?"

"No." Her single word was spoken so softly she was surprised he heard it.

"As I thought." He let out a heavy breath, reached out, and picked up the crow bar at his feet. "So I had to put plan B into action." He crammed the edge of the bar into the top of the old barrel. Then, with a grunt, he pried the lid off. The room was filled with a loud crack as the wood gave away beneath his strength.

"Plan B?" Meg worked to sound interested, but now she wanted to know everything so that when—not if—she escaped him, she could tell Quint and Officer Humphreys.

He leaned the barrel over and let wine spill out on the floor before he replied. "I planned to just find the treasure, take it, and disappear. Hell, I wouldn't even have to disappear. I could just turn in my notice. The treasure may be nothing more than a legend to everyone else, but I know it's here. And when I get my hands on it, no one will be the wiser. Then I can have it all." He reached into the barrel and more wine sloshed out. Apparently, there was nothing but liquid. He grabbed a nearby towel and dried his arm before he spoke again. "And despite the fact that I would have loved to share it with you, Megan, I do believe it's a bit late for that."

He pointed his finger at her as if she were a naughty child. "Unless you're open to killing Melanie and Quint. We could make it look like a love affair gone wrong, and you could live here with me as Mistress of this Manor for the rest of your life."

She was terrified at his offer. "No." She had to force the word out.

"I thought not. And it's too bad for everyone involved."

"So Melanie caught you down here?" It was another tactic to stall for time.

"She caught me opening the barrels."

"Do you really think the treasure's down here in the barrels? After all, Quint found paintings hidden in the floor. Maybe that's where more treasure is hidden." Meg had to ask trying to give him a new direction to take beside any idea of killing her or Melanie. Her instincts told her time grew short. If she were going to do something to save herself and Melanie, she had to do it soon. For the moment, she just kept him talking. "There could be a million places in his house to hide treasure, all sorts of hidden rooms. Besides, Quint said there was nothing but wine in these barrels." She thought of the small dressing room hidden in her apartment. It had remained untouched for a hundred years.

"There is, I've broken open over a dozen of them. But I've got a couple more hours to look. Then, of course, I have to decide what to do with you and Melanie." He paused and looked straight at Meg. "I'll be honest with you. I've considered staging a sensational murder." He chuckled. "I could even let your husband take the fall, just like what happened to the original owner. That would be better than a murder mystery dinner, don't you think?"

He talked about murder as though he was discussing a new entrée on the menu, and his words formed a lump in Meg's throat large enough to choke her.

Meg stared at him, though she wanted nothing more than to close her eyes. "I'd prefer the murder mystery dinner."

"Just think." He spoke as if she hadn't said anything. "You and Melanie down here, cut open just like Joshua Montgomery's wife, Ellen, found at the bottom of the stairs by your own husband. I could even put you both in the same spot Ellen was found, and I would be most helpful to the police when I tell them about the way you accused Quint of scaring you into moving in here."

"You heard that conversation?" He'd been eavesdropping? Anger roared through her.

"Only part of it, although it was a very interesting part. Sound echoes and bounces through these tunnels. I do say, though, Quint was so hip on whispering in your ear so much of the time, it must be the romantic in him. Too bad the two of us couldn't be together, Megan. I would like to whisper in your ear." Brad smiled at her, and she would have loved to slap that smile off his lips. "Your argument helped out a great deal, however. Thank you very much for maneuvering things into my favor, Megan."

Just like the servants testified that Joshua Montgomery and Ellen argued...

Meg had to do something, anything, to keep this from happening. Again.

While she twisted against the binds at her wrists, he went on, "I think it won't be too much longer before this Manor is mine, although I am a little upset that you won't get to be mistress with me. You will, however, get to live in the house's history, so that's something."

He maneuvered another barrel closer, rolling it side to side before prying the top off with the crow bar. The old wood creaked loud enough to echo off the tunnel walls. Too bad no one else could hear it.

"More wine. Looks like white this time." Brad stuck his hand into the rich liquid and reached in all the way to his shoulder.

"What if there's no treasure? What if all that's hidden is the paintings Quint found?" Meg asked, determined to keep him talking.

"There has to be," he insisted. "And I'll bet your dear husband knows where it is. How else is he coming up with enough money for the continuous renovations?"

"The restaurant's doing well..."

"Not enough to give him the one million it's going to take to get that pool up and running, and that's what he plans to do next."

She didn't want to argue with him about it, so she let the topic drop.

"So did you get that scar on your arm from crashing through the door of my shop when you attacked me last month?" She wanted to know. Not only did she want to keep him talking and stall for time, but now she did want to know everything. She glanced at Melanie and noticed that Melanie had worked the tape on her mouth free.

"Yes, lucky for me, it was the only cut. It was a good thing your door was single paned, and I wore that nylon suit and a ski mask, or I could have been hurt." He wiped his arm with the towel he'd had tucked into the top of his jeans. "Oh, Meg, things could have been so different."

"How so?"

"We could have been together. We could have been happy. Now it seems that all I'll get is perhaps a single kiss before I stage your murder, frame your husband, and set things into motion."

"I don't think so."

Meg turned at the sound of Quint's voice. He stood there. He looked so calm, but Meg saw the tension in his expression and the way the vein at his neck pulsed. He obviously heard enough to know of Brad's plans. She twisted against the ropes and felt them loosen. Freedom felt close.

Never in her life had she ever felt so torn. She was glad to see Quint, but at the same time, she was terrified for him. He had just walked into a trap.

"Don't think you can mess up any more of my plans." Brad's smile was frightening.

To Meg's horror, Brad moved behind her in a flash. In the same instant, he pulled out a knife—a very large knife she hadn't even known he'd had. He held it to her throat. The touch of the cold steel made her breath catch and her heart race. Terrified to move even a centimeter, she fought down the shiver threatening to worm its way up her back. After a long moment, she forced in a breath, just enough to keep dark spots from dancing before her eyes. It was all she could manage given her tight chest and the lump of terror lodged in her throat.

"I think we'll have to change this simple murder to look like a murder-suicide. It won't have the glamour and sensationalism of a trial, but it will still make great headlines and draw people to this house." Brad still smiled confidently.

Quint shrugged as if Brad's knife on Meg's throat meant nothing. Meg wanted to scream. She fought the urge to twist the ropes on her wrists and work to escape. But she didn't dare move.

"You're wasting your time if you think you'll find the treasure, though. Meg and I already found it."

Meg couldn't believe how convincing Quint lied. She swallowed, and the cold knife bit into her skin.

Quint didn't look at her as he spoke. He kept his hard gaze on Brad. "And if you hurt her or kill us, you'll never know where it is."

She couldn't breathe. She stared at Quint, unable to say a word or contradict his lie.

I love you, she thought over and over.

She wished she'd told him about the baby. It was, after all, what he wanted. And now, she wanted it, too.

Tears flowed unchecked down her cheeks.

"With all of you out of the way, though, I'll have plenty of time to hunt for it." Brad was insane.

Brad grasped her arm. Slowly, he pulled Meg to her feet, holding her in front of him. His hands on her were cold, colder than the terror that gripped her.

Quint's gaze hardened. "If you harm her, it will be the last thing you do."

Meg didn't understand how he could be so calm when it took everything in her to keep her from shaking all over.

Then many things happened at once.

Quint rushed at Brad.

Melanie screamed. The sound of it echoed through the cellar.

Meg managed to slip her hands from the ropes at her wrists, struggling against Brad, desperate to get away from his knife.

Burning fire erupted in her stomach. Hot flame licked into her gut.

There was heat and pain. It was worse than any pain she'd ever known before. It started in her abdomen, radiated through her body, and kissed her fingertips. She screamed. Her knees gave out, and she landed hard on the cold stone floor.

Meg heard Quint's anguished cry and wondered if he were in pain, too. She didn't understand why she didn't have the strength to turn and look at him. Cold gripped her with sharp talons, but something warm and sticky coated her robe.

Then the lights went out.

Terror gripped her. She would have screamed but the darkness was so thick she couldn't breathe, much less scream. Her strength abandoned her.

She heard Quint call her name.

CHAPTER TWENTY-FIVE

Visions, like dreams, came to Meg. These were strange dreams, where she lived them, and at the same time watched them like an observer or a movie cameraman.

She was in a log cabin in the wilderness. How she recognized the single-room dwelling as home, she had no idea. The cabin was dark, lit by the flames dancing in the hearth, and by the single fat-dipped taper on a roughly constructed table. The door and the shutters were closed, sealing the small house to keep out the creatures and the coolness of the night.

Two men argued near the door.

"Jeremiah McGillin, you would do better to let me have her." The man who spoke stood closer to the door, his clothing more refined, cleaner, made of silk and velvet and linen in richly dyed colors of blue and deep green. "I already own everything else."

Jeremiah McGillin stood straight and proud, despite the fact he wore no jewels and his clothes were the color of nature, his pants brown, and his shirt not white, but not beige. All his life, he worked the land. It took many years to hack his farm out of the wilderness and build his home. The work rewarded him with strong legs and broad shoulders and powerful arms. He was a man unafraid to fight, when a fight was necessary.

And as far as he was concerned, this fight was necessary.

The woman who stood beside him was small and fragile. Yet, she stood proud with her shoulders back. Her long, thick hair was almost the same color as the fire behind her. Jeremiah held her elbow, as if he needed to keep her by his side. But he didn't need to keep her there, she wanted to stay. Months ago, she'd made her choice to go against her own father's wishes—her own father's gentleman's agreement—with the man who stood before them. She'd defied her father to run off in the middle of the night and marry *him*. He now wished that he had built a cabin with another room so that she need not witness this confrontation.

Meg was this woman, but now Meg's name was Flora.

"Flora." Stephen Windsor's tone softened as he turned his attention to her. The ring on her finger reflected the light of the fire. He stared down at it for a long moment before continuing. "Your father and I agreed, that makes our engagement official. You cannot be married to this man. That is a sin. Come away with me now, and we shall forget this ordeal. I give my word that I will not bring charges against him." He spoke as if Jeremiah weren't even in the room.

"No." Flora's reply was soft, yet firm. "Jeremiah is my husband in every aspect. Your arrangement was with my father. I agreed to nothing. I shall be nothing to you."

"You do not own this house, Stephen Windsor. Get out of my house before I toss you out by the seat of your fancy breeches," said Jeremiah.

Flora/Meg heard the way Jeremiah fought to control his anger. He always tried to keep her from witnessing his anger.

Windsor reached out and took hold of one of Flora's hands. "Your hands were once so soft, Flora." Then he looked again to Jeremiah, and his eyes hardened. "You would bring her to this barren place and work her until her skin is cracked and chapped, when you know she would have a life of leisure with me?" His voice rose with each word.

Flora pulled her hand from his grasp. "I would rather live with pigs than to have a life of leisure with you, Stephen Windsor. Refrain from touching me again, please."

Behind her, the fire crackled. Like the sparks and heat that came from the fire, tension filled the room. Flora didn't like the feel of it, just as she didn't trust Stephen Windsor. Windsor had tried before to lure her away, first with flowers then by physical force. Jeremiah managed to stop him at the end of the lane. She knew he regretted not killing Stephen Windsor for that unspeakable action. If he had killed him then, he would not have to face down the blackguard with his wife as witness.

"I said, get out of my house." Jeremiah's voice grew firmer.

His Kentucky rifle hung over the mantle, but Flora knew it was too far away and would take too much time to retrieve. Besides, she also knew Jeremiah would never take the chance with her so close.

Windsor refused to leave. "Her father and I had an agreement. She belongs to me."

"She belongs to no one but herself." Jeremiah took her hand. "She makes her own choice, and she chooses me. Now get out."

For a long moment, the house was utterly still. Even the fire remained silent. Flora held her breath. She didn't want her husband to fight this man in his own house, but she knew he would. She knew he would do whatever necessary to protect her, his wife, and the home they had built together these past months.

Stephen Windsor turned and reached for the door latch.

Flora let out the breath she held.

Within the vision, Meg watched, knowing in her heart a sense of doom hung over this small house. As Flora, like Flora, Meg let out a sigh of relief when Stephen Windsor turned to leave. Her heart caught when he turned back in a flash. "She can't choose you, if you're dead." Sharp, cold steel gleamed and reflected the firelight.

Flora screamed and the sound pierced the walls enclosing them. Jeremiah tried to push her away, out of danger.

She slipped from his grasp and before he could stop her, and stepped in front of him.

She heard the sound of the knife as it slipped into her. She screamed. Then came a bellowed cry of pain, a cry, she realized, that came from Jeremiah. He caught her as her knees buckled beneath her, and he lowered her to the cold floor. Already her blood spilled and covered her skirts, feeling warm but leaving her cold.

"You bastard." Jeremiah tried to stop the flow, but Flora felt it soak her clothes more.

She held on to him, her hands sticky with her own blood. "Jeremiah—I—love—you." She lay dying in his arms, and there was nothing either of them could do. As she spoke, her words were broken. "I'm so cold."

She felt the way he tried to warm her with his hands, tried to cradle her. "It should have been me. It should have been me," he said over and over. "No you, Flora. Not you and our baby…"

In the blink of an eye, Meg awoke in another place, a place where dusk and soft mist fell softly over the prairie. Wind blew across the plains and buffalo grazed a short distance away. In a teepee lit by the light of a fire, Quick as a Fox stared at the white trader. Meg was now known as Eyes of the Sky. She knew her husband never trusted the white trader, and she now felt her husband's disdain for the trader as strong as she felt the heat from the nearby fire.

"Eyes of the Sky is not for trade." Quick as a Fox spoke in his own tongue. He did not speak the white trader's tongue.

The white trader spoke enough of Quick as a Fox's tongue to be understood. "I will give you two horses for her."

"She is not for trade." Quick as a Fox glared at the white trader. "Leave. You insult me."

The white trader appeared to not understand his words. "Three horses." He held up three fingers.

Quick as a Fox glanced at Eyes of the Sky. Eyes of the Sky saw love and desire in his eyes. She knew he would never trade her; no matter how much was offered.

In the firelight of the teepee, Eyes of the Sky saw the knife the man pulled from his belt, and Quick as a Fox sidestepped quickly. Her husband was brave and strong, Eyes of the Sky knew her husband feared no fight with the man. Quick as a Fox was true to his name, and, again, he sidestepped the trader's strike. Quick as a Fox's brother had said he thought this trader was touched in the head with greed, and he was right.

The knife the white trader held sliced through the air again and again as the two of them danced about the teepee. Eyes of the Sky stayed at the far side of the teepee. During the struggle, the knife the trader held slipped from his grip. It sailed through the air like an arrow and found its mark in her belly where their child lived. The pain that gripped her was unlike anything she'd ever known before as she fell into Quick as a Fox's arms. The white trader ran from the teepee and was swallowed by the darkness. Quick as a Fox stared down at Eyes of the Sky and spoke his love for her. She wanted nothing more than to hold on to his love, but it was not strong enough to save her...

As Ellen, Meg recognized Joshua Montgomery. She recognized the wine cellar of Montgomery Manor. Neither Joshua nor his partner, Mr. Windsbrook, knew she stood just inside the room. She had left the Halloween dinner to come and find him. She found him arguing with Mr. Windsbrook.

Joshua stared at the man he had trusted for a decade. "Our relationship is dissolved, Windsbrook, now get out of my house."

"Half of this is mine. I helped create it." Windsbrook looked at him hard. "If you think I'll simply walk away with nothing, you are mistaken."

"I knew you would return," Joshua offered a bitter, crooked grin. "Why else do you think I took the precaution of hiding everything of value into new places where you couldn't get your dirty hands on anything? Hell, I've left my dinner party and to catch you in the cellar, obviously looking for the gold you thought was here before. I could kill you for entering my home uninvited, and no one would bat an eyelash."

Knowing Joshua, Ellen thought he wanted to do just that.

"Perhaps I'll kill you first."

The knife seemed to materialize from nowhere, taking Joshua off guard. Ellen thought it took all of Joshua's strength to maintain his balance and keep the knife from slicing him open as Windsbrook collided with him, sending the two of them back into a stack of wine barrels.

Ellen clamped her hand over her mouth to keep from screaming out. She didn't want to distract her husband. It was hard to watch as the impact knocked Joshua into the barrels. He fought well, she thought, despite the fact she didn't think he was suitable for fighting. He was a businessman; he made decisions and worked behind a desk. Her husband was a tall man, yet he was not as coordinated or as experienced in fighting as Windsbrook. Still, she was proud to see Joshua managed to keep himself on his feet and keep himself from getting skewered. He quickly got the hang of it. He got in a few punches, knocking Windsbrook off balance before sending him skidding across the cellar room into the stones of the opposite wall.

And right into her.

Hot pain filled her. She couldn't breathe.

Then she couldn't stand. She looked down to see Windsbrook's knife in her stomach.

Windsbrook stumbled away, stared at Ellen without a word then ran away through the stone doorway toward the stairs.

Ellen stared at Joshua for what seemed like an eternity. Joshua eased her to the floor. The stones were so cold. She looked down and saw her blood covering the lovely blue dress he'd bought for her, the dress that made her eyes look darker.

The pained cry he let loose brought the servants of the house and the guests of the party. She knew he thought of their baby so small in her womb, and he wanted nothing more than to save it and her. She felt nothing as he pulled the knife from her where the baby grew. The room grew dark. She heard the servants arrive. She heard Joshua say, "Oh, my Ellen, I'm so sorry…"

Then there was only darkness.

Quint held Meg in his arms and let the pain flow through him just as he had so many other times before. So many memories converged on him at once. Flora, Eyes of the Sky, Justine, the woman who had favored his sword with a ribbon from her hair, Ellen, countless others in other times, other places all formed the pain he'd been forced to bear for an eternity of lifetimes. Would he never be able to break this cycle and save the woman he loved? Why did he not deserve a life with her? Why did he not deserve to see his child born? What horrible crime could he have committed to deserve such endless pain?

He thought he could break the cycle if he kept her with him, and yet it was not to be. If he had not forced her to move in to the Manor, would she still be alive?

He knelt on the cold floor, just as he had in the past, and held his wife in his arms as seconds ticked by while her life ebbed from her.

Brad was gone. He didn't even have to look up to know that. The killer always ran away like the coward he was. The white trader, Stephen Windsor, Windsbrook, the others, they had all run while he had knelt with his dying wife in his arms, trying to keep her warm as she gasped her dying breath.

But this time, something was different. Quint knew it as soon as he felt the hand on his shoulder. He looked up into the soft eyes of Melanie Wirthington. He had a witness.

He also had the technology of the twenty-first century.

Melanie moved his hands to Meg's wound. "Keep pressure on it." She sounded calmer than she appeared. "I'll call 9-1-1. But I have to go upstairs, my cell doesn't get a signal down here. Will you be all right if I leave you?"

"All right?" His wife was dying as he watched, and Melanie wanted to know if he was all right.

"Just keep pressure. I'll get help."

And she was gone.

He looked down to find Meg looking up at him. "Quint?"

"Don't try and talk, honey, just stay quiet." He pressed on her wound and cradled her to his chest. "Listen to my heartbeat and know that I love you. Know that it beats for you, only you, Meggie." He felt tears on his cheeks, and when he looked down at her again, her eyes were closed.

Moments later, employees found him with his wife in his arms, murmuring his love for her. And the sound of paramedics wheeling in a stretcher was the most welcome sound he'd ever heard.

CHAPTER TWENTY-SIX

Meg opened her eyes and moaned against the pain that came to her with the light.

She moved in slow motion. Anything quicker brought dizziness that joined forces with the pain in her head. There was pain in her stomach, too; but it was different. It was more like a constant, dull ache, not the sharp pain behind her eyes from the light.

She took a deep breath, and the antiseptic smell of the hospital touched her nose. She looked down at herself and took in the form of her body beneath the covers on the bed. Quint sat on a chair next to the bed. Well, he didn't quite sit. He leaned forward and rested his arms and head on the bed near her knees. He was asleep. She heard his even breathing in the quiet of the room. Her arm was unusually heavy as she reached out a hand, and placed it on his head.

He woke in an instant and turned to look at her. Then, without a word, he reached out and took her hand in his. He brought her hand to his lips and kissed it.

"My stomach hurts." A whisper was all she could manage. She didn't tell him but it hurt to talk, too. Her mouth was so dry. She thought it was filled with sawdust.

"It's going to hurt for a while, *mon coeur*."

It all came back to her in an instant. "He stabbed me."

His gaze met hers and darkened. "Yes, he did."

"Where is he?"

Quint rubbed the bridge of his nose. "Beginning his long rot in jail."

"The baby?" She had to ask, although she was already certain it was lost. It was so small, so new. It couldn't survive. She felt empty. She couldn't stop the tears from forming. Then so many emotions hit her at once; sadness, guilt, and desire.

She hadn't known how much she wanted a baby, hadn't thought she was ready. Now that it was gone, she wanted it back.

"I'm sorry, Meggie. The doctors did everything they could, but they couldn't save you both. The baby was just too small, and you sustained too much trauma, lost too much blood. But the doctor said that after some time healing, you'll be as good as new. We can try again." He stood and drew closer, holding her hand until they were face to face. He gently rested his forehead against hers and held her for a long moment. Their tears mixed.

Meg didn't speak again until she'd the strength to find her voice. "It was just like Ellen."

"No, not just like Ellen. Ellen died. You didn't. I get another chance with you, Meg." His grip on her hand tightened as he spoke.

"I dreamed of her." Her eyes welled with more tears. "And I dreamed of an Indian girl in a teepee and people in a log cabin and a man with a sword and..." She couldn't remember the others, but she knew they were there within her thoughts, buried deep in her memories.

"You did." It wasn't a question.

"You loved them all, didn't you?" It was a stupid question, but she needed to ask anyway.

"Yes, as you always loved me. Just as I love you now, Meggie. I will always love you. And I'm thankful I was given another chance here and now to spend the rest of my life with you, thankful I didn't lose you as I always have in the past." The kiss he gave her was soft; his hand on her face possessive. "Will you do me the honor of spending the rest of your life with me?"

"Yes, my love." She looked up at him, blinking back her tears. "How do you think this happened, Quint? How do you think we've loved one another over and over, but never been allowed to be together?"

"I don't know." The honesty with which he answered touched her heart. "Perhaps I was meant all along to share my life with you. Perhaps we are two spirits meant to be together. I know I'm meant to be with you now, and that I can't live without you. I don't want to waste time questioning it any more. I know that each moment, each second I'm given with you is more precious than any gold, any diamond or any treasure I have hidden in our house, and I don't want to waste any of them."

He kissed her again.

She welcomed his kiss and gave her own back.

"Quint?"

"Yes?"

"Did you really find the treasure, or was that just a lie to stall for time?"

Quint smiled and squeezed her hand. "I'm holding the real treasure right here, right now. It wasn't lie, Meggie. You and I found the treasure when we found our love." He kissed her again.

Then he grinned at her, that crooked, familiar Joshua Montgomery grin. "But if you want to know where the gold is, I can show you when you get better."

"You know where it is?"

His grin grew. "I've always known, *mon coeur*. Always. After all, just like the paintings I placed in between the floor joists, I hid it."

Then he kissed her again.

EPILOGUE

"Why do you always need to show me hidden rooms in the middle of the night?" Meg's whisper sounded loud in the stillness of the hallway. The hall was warm, but gooseflesh still covered her bare legs. Her fuzzy slippers made not a sound on the carpet.

"Because during the day, there are too many people here. Besides, I find sneaking around our house at night when it's just the two of us very exciting." Quint met Meg's gaze through the dim light of the hall and grinned. "Don't you?"

"Staying in bed, making love with you sounds more exciting. And warmer," Meg replied. But she kept her hand tucked in his and matched his step. "If we're going to make these nightly hikes a usual thing, I should get a pretty nightgown in case we pass any guests sneaking out of the kitchen."

He looked her up and down as they continued down the hall. "You look just fine in my shirt. Don't waste your money on a nightgown."

"Can you give me a hint of what you plan to show me this time? Because I hope it's not another underground tunnel."

"Not exactly."

"Not exactly you can't give me a hint or not exactly it's not another tunnel?"

"You'll just have to wait and see, mon coeur."

At the stairs leading to the cellar, she still held his hand, but she stopped. "The cellar? I don't think I can go down there. I'm not sure I can go down there even it was daytime."

"I won't let go of your hand. It'll be okay. I promise."

Meg gathered her courage. After her near-death experience eight weeks before in the cellar, she hadn't been back. He squeezed her hand.

Then he leaned close and whispered in her ear. "The treasure is hidden in the cellar."

She stared at him a long moment, astonishment filling her like the water that now filled the swimming pool. She forced her mouth to close and licked her lips to bring to them some much-needed moisture. Without another word of protest, she allowed him to usher her down to the cellar. Once they were in the tunnels, she asked, "It's not hidden in the wine barrels, is it?"

"No."

Meg's heart picked up pace as they neared the place where Brad stuck a knife into her. Before she could tell Quint she thought she could go no further, he moved to the stone wall. Then he removed a loose stone to reveal a metal looped latch that stuck out between the stones. Meg would have never noticed that the stone was a darker color than the others if Quint hadn't pulled it free. He twisted the latch and the entire wall swung open. It was a large door covered with stone to match the rest of the tunnel wall and keep the door hidden.

The sconces on the walls nearby were enough to light the room inside. But it didn't take much light for Meg to see the rows of shelves. "Gold? Treasure?"

"Silver coins. Gold. Stock certificates. Sculptures. Art. All right here where Joshua Montgomery hid it."

Meg stepped into the large, secret vault and took it all in, her amazement leaving her speechless for a long moment. "This has been hidden here all this time?"

"Yes." Through the soft light, he met her gaze, his blue eyes sparkling. "Do you think you can keep this a secret?"

"Yes."

He leaned close and touched his lips to hers. "Remember when you wanted to christen the cellar?" he asked after ending the kiss.

Again, her heart raced but now it was for completely different reason. The terror of the cellar she'd felt before was forgotten with his kiss. The next thing she knew he pressed her against the stone wall. The cool stones against her back added fuel to the fire he set in her blood. He held both her hands above her head, his fingers laced through hers. And his kiss…

…was a kiss of forever.

The End

DEAR READER,

I'd like to take this moment to tell you how much I appreciate you reading *Montgomery Manor*. I hope you enjoyed Quint and Meg as much as I enjoyed writing their story. I have always been intrigued with haunted houses and the reasons people dare to enter them. I would love to own a house like Montgomery Manor with hidden rooms I could explore, especially if there was a bookstore on the premises! If you have not read *Hargrove House*, which is Book One, I encourage you to pick up a copy and step inside. I'm excited to tell you I will continue The Haunted Series. Book Three — *Camden Place* will be released in Fall 2016. Please be on the lookout for it. You can see all the books by Allie Harrison and Allie Quinn at: www.AllieQuinn.com

You can also find me on Twitter at ImAllieHarrison and on Facebook at The Official Page of Allie Harrison and Allie Quinn.

For all my news, stop in on my website and sign up for my newsletter.

Thank you again,
Allie

Coming soon:

The Haunted
Book Three — *Camden Place*

After a horrific attack, Claire Newman needs a fresh start, so when she inherits old Camden Place, she's more than excited to reach her new home in the heart of Charleston, South Carolina. The halls echo with history, and the air is filled with something haunting and magical — just what she needs to recover her once lively spirit. But after playing the grand piano in the music room, she discovers she's not the only resident of Camden Place. In fact, there is an entire group of people in the dining room enjoying a dinner party. One of them is handsome and unearthly, Quincy Camden. How could the original builder of Camden Place be sitting at Claire's dining room table when he died mysteriously in 1847? And why is he the only one at the party who can see her? Is Quincy a part of the future she's building in her new home? Can Claire change Quincy's future or save him from his fateful death? Or is she destined to join him at the ghostly party?

ABOUT THE AUTHOR:

Allie Harrison lives with her husband in Southern Illinois. When she isn't enjoying fun family time, games with friends, reading, crafts, music and winemaking, she's working to build fictional worlds and unforgettable characters. She also writes as Allie Quinn and can be found at AllieQuinn.com